GRAVE MISTAKE

A Johnny Ace Mystery

*Also by Ron Ellis, featuring Johnny Ace,
and available from Headline:*

EARS OF THE CITY
MEAN STREETS
FRAMED
THE SINGING DEAD

GRAVE MISTAKE

A Johnny Ace Mystery

Ron Ellis

HEADLINE

First published in 2001 by
HEADLINE BOOK PUBLISHING

10 9 8 7 6 5 4 3 2 1

British Library Cataloguing in Publication Data

Ellis, Ron, 1941–
  Grave Mistake
  1. Ace, Johnny (Fictitious character) – Fiction
  2. Private investigators – England – Liverpool – Fiction
  3. Liverpool (England) – Fiction
  4. Detective and mystery stories
  I. Title
  823.9'14 [F]

ISBN 0 7472 7224 7

Typeset by Palimpsest Book Production Limited,
Polmont, Stirlingshire
Printed and bound in Great Britain by
Clays Ltd St Ives plc

HEADLINE BOOK PUBLISHING
A division of Hodder Headline
338 Euston Road
London NW1 3BH
www.headline.co.uk
www.hodderheadline.com

To my new editor, Shona; my publicity lady, Pat, and my agent, Kerith, who look after me so well and are determined to make me famous as well as notorious. Johnny Ace would also add they are all extremely attractive but, in these days of rampant sexism, I could not possibly say that.

Chapter One

Saturday afternoon in mid-March. A stiff wind battled it out with a pale sun over Liverpool, whipping up waves on the River Mersey and sending litter scurrying round the alleys. People out on the streets wore anoraks and fleeces, something to do, I suppose, with the wind-chill factor that was turning a spring afternoon into an Arctic experience.

On Church Street, shoppers crowded into Marks & Spencer, C & A and HMV, sweeping past the security guards on duty at every door – a familiar feature of big-city retailing in the year 2000 when British street crime reportedly exceeded that of America.

On the pavement outside the stores, market traders were doing a roaring trade in cheap kitchenware, football scarves, T-shirts, handbags, fruit, flowers and household goods. The stores had been trying to have the stalls removed but, so far, without success. Round one to the little man.

Edwin Starr was due in town that weekend with his Motown Revue, *American Beauty* was filling the multiplexes on the back of nine Oscar nominations whilst Everton were down in London at The Bridge, facing a Chelsea side bereft of Englishmen.

Meanwhile, in the Tesco superstore in Formby, a young lady called Jo Smithson was busy doing some shopping.

Maybe she stopped at the cheese counter, maybe the bakery.

I don't know the details because not much of her shopping was recovered. I do know, however, that she spent some time in the liquor department because a carrier bag containing two bottles of champagne was found later on the back seat of her abandoned car.

Whatever it was she was celebrating, she never got round to drinking it.

Possibly the man was already stalking her as she walked round the supermarket. Saturday is a busy afternoon so the odds are she would have been unlikely to notice him in the crowded aisles.

If, indeed, it was a man.

She did reach her yellow Fiat Punto in the car park. A fair reconstruction of events would have her unlocking it with her remote control, which was found lying on the ground beside the nearside wheel, opening the rear door to put her shopping on the back seat. At which point she was abducted.

Who knows whether her assailant had a knife or maybe even a gun? Shooters were becoming commonplace in the city in the new millennium. Any retail outlet, building society or Post Office was fair game. Whatever it was, Jo Smithson had been scared enough to drop the rest of her shopping and leave her unlocked car behind in that car park to go . . . where?

I said she left her shopping. Apart from a spilt jar of Branston pickle and a peach toilet roll lying on the ground, nothing was found. I guess somebody went home with a few bags of unexpected 'freebies' that afternoon.

At five o'clock, Jo's father, Leonard Smithson, received a phone call. It was simple and to the point. It ran along the usual lines of 'We have your daughter. Don't contact the police or she's dead meat.'

It looked like a pretty straightforward snatch, with the anxious father having an even-money chance of getting his daughter back alive, whether or not he contacted the Law.

In the event, it turned out to be anything but straight-forward.

Leonard Smithson didn't phone the police. Instead, he rang an old friend of his, my partner Jim Burroughs.

Jim and I had set up a private investigation agency a year or so before, renting offices in Dale Street in the heart of the city's commercial centre.

I'd already been involved in a couple of cases, which had given me an appetite for the work, and I had time on my hands. Thanks to the new technology, my daily show on local radio didn't take up more than a couple of hours. I prepared most of it at home, and, although I also had an interest in the property business, renting out furnished flats, I had a manager to look after that. When Jim decided to take early retirement from the Merseyside Police, where he'd made Detective Inspector, it seemed the time was right for us to join forces.

Jim was at home, listening to the end of *Sports Report*, when he took Smithson's call. He arranged to meet the man at our office in an hour and then immediately rang me.

I was in my flat in the Waterloo Dock, all set for an evening at home. I'd cracked open a fourpack of Scrumpy Jack cider, had an Indian takeaway booked for an eight o'clock delivery and I'd collected a large marrowbone from the butcher for the dog. It was his night in too.

'I think you should be there, Johnny,' Jim advised. 'You know who Leonard Smithson is, I take it?'

Who on Merseyside didn't? Leonard Smithson was a high-profile local figure. He'd served his time as an electrician in the late 1950s and, upon qualifying, had started his own firm. He soon had over twenty people working for him.

His next move was into wholesaling and, by the mid-1970s, LS Electrics had become one of the biggest outfits in the city. In 1985, he had the foresight to recognise the potential of the mobile phone industry and he set up a subsidiary company dealing in mobiles, opening offices all over the country and hitting paydirt when they became the biggest consumer growth product of the next decade.

In the late 1990s, he turned his attention to another boom

industry. Leisure. He bought a tumbledown warehouse near Duke Street and turned it into the most palatial nightspot in the city. Entry was strict, he had his own team of doormen, and Nirvana soon became the fashionable place to go for sophisticated clubbers.

The media loved him. He was the archetypal professional Scouser, always there with an opinion on anything connected with Liverpool, carefully worded into cute sound-bites that delighted TV and radio presenters who entreated him on to their shows at every available opportunity.

'They couldn't have chosen a better target,' I said. Smithson was a climber with a bullet in the *Sunday Times Rich List*. 'A young heiress whose old man wouldn't miss a few grand from the petty cash.'

'It isn't cash they're after,' replied Jim ominously. 'Try and get here for seven, will you, Johnny?'

I phoned the takeaway to cancel the meal then filled a fresh bowl of water in the kitchen for Roly and gave him the bone from the fridge.

Roly is part lurcher and part deerhound; I inherited him by accident on another case. He's boisterous and wilfully disobedient, and I sometimes feel like turning him in to the animal rescue centre but he has such a winning smile I always end up forgiving him, even on the occasions when he eats my dinner. He wasn't smiling now, though. He doesn't like being left on his own.

That's the trouble with women and dogs. It's hard to get away from them yet you wouldn't be without them.

Leonard Smithson and Jim were already at the office when I arrived. Smithson was a short, stocky man, whose black hair owed more to Clairol than nature. In the 1970s he would have worn a medallion. The diamond Rolex, mohair suit, florid face and extended stomach bore evidence of his rich lifestyle but his expression betrayed a tragic mixture of anger and fear.

'Have you any idea at all who could be behind this?' I

asked him. 'Someone you've crossed in business, someone who knows you've got money?'

'Everyone knows I've got money, for God's sake, but, yes, I know exactly who these people are – and it's not money they're after.'

I raised my eyebrows. 'Then what?'

'They want Nirvana.'

'Your club?'

Smithson explained. 'A security firm called Conqueror has been pestering me these past few weeks. Basically they want to control the door at the club and the price for this "insurance", as they call it, is scandalous, as you can imagine.'

It was hardly a new notion. Back in the 1960s, when I'd been playing drums with The Cruzads and we worked the city's nightclub circuit, I'd seen a club owner armed with a loaded shotgun lock himself in his steel-lined office when a gang stormed his premises. The doorman had tried to stop them. 'Sorry lads, I can't let you in, you know that. Boss's orders.'

They impaled the poor sod on the iron railings outside the club. 'Nothing personal, Albert,' they said. The spike went in through the soft nape of his neck. He didn't die and he didn't exactly lose his mind but, in subsequent conversations, he would laugh in the wrong places and he never worked again.

In those days, they called it protection.

'How do you know it's the same people?'

'Last night, I got a phone call from their main man, Harry Mottram, the managing director of Conquerer. He's bad news, an evil man. It's not enough for him to take a cut from the door. He's now after the club itself. Made me an offer there and then.'

'At the going rate?'

'Less than half what it's worth. I told him to get stuffed. He said he was going to fax me a contract for the sale and I had to fax it back to him, signed, before midnight or the price would be halved. He also said, if I didn't send it, I'd regret it in other ways. I didn't know at the time what he meant by that.'

'So you refused to pay?' I asked Leonard Smithson.

'Too right I did. I have my own team of men on the door, I thought I was well protected.'

'Until this happened.'

'Yes. An hour or so ago, I received a phone call reminding me to return the contract, signed, before midnight tonight and Joanna would be set free. We had no idea she was missing. Just thought she was a bit late back from the shops.' Smithson hesitated for a moment, swallowed noisily, then drew out a piece of paper from his pocket and threw it on to the desk. 'There's one other thing. They told me on the phone to watch out for an e-mail. Here was what they sent.' He watched me carefully as I picked it up. 'This will give you an idea of the sort of people we are dealing with. My daughter had beautiful long blonde hair, Mr Ace.'

I looked at the image on the paper and was suitably shaken. It was a head and shoulders picture of a comely young woman with full red lips, a retroussé nose and large eyes which would have been attractive had they not, like her mouth, been wide open in terror.

There were no clues as to where it had been taken, other than it was indoors and they had probably used a digital camera and put the picture straight on the computer.

There was one significant detail in the photo that stood out with horrifying starkness.

Joanna Smithson's head had been completely shaved.

Chapter Two

I passed the photo wordlessly to Jim who looked equally shocked.

We established a few facts. Joanna was twenty-two, an only child, and she still lived at home in the Smithsons' newly built five-bedroom mansion in Blundellsands. She was in her third year of an Organisation and Management degree at Edge Hill in Ormskirk, which was once a teacher training college but now formed part of Lancaster University.

'It seems to me they send everyone to university these days,' sighed Leonard Smithson. 'I left school at fifteen and was none the worse for it.'

'Probably better off,' I said, 'but the government has to keep the unemployment figures down somehow.' Sending them off to war isn't a vote catcher any more. Modern kids would tell Kitchener to get stuffed. They save their fighting for football grounds. 'When exactly did you last see your daughter, Mr Smithson?' This wasn't the time for political discussion.

'She was at home all morning. She had lunch with me and my wife, Brenda, who, incidentally, is going frantic.'

'And is your home well protected, like your club?'

'Like Fort Knox. State-of-the-art cameras and alarms. Remember, I'm in the electronics business.' His voice faltered. 'But they didn't take her from there, did they?'

'Then where . . . ?'

'After lunch she went out shopping, to Tesco's in Formby.'

'In her own car?'

'A yellow Fiat Punto. It was her pride and joy. I bought it for her twenty-first. As soon as I received the phone call, I drove there to look for her. The car was still in the car park. Lucky nobody had driven off with it.' He told me about the shopping. 'We were having some friends round tonight for a drink and some supper to celebrate my wife's birthday. Hence the champagne.'

'This is why you should contact the police,' pointed out Jim. 'The kidnappers are bound to have left evidence somewhere on the vehicle for Forensic to work on. These days, with DNA testing and suchlike, the police should easily be able to trace them.'

'By which time, they might have killed Joanna. If these people think the Law are involved . . .'

'They needn't know.'

'Come on, Jim. It's like police protection for witnesses. When it comes down to it, it means bugger all, and you know it.'

I checked my watch. The message had said he had till midnight and it was already almost seven. 'We've just over five hours to go to their deadline.' I looked at Jim. 'Can we trace the number?'

'It was a mobile with a fax facility,' answered Smithson.

So much for the age of wonder technology when everyone is supposed to be instantly traceable.

'We can pinpoint his whereabouts to within a hundred yards if you have the number,' insisted Jim.

Smithson snorted. 'He could be anywhere. On a crowded train in Scotland heading for the Isle of bloody Skye.'

'Not Skye,' I said, 'not with the mountains. It's bad enough trying to get a signal in Formby. But I take your point.'

'Come to that,' said Jim, 'he could have left his mobile miles away, switched on to diversion or given it to some-one else.'

'Even if he's kept it himself, as soon as I send the fax he's waiting for, he'll switch the thing off altogether anyway.' His face hardened. 'Tell me, if I don't play ball and sell them the club, do you think they would really kill her?'

'Possibly,' I replied. 'It's hard to tell but, if they were prepared to kill her at all, I'd say there'd be just as much chance they'd do it even if you went along with them and signed that bit of paper. Young Jo'd always be a liability, a potential witness against them.' I didn't like to frighten the man, but, 'They might think the few extra years for murder were worth the risk.'

Smithson grunted. 'That's assuming they were convicted, of course.'

'Quite.' Given the current state of British justice I didn't hold out too much hope of that happening.

There was a silence while we all pondered the unthinkable. No daughter, no club, no arrests. A triple whammy.

The only difference would be, if Smithson *didn't* accede to their demands and his daughter died, the blame and the guilt would be shifted on to him and maybe he wouldn't be able to live with that.

'And you still don't want to involve the police?' I asked, looking across to check Jim's reaction. I could see it was difficult for him, as an ex-DI, to accept this. I had no problem with it myself. I'd seen too much corruption in the Force and too many cock-ups by inadequate policemen who would have had difficulty holding down a job picking mushrooms. I wouldn't have trusted our boys in blue to trace a lost parrot, much less deal with a crime that put someone close to me in danger. Rescuing damsels in distress was definitely not their forte.

'I'd be signing Joanna's death warrant if I did. But I know Jim's straight and he tells me that you, Mr Ace, are unorthodox and not a little ruthless, which is why I have come here to get my daughter back.'

I wasn't sure what Jim had meant by 'unorthodox and ruthless'. Admittedly, a couple of people who had tried to kill me in the past had stopped breathing rather suddenly, but on both of these occasions the situation had been one of 'them or me', which I felt morally justified the outcome. To hear Jim talk, you'd have thought he was offering Smithson someone from the Russian Mafia.

'We'll do what we can,' I promised him. The obvious first step was to find out where the girl was being held. 'Have you had any indication at all as to her whereabouts?'

'Not a thing other than the mobile number.'

I changed tack. 'Has Joanna got a boyfriend?' A possible accomplice.

'She's been going out with this lad called Toff for a few months.'

'Toff? Ex-Eton, is he?'

'You're joking. He's a scally. His name's Christopher. There was another Chris in his class so he got "Toff" and it stuck.'

'Is he at the same college?'

'No. He's a waiter somewhere in town.' Smithson's tone conveyed the impression that waitering was not a profession he would have chosen for a future son-in-law. You often find this. People who start out from nothing prefer their children to join them on their climb up the social ladder, become or marry chartered accountants and join up with the Rotary and the Lodge. Waiters came into the category of undesirables like musicians and brickies who might drag the whole family back down to the gutter.

'You don't think he's got anything to do with it?'

'I doubt it. He's not bright enough.'

Jim broke in. 'So what exactly do you want us to do, Lennie?'

Smithson's answer couldn't have been more simple. 'Get her back.'

'We don't know where she is,' I objected.

Jim Burroughs took my side. 'Lennie, Johnny's right. What can we do on our own? I think you've got to bring in the Law.'

'Wait just a minute.' I had had an idea. I turned to Leonard Smithson. 'Who's the guy in charge of Conqueror, did you say?'

'Harry Mottram.'

'Where's he live?'

'He's got a mansion near Mobberley, not far from Manchester Airport. Well out of town.'

'I know it. Dave Dee lives somewhere round there.' Dave Dee, Dozy, Beaky, Mick and Titch played The Cavern back in the 1960s and they were on the bill in 1966 when Harold Wilson performed the re-opening ceremony. Dave Dee is now a magistrate in Macclesfield. Would you credit that?

'Isn't that where that Swampy character buried himself, protesting against the new runway?' asked Jim.

'I believe it is.' Smithson suddenly became excited. 'She's going to be there, isn't she? I've got a shooter at home, let's get round there.'

'Calm down,' I said. I could see why he'd been successful in business. Instant decisions and ready to back them up. It didn't work quite like that though in kidnap cases. 'He's hardly going to take her there, is he? Not shitting on his own doorstep.'

That stopped him in his tracks. 'You're right, of course. He wouldn't drag his own family into it.'

'No, but we might.'

'What do you mean?'

'Has Mottram got kids?'

'Don't know. Why?'

'He'll have a wife though?'

'Yes. Young blonde piece. I've seen pictures of her in *Cheshire Life*.'

'If we could get our hands on her, we could offer him a swap. His wife for your daughter.'

Jim emitted a loud groan. He was probably still assimilating the fact that his chum possessed an illegal weapon.

'For God's sake, Johnny . . .' but Smithson cut him short.

'He's right. The man is fucking right. We'd have something

to bargain with. He wouldn't dare harm Jo if we had his missus.'

If Jo wasn't already dead, I thought, but didn't say it.

'Don't talk crap.' Jim was almost foaming at the mouth. I feared for his angina. 'It's against the bloody law for a start. You can't just walk into a man's house and seize his womenfolk. That went out with the Vikings.'

'I suppose you're right,' I admitted reluctantly. I thought the theory was good though. 'Maybe if all else fails.'

'Get back to reality, Johnny. You're living in a bloody fantasy world.'

I've often been told that and, what's more, it's probably true. Most of the time it's never seemed to me to be a bad thing, but in this case, I had to agree. It was more likely to be suicidal.

Luckily, I never got the chance to put the idea into practice. At that moment, Leonard Smithson's mobile phone rang. He whipped it out of his inside jacket pocket and barked into the mouthpiece. 'Yes?' As we watched, a look of elation spread over his face. 'Jo, is that you?' A pause. His expression changed to one of incredulity, then horror. I could hear a shrieking at the other end of the line. 'Whereabouts are you?' Another pause. 'Stay right there. We'll come and pick you up. Don't worry, sweetheart. It'll be all right.'

He turned to us. 'Joanna. She's got away.' He started to babble.

'Steady on,' I said. 'Sit down a minute and take it slowly.'

He drew a hand over his perspiring forehead and half collapsed into a chair. 'They've been holding her in this house in Bootle. Two men. One of them left a few minutes ago leaving her alone with the other.' He started to cry. 'She thinks she might have killed him.'

Chapter Three

The girl wasn't wrong.

The address she gave us was that of a terraced house at the bottom of Stanley Road, overlooking North Park. Most of the three-storey houses in the row had been coverted into flats but this particular one was still in single occupation.

It took the three of us fifteen minutes to get there in my car. Joanna had locked herself back in the house as Jim Burroughs had instructed but she answered the door as soon as we knocked. She was shaking. Tears mixed with blood were drying on her cheeks, her sweater was ripped exposing her white bra, and more blood covered the front of her beige combats. With her bald head, she presented a horrific sight, like a discarded model from Madame Tussauds waiting to be melted down.

'He's on the top floor in the front room.' She choked the words out.

Leonard Smithson held his arms open and she ran into them, sobbing. 'There there, it's going to be OK, sweetheart,' he whispered.

I left them to it and ran up the steep stairs to the top floor. Jim was already there, bending over a body.

'Brown bread?' I enquired, but I hardly needed to ask. The crimson pool beneath the matted brown hair, the vacant expression of the open eyes and the slack-jawed mouth told their own story. The corpse was in its early thirties, white, wearing denims, trainers and an Umbro T-shirt, which matched the grey pallor of the skin.

'She must have clobbered him with that.' He pointed to a large stainless steel paperweight lying beside the corpse, encrusted with blood.

'Good for her. One less gobshite on the streets.'

Jim spoke quietly. 'This is serious, Johnny. She could go down for this.'

'Come off it, Jim. Trying to escape from a kidnapper, self-defence . . .'

'You're forgetting Tony Martin, that farmer from Norfolk who got life for shooting a burglar.'

'Course I'm not, it was scandalous. In any other country he'd have got a bloody medal for it.'

'We're not in any other country and if you get a jury of liberal do-gooders, anything can happen. Remember, the criminals are the victims these days.'

'So what do you suggest? We get rid of the body and pretend we've never been here?'

'Don't be a pillock.' He was back wearing his policeman's hat. 'You know quite well we can't do that. Besides which, we'd be leaving all the evidence behind – the girl's bound to have left prints. Not to mention the deceased's accomplice who, incidentally, could return at any second. No – there's only one thing to do. She dials 999 straight away.'

After one last glance at the dead man, whom neither of us recognised, we returned downstairs to where Leonard Smithson was holding his daughter. She was still shaking and crying.

Smithson raised his eyebrows. 'Is he . . . ?'

''Fraid so,' murmured Jim. He addressed Joanna. 'Look, love, you're going to have to phone the police, get them down here. Don't say the man's dead, just that he's injured and you want an ambulance but most of all, tell them you're frightened the other man will come back. Emphasise you're in danger.'

Her hands trembling, she detached herself from her father's

arms and extracted her mobile from her pocket to make the call. Smithson turned his attention to Jim and me. 'We've got Mottram now.' He sounded quite excited. 'How long will he get – there's kidnapping, extortion, assault?'

'Hang on,' I said. 'I wouldn't bank on it. Even if they catch the other bloke, he'll know better than to shop Mottram.'

'He won't stand by and take all the blame, surely?'

'He will if the alternative is an early bath at the crem.' Smithson's face fell. 'Whereas Mottram will doubtless offer to look after his family whilst he's inside.'

'But we've got the evidence to send Mottram down.'

'What evidence?' Jim demanded. 'Did you tape his phone call?'

'No, but I have his e-mail.'

'Anyone could have sent it.'

'What about his fax?'

'A contract to sell him the club? I can just hear him in court. "Purely a business deal, m'lud."'

Smithson looked suddenly weary, like a jogger whose Lucozade bottle has run dry ten miles into a marathon. 'So what are you saying? Mottram gets away with it?'

'This time, perhaps, but look on the bright side. You've got your little girl back safe and sound. Her hair will grow again and she's lucky she hasn't been seriously injured. One of the men who abducted her is dead and the other will go inside for a very long time when they catch him. It ain't all bad.'

'What if the other man comes back?' cried Joanna.

'He'll hardly be likely to come in when he sees the police car outside.'

It was twenty minutes before the Law arrived and there had been no sign of the second kidnapper. 'They're here now,' Jim exclaimed, responding to the sound of a siren.

'At last,' I murmured. 'They probably stopped for a sandwich on the way.' The car screeched to a halt outside. Jim gave me an angry glare. He's very touchy about any aspersions cast on his ex-colleagues.

A uniformed sergeant accompanied by a constable ran up to the front door. Jim introduced himself as ex-Force. 'He's upstairs in the front room. I'm afraid he's dead.'

'I'll get on to the station. They'll want an SOC team up here right away.' The sergeant pulled out his radio and rang the station. 'It would be Saturday night of all frigging nights. As if we haven't enough on.'

'Where's that ruddy ambulance?' asked the constable. He had greying hair and was not far off retirement. He looked bored, a lifetime on the beat, seen it all a thousand times before, been there, worn the helmet. As he spoke, a white vehicle drew up outside with more blazing sirens. Already, a cluster of neighbours was forming on the pavement.

'Right on cue,' I said, going down the hall to let them in. Joanna stayed in the back room holding on to her father's arm. The constable remained with them. Possibly he thought the girl might do a runner.

Jim led the way upstairs, followed by the sergeant. I ushered up the paramedics in their wake although we knew there was nothing they could do. Dead was dead.

Within an hour, the house was crawling with CID and Forensic people.

By good fortune, the inspector who arrived to take charge of the case was an old colleague of Jim's and Jim was able to fill him in briefly about what had happened and how we came to be at the house with Joanna's father. 'A nasty business, Clive,' he concluded. 'By the way, I don't think you've met my partner, Johnny Ace. Johnny, Clive Ormesher.'

Ormesher was an amiable man, mid-thirties and muscular with large teeth, thick blond hair to his collar but cleanshaven. Richard Branson meets The Chippendales. I wondered if he waxed his chest.

A young woman with bright red hair marched purposefully up the stairs carrying a black Gladstone bag.

'The new duty pathologist,' explained Ormesher, seeing Jim Burroughs's raised eyebrows. 'Dr Vivian Crabtree. Just moved over here from the Midlands. Not a lady to tangle with but very efficient at the job.'

She didn't have to be too clever to work this one out. Death caused by a blow to the temple, the weapon a steel paperweight.

We all trooped upstairs again. Nothing had changed. The body wasn't going anywhere. Ormesher turned to Jim Burroughs. 'Do we have a description of this other man?'

'You need to ask Joanna,' he said. 'We hadn't got that far.'

Back downstairs, Ormesher spoke gently to the trembling girl. 'Take your time, young lady. How tall would you say he was?'

Joanna pointed to me. 'About the same size as him.'

'Six one,' I said.

'Hair?'

'A number two.'

'What?' asked her father.

'Like David Beckham,' I explained. 'They used to call it a crew cut.'

'Except a bit shorter than a crew cut if it was a number two.' Clive Ormesher was obviously au fait with current hairstyles. 'Any distinguishing features?'

She thought for a minute. 'He wore a gold stud in his right ear and he had a scar in the cleft of his chin.'

Ormesher was writing it all down. 'That's good. Now, did you notice what he was wearing?'

'T-shirt, jeans and trainers.'

'Was he fat or thin?'

'Very thin. And he had a slight limp.'

'Accent?'

'Broad Liverpool.'

Of course. Another Scouser giving the city a bad name. Wherever in the country you go, mention you're from Liverpool and some joker will make some crack about hiding the cutlery as if no lowlifes ever came from Torquay or Chipping Norton.

'If only all witnesses were as observant as you,' smiled Ormesher pleasantly, shutting his notebook.

And then he charged her with murder.

Leonard Smithson nearly went apoplectic. Joanna screamed and burst into tears. 'You can't do that,' her father roared at the inspector.

'I have no choice,' replied Ormesher. 'Your daughter has admitted she killed the man. I suggest you get hold of your solicitor immediately, sir. Meanwhile, you may accompany her to the police station, of course.'

'Just a formality,' Jim assured his friend quickly. 'I'm sure they'll decide there's no case to answer.' I said nothing. Neither did Ormesher. 'What the police will want to do is catch the kidnappers.'

'And the man behind them.'

'That too.'

'What about this other kidnapper? If we find him, Joanna's in the clear. Jim, can't you trace him?'

'I'd leave it to the police now, Lennie. They've got the resources.'

'Christ, I'd better phone the wife now and let her know Joanna's safe. Talk about the good news and the bad news.' Smithson gave a hollow laugh then turned to me.

'It seems I was a little premature in hiring you, Jim. Thanks for coming along and everything. Let me know what I owe you.'

'Forget it, Lennie. And if there's anything more we can do . . .'

'I don't think so.'

I disagreed but kept quiet. I could see several loose ends here that needed tidying up. Harry Mottram for one.

We hung around a few more minutes whilst the ambulance took the body to the mortuary for the post mortem and Leonard Smithson accompanied his daughter and the officers to the police station. Joanna seemed to have relapsed into a state of shock and, had it been up to me, I'd have been inclined to turn her over to the paramedics. But it wasn't up to me.

'She held up well, considering,' commented Jim. 'Lucky she wasn't badly hurt. They could have raped her, scarred her for life. As it is, a decent Irish and she'll look as good as new.'

Irish jig – wig. Right. Jim's taken to using Cockney slang rather a lot lately. I put it down to watching too many re-runs of *Minder* on Granada Plus.

'Do you think Mottram will try again?' I asked, as I drove Jim back to the office to collect his car.

'Try what?'

'I don't know. He still wants the club, doesn't he?'

'He'll hardly go for the girl again.'

'Probably not, but I doubt he'll give up that easy. I think there's more to come in this case.'

And so there was – but not immediately and not in the way I envisaged.

Chapter Four

I went back home. It was nearly eleven o'clock and I was ravenous. I eyed Roly's half-eaten marrowbone enviously. He growled.

I checked the answerphone. There was a message from Maria. Was I coming round later? Victoria's first tooth had come through; she thought I might want to see it. The message was timed at seven-thirty.

I hesitated, picked up the receiver and held it for a moment.

I was still finding it difficult to adjust to our new situation.

Our daughter had been born three months ago. Despite her mother being forty-two – what the midwife called an elderly primate – she was a healthy baby, weighing in at 6lb 8oz. She had black hair like Maria but my green eyes. She was gorgeous and I was besotted with her.

But enough to marry her mother?

I'd been going out with Maria for four years. She works in the Picton Library and has a son, Robin, from her long-dissolved marriage. It'd been a good relationship but now, inevitably, it was moving into uncharted areas. But we'd managed to work out a system that, so far, was acceptable to us both. Not what Maria really wanted, perhaps, but something she could live with.

For the time being.

I'd always told her that marriage wasn't on the menu for me. I might stay with her a lot of the time, even most of the time, but I was still keeping on my own place. I needed my own space, my own independence.

Then there was Hilary. Hilary and I have been lovers and friends for over twenty years. I couldn't walk away from that. Maria had been prepared to accept Hilary before the baby was born. Now it was a different ball game.

'I don't mind you seeing her,' she'd said, not unreasonably, at the Maternity Hospital. I'd been there at the birth. 'I know you've had her a long time, but from now on, you don't sleep with her any more.' The baby lay in her arms, not yet an hour old. Maria didn't take long to lay down the rules. 'Or you don't see us again.'

I couldn't argue with that and so far I had kept to it.

I replaced the receiver. I didn't feel I wanted a night of suburban domestic bliss right now, so I picked up my leather jacket and walked down to the Masquerade Club on the other side of the Pier Head.

Saturday Night is Cabaret Night said the posters outside. *Tonight – The Fabulous Smith Sisters. All the way from the USA.*

'Never heard of them,' I remarked to Tommy McKale, the owner, pointing to the billboard as we went in. Tommy nodded the doorman to let us through and Dolly in the paybox waved cheerily. Dolly is eighty-six but she doesn't look a day over seventy-five, obviously the result of her latest face-lift. She seems to have them most years. I often wonder why she bothers. Who wants to look seventy-five? Make it thirty-five or forget it.

'Julie, Mel and Kath,' Tommy said. 'They're all from the Dingle really but they went to New York last month on a shopping weekend so nobody can dispute the advertising.'

Nobody in their right minds would have disputed anything with Tommy McKale unless they fancied risking a one-way trip to the bed of the Mersey.

The Masquerade's hardcore membership is comprised of gangsters, perverts and remedials – people who, for one reason or another, are unlikely to gain admittance to any other club in the city.

No criminal charges have ever been brought against either of the McKales, Tommy or his brother Denis, although they are popularly believed to be the brains behind many of the city's underworld activities. The source of their income has exercised the best brains of Merseyside Police for years but the inward flow of money continues unabated.

'What are they? Spice Girl sound-alikes?'

Tommy laughed. 'No, nothing like that. These sound more like the Andrews Sisters. Remember them?'

'Before my time, Tommy. Christ, they were going before the war. Won't their act be a bit old hat for today?'

'Maybe. They don't sing too good either but they have one advantage over the real Andrews Sisters.'

'What's that?'

'They come on stage topless.'

'They're not in their eighties as well, are they?'

Tommy chuckled. 'Early twenties, Johnny. It's what they call niche marketing. With so many social clubs closing down, we've started to get a lot of crumblies down here of a Saturday night, pensioners who like to hear all the old songs.'

'But why do they have to be topless?'

'That's mainly for the regulars. They couldn't give a shit about the singing, they just like to see a bit of flesh. So this way we cater for two markets with the one act.'

'But don't the pensioners object to the nudity?'

'Not at all. They're used to seeing couples shagging on television every day so they take it for granted now. They think it's the norm.' He looked at his watch. 'The girls are on again in a minute – come through and have a shufty.'

He led the way to the bar and ordered us both a drink, cider for me, isometric orange for him. Vince was doing the honours. He wore a gold chain singlet and a pair of cutaway navy shorts.

'How's the baby, Johnny?' he asked.

'Cut her first tooth,' I said in a tone of voice that rated it at least the equivalent of a moon landing or Everton winning the Premiership. 'And she's only three months old. Usually they're six months at least.'

'Ooooh,' exclaimed Vince admiringly. 'The clever thing. What is it you've called her? I've forgotten.'

'Victoria.'

'After the railway station?'

'No. After the Queen.'

'Do you think you'll marry Maria?' Tommy asked.

'Tommy, I got past forty without being married so I must have known it wouldn't suit me.'

Vince beamed. 'When I got to thirty and wasn't spliced, everyone thought I must be straight. All my chums were married.'

'Yes, but to each other,' I said.

'Nothing wrong with that, dear,' said Vince. 'The church welcomes gay marriages now.'

'That's because most of the vicars are that way inclined.'

'Anyway, that was all before I met Rupert and settled into connubial bliss.' He smiled, showing off a jewel newly embedded in his front tooth, and rubbed his designer stubble reflectively. 'We're thinking of having a baby ourselves, me and Rupert.'

'With a bit of help, I trust.'

'Rent-a-Womb. Surrogate mothers lending their bodies as a vehicle for a new life in exchange for hard cash. The black economy at its most fruitful, in every sense of the word.' Vince guffawed. 'We're going to use Rupert's sperm for the first baby and mine for the second.'

Tommy McKale shuddered. 'Why don't you go out and buy a bloody baby at Tesco's. That's what it's coming to.'

Vince grinned and went off to serve a customer. The mention of Tesco made me think of Joanna Smithson. I told Tommy all about the events of the day.

23

'Sounds like a heavy scene,' he said. 'The girl did well. They'll have a job pinning anything on Mottram though.'

'You reckon?'

'I do. He'll be too smart.'

'You know him then?'

'I know of him. He's not from these parts, he only arrived in town a few months ago but, by all accounts, he's seriously bad news.'

'Where's he from, then?'

'Newcastle, so they say. Things got a bit hot for him on Tyneside, something to do with a girl getting raped and killed. The Law had nothing on him but one of the Geordie outfits ran him out of town and he ended up trying to muscle in on the scene here.'

'He's not been after either of your places, has he?' As well as the Masquerade, Tommy and his brother also own a leisure club, converted from an old boxing gym.

'No chance. He's too clever to tangle with any of the local outfits but Smithson's a different case. He's fully legit so he's vulnerable. I'll tell you another thing. Mottram won't like one of his men being taken out like that. He'll be looking for revenge.'

I didn't like the sound of that. Leonard Smithson needed to be warned. Not to mention Joanna.

'Enough shop talk,' said Tommy. 'How's things with Hilary? I miss seeing her with you.'

'Not wonderful.' When I'd told her about Maria expecting the baby, she'd been devastated. Then she was angry, said Maria had done it on purpose to trap me and I shouldn't fall for it. I'd assured her that it wouldn't make any difference and we'd still go out with each other regularly, and we had.

But only until Victoria was born.

Since then, I'd only seen her once. We went out for a drink but she didn't stay over as she normally would have done. I made an excuse for it not to happen without actually telling her that it would never happen again. She made no comment, but I knew the issue would have to be resolved one day.

'You can't expect them to be,' said Tommy. 'You're going to have to decide now, one way or the other, aren't you?'

I knew he was right. I also knew that, in reality, there was no choice. I just didn't want to make the decision yet.

'And what about that other bird you were shagging, up at the Bamalama?'

'Shirley, you mean? She's just a mate, Shirley. I haven't seen her for weeks. She's still living in one of my flats but I've not been round there since the New Year.'

Shirley and I had been friends for a long time and we'd spent occasional nights together over the years, when circumstances suited, but all that was now consigned, as the politicians are fond of saying, to the dustbin of history.

We were interrupted by the start of the cabaret. 'Here they come,' announced Tommy. 'The Smith Sisters. See what you think.'

I was pleasantly surprised. The girls themselves were stunners and their singing was actually quite good; in fact, their harmonies would have got them into any barbershop group in the country, whilst their semi-nudity gave new meaning to their rendition of 'Tea for Two'.

I stayed to see their act through then stuck around drinking for another hour. Tommy had booked a new DJ, a sixty-year-old weirdo called Remus who wore a red drape jacket, drainpipes and an Elvis pompadour wig. He played 1950s rock'n'roll which enticed the bevvied pensioners on to the dance floor to coax their geriatric limbs into grotesque parodies of the jiving they'd done in their Teddy Boy days. Not a pretty sight.

You had to hand it to these ageing rockers, they were certainly game old buggers. I figured it must be this grey power the media kept talking about. Sixties legends like Tom Jones and Engelbert Humperdinck had all been back in the charts recently. Indeed, the week before, I'd been at Ainsdale

Pontins to see another ageing pop star, P.J. Proby (sixty-one), trot out his old hits to a sell-out crowd. Hysterical women threw their knickers onstage, reminiscent of the old Tom Jones shows, except, judging by the average age of the audience, they were probably incontinence knickers and I thought the senescent crooner ill-advised to wipe his brow with them.

At 2 a.m., I decided to call it a night.

'Don't forget to watch out for Mottram,' Tommy warned me as I was leaving.

'I won't.'

I went back to the flat and woke Roly for his early-morning walk round the Pier Head. He wasn't ecstatic about it but came anyway although he made a point of yawning noisily at regular intervals. The wind was still blowing across the river but the sky was clear and I could see the sails of Bidston Mill silhouetted against the moonlit sky.

Tomorrow, I thought, I would go round to Maria's.

It was several weeks before I gave any more thought to Joanna Smithson.

Chapter Five

'Dogdirt,' exclaimed Jim Burroughs. 'That's all the general public seem to care about.' He held up the morning's *Daily Post*. 'The public services sector is falling apart, the schools, the hospitals, the railways and the police, they're all a shambles, petrol prices are sky high, they're closing fire stations right left and centre yet nearly every letter in here is about dogdirt.'

Roly looked up from his position on a blanket under the desk as if to say, 'Not guilty, pal,' yawned, and went back to sleep.

'I suppose coming home with shit on your shoes has more immediate impact than cuts in the fire service,' I replied. 'Especially if you have wall to wall carpeting.'

I was sitting at the computer, trying to locate a Mr D.I.G. Blease in connection with a new case. I'd checked through various directories, registers and electoral rolls but, so far, I'd been unable to track down his whereabouts.

We were well into July and the rain and winds continued unabated as if someone had forgotten to order summer. I wondered what had happened to that global warming everyone had been looking forward to.

England's football team had been comprehensively slaughtered at Euro 2000, at the same time as their supporters were busily laying waste to Belgian city centres. Tiger Woods had won the US Open by an unprecedented margin of fifteen holes, Pete Sampras was Wimbledon Singles Champion for a record seventh time and the Williams sisters looked like doing more for young black America than anyone since Muhammad Ali.

At the agency, we'd been pretty quiet. The Leonard Smithson case had been hibernating for several weeks but things were now starting to happen.

The man Joanna Smithson had killed had been named as Tony Dewhurst, a thirty-six-year-old career hoodlum well known to the police, with a string of offences ranging from burglary and Social Security fraud to illegally possessing a firearm and GBH.

Unfortunately, after extensive enquiries, and despite Joanna's excellent description, the police had so far been unable to trace his accomplice. All known associates of the dead man were traced and interviewed but they all denied any knowledge of Dewhurst's activities and every one of them had unshakable alibis for the Saturday in question.

Even his closest relatives, his wife Christine and his widowed father Roland, an ex-con himself, professed to have no idea for whom he was working or what he was doing in Bootle.

As Tommy McKale had predicted, no action was taken with regard to Leonard Smithson's claim that Harry Mottram was behind the kidnapping. There was not the slightest piece of evidence to back it up. No connection of any kind could be found between Mottram and Dewhurst.

To be fair, the police did speak to Mottram who expressed surprise and regret when it was suggested to him that he might have been involved in the abduction. As a law-abiding citizen, he regarded it as an 'abhorrent act' and hoped the police would quickly bring the perpetrators to justice.

Mottram agreed that he had made Leonard Smithson an offer to buy Nirvana, but maintained it was a legitimate business deal. Since the kidnapping, there had been no further approaches regarding the transaction, which suggested

Mottram had abandoned his attempt to buy the club. Nor had there been any hint of reprisal from any quarter against Joanna or her family in regard to the killing.

The most disturbing aspect of the affair was the fact that the CPS was going ahead with the charge of murder against Joanna. Naturally, her father had hired the best counsel, and public opinion was right behind the unfortunate girl, but it was an ordeal that most people thought she didn't deserve to face.

'I must admit I thought they would have caught the other man by now and cleared the girl,' said Jim. 'Instead, it's all gone a bit pear-shaped and I'm getting worried.'

So was I, if only because I couldn't believe the CPS would go ahead with such a controversial prosecution if they didn't think they had a more than even chance of winning.

Joanna had appeared in the Magistrates Court back in March and had been committed for trial at the Liverpool Crown Court, the same court where Ken Dodd had once been famously acquitted. She was remanded in custody in the interim, bail being refused on the grounds of the gravity of the charge.

Now the day of reckoning had arrived. The trial was due to open this afternoon at 2.30 p.m. It was expected to be over by the end of the week. Jim Burroughs and I were both being called as defence witnesses, along with Leonard Smithson.

Meanwhile, I had the morning to continue my search for a missing goalkeeper.

A couple of weeks before, amidst all the junk mail and catalogues, we'd received a handwritten letter, something you don't see too often nowadays. E-mail must have rung the death knell for ink manufacturers.

The letter was a request from a Mr Norris Pond, asking if he could hire us to trace one David Blease, a footballer who'd once played for a now extinct local team called the Wavertree Corinthians. Hardly the stuff of *Miami Vice* or *LA Confidential* but the bills had to be paid somehow.

Apparently, Mr Pond was a founder member of the Corinthians, a club formed in 1975 by a group of lads who played for a Sunday-morning pub team in Wavertree. Their aim had been to try and bring back the spirit of amateurism and sportsmanship to football that they felt had got forgotten amidst the cynical professionalism and commercialism of the modern game.

Some hope. I didn't ask him if they'd ever actually won a match against these cynical professionals, but the club had kept going for an unlikely seven years so I guess they must have managed the odd draw.

Now, Mr Pond was compiling a history of the club together with a potted biography of every player who had turned out for them during their brief existence.

Histories of football clubs have become an unexpected success story in publishing over the last few years. Geoff Wilde and Michael Braham produced the definitive book of the genre in 1997, recording the life histories of 664 players who had turned out for Southport FC between 1921 and 1978 when the club was voted out of the Football League.

Norris Pond was working from a much smaller cast list but, even so, he had been remarkably successful, tracing no less than eighty-nine men, alive and dead, who had worn the Corinthian shirt.

'There's just one man I need to contact to complete the list,' he told me when he came up to the office. He was a big man, in his early sixties, barrel-chested and florid-faced. He walked stiffly, like many ex-footballers whose arthritic joints bear witness to years of heavy tackling. His hair was grey and crinkly. In a 1950s skiffle group he could have doubled as a washboard.

The missing man was David Ian George Blease or 'Digger' as he was inevitably called on the football field.

'He played in goal for us in 1979 for half a season then he cried off one Saturday with an ankle injury and we never saw him again,' Pond recalled. His memory was excellent. He gave me Blease's last known address and phone number. 'He was a window cleaner by trade, but that's all I know about him.'

I wasn't optimistic; the chances of finding this fellow were slim. 'It's twenty years ago, Mr Pond.'

'Oh, he's not at that address now. I've been round, obviously. Like I say, I traced all the others and it wasn't easy, I can tell you. It's so annoying to be beaten by just one name but in the end I decided I'd have to hand over to an expert.'

I wasn't sure I was the sort of expert he was thinking of but it was worthwhile having a go. We'd nothing else on and, for a start, I could broadcast an appeal on my radio programme. Some listener out there might know Digger Blease, Wavertree's one-time answer to David Seaman.

However, that had been over a fortnight ago and there'd been no response. I was drawing blanks at every turn.

I'd found out from various records that David Blease was born in Liverpool in 1954, son of Alan and Judith Blease. His father was a lathe operator and his mother a housewife. Both of them were now dead. David had married an Iris Brocken in Liverpool in 1974 but I couldn't find any evidence of any children registered.

Jim was able to confirm that Blease had no criminal record and the last licence he had held for a motor vehicle was in 1979 when he owned a Hillman Minx and lived in Wavertree, near the Corinthians' ground.

After which, he disappeared off the face of the earth.

Chapter Six

'What I'm going to have to do,' I said, 'is call on some of Blease's old team-mates and see if they know what happened to him.'

Jim looked doubtful. 'Pond will have tried that already. Remember, he said he'd spoken to all the other players.'

'But if they were among the first he interviewed, he wouldn't have known at the time that he couldn't trace Digger so the subject wouldn't have come up.'

'He'd have gone back again later, surely.'

'Possibly,' I conceded, 'but I can't think of any other angle. Besides, one of them might remember something they didn't mention at the time or perhaps Pond got up their nose and they didn't want to co-operate. Either way, it's worth a try.' I'd exhausted all other avenues of enquiry I could think of.

I picked up the address book Norris Pond had left me. It contained addresses and contact numbers listed beside each player, together with the dates they'd played for the club. I was looking for people who were there the same season as Blease. There were seventeen of them, it turned out – three of whom were dead. Two car crashes and cancer. In the case of the dead ones, Pond had spoken to relatives who had been able to fill in most of the gaps in his records.

'Leaving just fourteen of "The Team of '79" still breathing,' I said, picking up the phone. 'Here goes, let's try Norbert Wharton, 1978–81.'

The ex-Corinthians sweeper answered my call in person and

assured me he was quite happy for me to go round and talk to him at his Litherland home. I said I'd be there in half an hour.

'Don't be late for court,' warned Jim.

'I won't, don't worry. Tell you what, I'll meet you in Richie's Butty Bar at one.'

'Good idea. It's your turn to buy the lunch.'

As I stood up, a deep snore came from under the desk followed by a long sigh. 'I'll leave Roly with you,' I told Jim. 'He obviously needs the rest.'

Norbert Wharton lived in a neat row of semi-detached houses in a street behind Secrets disco. In the glory days of the 1970s, when the city boasted venues like The Wookey Hollow and The Shakespeare, Secrets had been Allinsons, where patrons could have a meal and watch top American cabaret stars like Gene Pitney and Lovelace Watkins.

Long-gone days. Today's teenagers wanted dance, DJs and drugs, and forget the food.

Wharton's house needed a coat of paint and his front garden was overgrown. He answered the bell in his dressing gown and slippers. I put him in his early sixties, fat, squat and very unfit. His jowls had dropped and spread all round his neck, giving him the appearance of a wax candle that had been left too near the fire. It was hard to imagine him as a one-time athlete.

'Had a late breakfast,' he wheezed, by way of explanation for his attire. 'Call me Nobby. The wife's at work. Can I get you a beer?' He ushered me through to the kitchen at the back of the house.

I accepted a can of Boddington's draught bitter and he took the same. The table was full of dirty dishes but he ignored these and settled us on two wooden dining chairs.

I explained my mission and he told me about his brief career with the Wavertree Corinthians.

'I was with them for three seasons, the twilight of my soccer career such as it was. The nearest I came to fame was a trial with Wimbledon when I was seventeen. They didn't take me on.'

'So you were never a pro?'

'No, part-time all my life. I'm a painter and decorator by trade.'

'Really?' He didn't seem to see any irony in that, although the shabby décor of the room was in keeping with the ill-kept exterior. 'Who have you played for?'

'Oh, I've been at a lot of clubs. The highest I got was the Isthmian League. I was turned forty when I joined the Corinthians – on my last legs, you might say. They were only local, played in a Sunday league, mainly against pub clubs. Pondy was the manager and he played centre-half. Built like a brick shithouse he was, but never dirty. Just the opposite. He was obsessive about fair play. Of course, what happened was, the other teams thought we were a bunch of softies and kicked the bollocks off us. I don't think we won more than a dozen games in all the time I was there.'

'As many as that?' I said.

Nobby Wharton laughed which brought on a fit of coughing. 'Yeah, nearly as bad as England.'

'Probably better,' I agreed, and we took a minute out to grumble about the current state of the national game. I said I wished Terry Venables was still England's manager, even if he had been a friend of the Krays.

'Was he?'

'So they say. I don't know if it's true or not.'

Nobby said drily, 'They should have given the job to the Krays. Nobody would have dared beat *them*.'

'So what can you tell me about Digger Blease,' I prompted. 'You do remember him?'

'Digger? Of course I do. He was the goalie and he was terrible. Mind you, he was only five foot six. He was a window cleaner by trade. I told him he should bring his ladders with him to give him any chance with crosses. It was like giving the opposition a two-goal start.' He took a swig of beer and wiped his mouth with the sleeve of his dressing gown. 'I ask you, a fellow his size fancying himself in goal.'

I said, 'A marginally better choice of career than basketball, I suppose,' but the remark went over Nobby Wharton's head and he merely shrugged. 'Did Norris Pond ask you about Blease?'

'Not at the time. It was six months ago when Pondy came to see me but he rang up some time later to say he couldn't trace old Digger. I told him the same as I've told you. I've heard nothing of Digger since and I doubt if I'd know him today if I passed him in the street. People change. It was over twenty years ago. I mean, look at me now compared to then.'

I didn't know what he'd looked like then but I guessed it would be a lot different to his present appearance. 'Have you got any photos of the team with Blease on?'

'Do you know, I think I might have. We had a club photograph taken at the start of the 1979 season.' He raised himself to his feet slowly and creaked over to a cupboard in the corner. After a few minutes sorting through piles of dusty papers, he brought me a faded newspaper cutting containing a smudged photograph of a group of longhaired men kitted out in striped shirts and dark shorts.

'That's me at the back next to Pondy.'

I wouldn't have recognised either of them. Nobby was slim with frizzy, shoulder-length hair and could have passed for one of The Pretty Things, whilst Norris Pond was blond, lithe and muscular like a Swedish version of Tarzan. I thought of how they both looked now. No wonder the Government was running an 'Eat Healthy' campaign.

Nobby stuck a podgy finger on the page, pointing to a much younger player. 'That's Digger there, in the green jersey.' I didn't bother to point out it was a black and white photograph.

'He looks taller than five six,' I said, studying the picture carefully. 'He's towering over the guy next to him.'

'We stood him on a box, that's why.'

'That explains it.' Hollywood used to do the same with Alan Ladd. 'Any idea why he suddenly disappeared in the middle of the season?'

Nobby rolled to one side, scratched his bottom and cleared the phlegm from his throat noisily. 'They did say at the time that it was woman trouble. He'd been carrying on with this posh married piece in Childwall that he met on his rounds. Apparently, she liked a bit of rough but then her old man found out and rumour had it he went looking for Digger.'

'And at five foot six, Digger wouldn't want to argue.'

'He was a Corinthian anyway, he wouldn't fight dirty.' Nobby gave a toothy grin. I wondered why the Corinthian moral ethic didn't stretch to cover adultery. 'He did the sensible thing and scarpered. He had no ties, you see, he could go anywhere.'

'And you've no idea of this woman's name or anything?'

'No. It was just a rumour, like, but knowing Digger there was probably a lot of truth in it.'

'Was Digger not married himself?'

'Had been but she'd thrown him out years before. He lived on his own in a flat somewhere Wavertree way. Had to get it where he could,' he added philosophically, as if this should excuse him from being beaten up by irate husbands.

'Did nobody from the club go round looking for him when he didn't turn up for a game?'

'Oh yes, but he wasn't there. He'd cleared off from his flat and we never saw him again. Alan Hollamby went in goal from then on. He was six foot three so it worked out better in the long run.'

'How much did the players mix socially?'

'Not much. We'd have a drink after training.'

'How often was that?'

'A couple of nights a week. That was about it.'

'Did Digger Blease go around with anybody special?'

Nobby thought for a minute. 'He used to be quite pally with Wally Tennant. Wally played wing half, had his own plumbing business in Garston. It's still going as far as I know. When the club first started, of course, everyone was mates together but I wasn't around then. I only joined in 1978, three years down the line.'

And four years later, the whole operation was wrapped up. 'Did you stay till the club folded?' I asked Nobby.

'No. I left in the middle of their last season, November 1981. I'd had a few bad knocks and my knees were knackered so I packed it in and took up serious drinking instead. I still watch football on Sky,' he said apologetically. As if that counted. 'I'm a Liverpool fan myself.'

I confessed to being an Evertonian.

'Oh yes? I heard a rumour they were getting Duncan Ferguson back from Newcastle. If you ask me, they'd be better off with George Sephton.'

'Not Liverpool's PA announcer?'

'That's George. "The Voice of Anfield" they call him.'

'But he's twenty-two stone at least.'

'I bet he'd last more games than Ferguson though.'

And on that note we parted. He couldn't tell me any more about Blease. I asked him if I could borrow the photo to take a copy and he said I could keep it. He wasn't nostalgic about the Corinthians. I thanked him and drove back into town.

Wally Tennant would have to wait. This afternoon I had an appointment in court.

Chapter Seven

Richie's Butty Bar is in Paradise Street just down the road from the Crown Court and also a few doors from Radio Merseyside, which means you get a fair sprinkling of media people in. Billy Butler was just leaving to prepare his afternoon show as I arrived and Jim came in a couple of minutes later. I ordered a tuna salad sandwich on brown, while Jim went for the sausage, egg, bacon, fried bread and black pudding option. Good thing his wife Rosemary wasn't there, not to mention his cardiologist. I didn't like to speculate on what he would say.

'Any joy with Blease?' Jim asked, tucking in.

'Not much. This Nobby Wharton reckoned he was chased out of town by a jealous husband.'

'But he doesn't know where to?'

'No, but he put me on to a chap in Garston called Wally Tennant that Blease used to knock about with. I'll try him next.'

'It'll have to be after the trial.'

We were inside the Crown Court for two but by the time the judge had started the proceedings and the jurors had been sworn in, it was past three o'clock.

At first glance, the jury looked a mixed lot. Four of them were women, two of the men were black, three were youths well under thirty whilst one old man looked like he'd been carried in from a nursing home. The other two were the sort that could well have been in the dock themselves.

The counsel for the prosecution was one Quentin Beaumont, a bear of a man in his early thirties with a black moustache that was not quite hirsute enough to conceal the permanent sneer on his lips.

His opening speech, outlining the case for the prosecution, lasted barely half an hour but the content of it confimed Jim's worst fears. He went for the jugular from the first sentence.

'Let me start, members of the jury, by emphasising one important point of which there can be no doubt. Joanna Smithson did kill Anthony Dewhurst, that is an established fact. The reason why she committed this terrible crime is a matter of dispute, but I hope to be able to clarify the situation for you and show that the charge of murder is the correct one.

'The defence,' he went on, 'will tell you that this young lady was kidnapped and held to ransom – but where is the evidence for this? On a busy Saturday afternoon, in broad daylight, not one person in Tesco's car park in Formby, where she claims to have been abducted, saw anything amiss. Nothing untoward was recorded on any of the CCTV cameras. The van in which she was apparently transported from the car park to the house in Bootle has never been found.' He allowed himself a sardonic smile. 'And it will not surprise you to know that the defendant has been unable to supply the police with either the registration number or the make of vehicle.

'Neither, despite extensive police enquiries, has a mysterious second man been traced, a man who supposedly assisted the deceased in this mythical crime. In fact, the police have found no evidence whatsoever of anything remotely connected with a kidnapping, not even a ransom note.'

Jim and I exchanged concerned glances. Beaumont was putting forward a persuasive argument. He went on to offer his alternative scenario and I could see the jury lapping it up.

'Let me suggest to you what really happened that afternoon.'

Joanna, he declared, had bumped into Dewhurst in the car

park as she was putting her shopping in the car. Far from being a stranger to her, Dewhurst was an old acquaintance. He invited her to go with him to his house in Bootle. She willingly agreed, forgetting to lock her car, which was later broken into, so accounting for the missing shopping.

'He's thought of everything,' said Jim grimly.

According to Beaumont, some time after arriving at the house, Joanna and Dewhurst started to have sex, but something happened and a row broke out between them.

'Possibly,' mused Beaumont, 'Miss Smithson changed her mind.' He referred to a set of handcuffs that had been found at the scene and wondered whether the deceased had proposed something a little more adventurous, something perhaps a little kinky, and it had not been to Joanna's liking. 'Though hardly a reason to murder him,' he added. 'She could have just said no.'

'Very clever,' whispered Jim wryly. 'Joanna's only piece of evidence to back up her kidnap claim and he turns it into a bondage session.'

I agreed. Beaumont was good. I'd observed his constant use of emotive words like 'kill' and 'murder', which all helped bolster unfavourable images in the minds of the jurors.

'Or maybe they just had a tiff about some trifling matter. Whatever the reason,' Beaumont continued, 'the row escalated, there was a struggle, she was angry, she grabbed the nearest heavy object, a paperweight, and hit him with it as hard as she could.' His voice speeded in a crescendo then boomed out the final words. *'Hard enough to kill him.'*

A gasp ran through the public gallery. I could imagine Quentin Beaumont on the stage of the National Theatre playing King Lear, but then, barristers and actors have much in common.

'I put it to you that the whole episode of the kidnapping is a fabrication, concocted by the defendant for one good reason.' He paused for effect. 'To justify her heinous deed. Imagine the scene. Her lover is lying on the floor, dead, and by her own hand. It doesn't require a genius to realise that protecting yourself against someone who was trying to harm you seems a little less wicked than viciously killing them during an argument. It also has the extra benefit of making a plea of self-defence more plausible.'

'What about having her head shaved?' whispered Jim. 'Are they saying she did that herself?'

Beaumont might almost have heard him. 'And now we come to the crowning act of deceit. To make her unlikely story more believable, she cuts off her own hair and claims it was done by her "assailants". As you can see for yourselves, her new look is not so out of keeping with her general appearance that it would cause her much hardship.'

He gesticulated to the ring in Joanna's nose and the tattoo on her left shoulder. The defence counsel jumped to his feet to object but the point had been made.

'She then phones her father and tells him what has happened.'

Beaumont contended that Leonard Smithson agreed to go along with his daughter's fake story, even to the extent of involving a reputable firm of enquiry agents who would act as witnesses to substantiate his account of events.

'Making us out to be stooges,' seethed Jim.

The one piece of physical 'proof' of Joanna's capture, the e-mail photo of her shaven head, was taken later, Beaumont declared, by Smithson himself and printed out on his own printer.

The prosecution called only one witness. Detective Inspector Clive Ormesher, in his role as arresting officer and later interviewing officer, told the court how he arrived at the scene of the crime and found the body of Anthony Dewhurst in an upstairs room.

'And the defendant was on the premises?'

'Yes. It was she who summoned the police.'

'And did she admit to killing the deceased?'

'She said she'd been forcibly taken to the house by

41

two men and—' but Beaumont was not prepared to let him finish.

'Just answer the question please, Inspector. Did the defendant admit to killing Anthony Dewhurst.'

'Yes.'

'I believe you made rigorous efforts to trace this second man that the defendant maintains abducted her?'

'We did.'

'And what was the result of these efforts?'

'We could not trace him, sir.'

'Thank you, Inspector. That will be all.'

He sat down and Joanna's barrister, Ifor Jones, stood up. I wasn't impressed. He was an ascetic-looking man with small wire-framed glasses beneath his grey wig and he had a nervous stammer, which didn't inspire confidence.

'Inspector, did Miss Smithson tell you why she attacked Mr Dewhurst?'

Ormesher looked relieved that he was being given his chance to speak and he proceeded to put forward Joanna's account of events as detailed in her statement.

Unfortunately, however, his efforts were doomed to failure, simply because Beaumont had got there before him and scathingly pre-empted everything he said. By the looks on their faces, I could see that most of the jurors thought the same.

No more witnesses were called after Ormesher. A statement from Dr Vivian Crabtree, the pathologist, confirmed that Tony Dewhurst had died around 19.00 hours from the blow to the head from the paperweight.

At which point, proceedings were adjourned until the following day.

'What do you reckon then, so far?' asked Jim. We were walking up Castle Street on our way back to the office.

'Pretty horrendous, wasn't it?'

'Beaumont's a clever sod. Dismissing the kidnapping as an accepted fact then offering a plausible alternative.'

'What do you think happened to the van?' I said. 'The one they took Joanna to the house in?'

'I reckon the second man took it away, along with the laptop they used to send the e-mail plus whatever weapon they used when they grabbed her in the car park. Getting rid of all the evidence in one go.'

'Except for the handcuffs.'

'And he even turned them to his advantage.'

It didn't ring true to me. 'But wait a minute. There was no vehicle outside the house when the police arrived and Joanna's car was still at Tesco's – so how are the prosecution going to explain how Joanna and Dewhurst got to the house?'

'Taxi, maybe? Don't forget, they're saying she went with him willingly.'

'I suppose. Funny the CCTV cameras saw nothing.'

'Not really,' said Jim. 'They can't be everywhere at once and she had parked at a remote spot, apparently to keep her car in the shade.'

'The big hole in the prosecution case,' I said, 'is the time element. Smithson rang you just before six, we met him at the office within the hour and Joanna called just after seven. If we can prove Dewhurst didn't die until at least seven, and we know he didn't, then the prosecution case collapses.'

'Their interpretation may collapse,' Jim warned, 'but not the whole case. At the end of the day, don't forget, she did kill the man. The defence, of course, will say she was forced to kill him to save her own life but it's really about how much doubt the prosecution can implant in the jurors' minds. If Beaumont can convince them she killed Dewhurst in anger rather than self-defence, they could go for murder although manslaughter is more likely to stick.'

'Surely she'll be found not guilty anyway?'

'Like I say, it depends on the jury and what they believe. I mean, who'd ever have thought that a middle-aged lady schoolteacher would be in the dock for slapping a pupil who was attacking her? Not a young child, either, but a teenage youth who they conceded was violent. Yet that's in all the papers today. What's more, she was found guilty! Can you believe it? These are strange times we're living in, Johnny. The roles of criminal and victim are being reversed.'

Roly was waiting for us at the office. 'Not much else we can do today,' I said. 'He needs some exercise so I think I'll walk him to the radio station.' I liked to get to the studio in good time.

'Before you go,' said Jim, 'I want to ask you a favour.'

I didn't like his tone. 'Oh yes?' I said guardedly.

'We've got a gig on Sunday night and the drummer can't make it. I wondered if you'd stand in.'

Jim has reformed his old group, The Chocolate Lavatory, which had been one of 300 or so unknown Merseybeat bands playing around Liverpool in the 1960s. Unsurprisingly, in view of their lack of musical prowess, they remained unknown until they split up a few years later and that should have been that. However, in the late 1980s, a few of the old groups got back together to play for the Merseycats charity organisation and, suddenly, it seemed every ageing, balding ex-musician was digging his guitar out of the loft and going back on the road.

I'd long ago sold my drum kit that I'd had from my days with The Cruzads so I had a readymade excuse to decline but Jim was ready for that.

'You can borrow Pete's kit, of course.'

'Where are you playing?'

'The police club in Fairfield, where else? Nice little venue.' It would be for Jim. All his old colleagues would be in there to cheer him on. 'We're doing a few country numbers these days, more suited to our age group. I wouldn't ask, Johnny, but we're desperate. Can't let the guy down.'

'I'll think about it.'

'Well hurry up, it's Monday today, it's only six days off.'

Ken, my producer, collared me at the radio station. There'd

been some reaction to the previous night's phone-in when a listener had suggested a public stoning of serial killer Dr Harold Shipman. 'They could charge a pound to throw a stone, the proceeds to go to the victims' families,' she enthused. 'Preferably using small stones.'

More money and a slower death. Is it me or are women getting more aggressive these days?

'You shouldn't let them say those things on the air,' grumbled Ken. 'It stirs up an unhealthy bloodlust amongst the public.'

I played a track from Bill Wyman's Rhythm Kings new CD, *Hole in the Wall*. Bill told Spencer Leigh that a lot of the old blues joints in the 1940s and 1950s were referred to as 'holes in the wall'. I put on Amos Milburn's 'Chicken Shack Boogie' (1948) next, which proved his point. You can't beat the old R & B singles or 'race records' as they were called at the time. They were the sounds that fuelled the 1960s British Beat boom.

The show over, I drove across to Blundellsands where Maria had a meal waiting for me. Victoria was in bed asleep. I went up to see her lying in her cot, eyes tightly shut and her tiny left thumb tucked between her lips.

'She's got your smile,' said Maria, coming up behind me. 'God help the boys when she's older. Talk about putty in her hands.'

'My smile, eh? Didn't work with you though, did it? When were you ever putty in my hands?' I grinned and put my arms around her.

Things had been pretty good between us lately. I stayed over at hers most nights and I hadn't seen Hilary for more than a month.

But that was shortly about to change.

Back in February, I'd promised to take Hil to the Summer Pops Legends of Rock'n'Roll concert at the Kings Dock, just two days from now. Luckily, Maria wasn't a big Jerry Lee Lewis fan so she was quite happy for me to go, as she thought, on my own. But I'd already given Hilary the tickets to keep hold of, which meant I couldn't change my mind.

Although Maria had accepted that I would still see Hilary occasionally, her name had not been mentioned for a long time. Perhaps she assumed I'd given her up. In which case, it didn't seem prudent to mention I was taking her to the concert, however innocent it might be.

'How did the trial go?' Maria asked as we went back downstairs to eat our meal. Maria had made coq au vin with spinach and cauliflower cheese.

'Not good. The prosecution ridiculed the notion that Joanna was kidnapped. They're trying to make out she went with Dewhurst of her own free will for an afternoon of passion.'

'You're joking?'

'No. Then they say the two of them had a row and Joanna clobbered him with the paperweight. In other words, the only thing the jury has to decide is did she actually mean to kill him or was she only intending to hurt him? Murder or manslaughter.'

'But that's preposterous.' Maria knew all about the case. 'What about the abandoned car and the other man?'

'All bollocks, no proof. They even claimed she shaved her own hair off to fool them.'

'Surely not? As if any girl would do that.'

'The trouble was, Joanna has tattoos and a ring through her nose.'

'What's that got to do with it? So do most young girls nowadays.'

'I know, but to the older generation it smacks of punk rock and The Sex Pistols. The prosecuting counsel made Joanna out to be a female Sid Vicious. Remember, judges live on another planet. They ought to be made to spend a week on a sink estate to see how real people live.'

'You said that on the radio once.' Maria always listens to my show.

'And I still say it. What made it even worse, Joanna's hair

hasn't grown back properly yet and it looks spiky which didn't help. Again, part of the image.'

'I just hope the defence counsel's good then.'

So did I. I didn't like to think of the outcome if he wasn't.

Chapter Eight

The Crown Court was crowded when Jim and I arrived the next morning. Not surprisingly, it was a trial that had aroused an enormous amount of public interest. The press was there in force.

Leonard Smithson joined us in the vestibule. He was looking haggard. The strain of his daughter's imprisonment and the trial had obviously got to him. After introducing his wife Brenda, an older version of Joanna with a lined, anxious face, he took us to one side. 'I can't help thinking there's something behind all this,' he said to Jim. 'More than just the kidnapping and Nirvana, I mean.'

'Like what?'

'I reckon this is a personal vendetta against me. Take this court case. It's nothing more than a persecution of Joanna.'

'That's the police,' I broke in, 'not Mottram. Mottram can hardly have planned for her to kill Dewhurst.'

'I suppose not.' But Smithson looked doubtful.

'You're getting paranoid,' Jim said sympathetically. 'Look, by the weekend, Lennie, this should all be over. Joanna will be free and you can take the family on holiday and forget the whole thing.'

Smithson seemed appeased by this but it wouldn't have reassured me. Whenever people start uttering platitudes of the 'don't worry, everything will be all right' variety, that's when I really start to get frightened.

Maybe Smithson was right. Maybe money wasn't behind

this. But if that was so, then whom had he upset? And what would they do to him next?

I hadn't time for any more speculation. The usher called us into court and the trial recommenced.

Ifor Jones opened his case for the defence and he put it succinctly and accurately. He named Mottram as the instigator behind the kidnapping, he told about the contract to buy Nirvana at an inappropriate price and the threatening phone call followed by the horrific e-mail photo of Joanna. He explained how Smithson had called on the services of Ace Investigations and described the scene that awaited us in Bootle when we arrived in response to Joanna's frantic phone call.

His big mistake was to call as a witness Joanna's boyfriend, Christopher Melia, the boy known as Toff. Jones's intention, which was perfectly laudable, was to show that Joanna would never have agreed to go willingly to the house with Dewhurst because she was faithful to Toff, thus discrediting Beaumont's sexual scenario. The snag was, Toff didn't make the ideal witness.

He shambled into the court wearing a T-shirt, jeans and a thin black jacket, a nervous expression on his face.

Ifor Jones did no more than ask him how long he'd been taking Joanna out, but that was enough.

'Six months.'

'And was it an exclusive arrangement?'

'Pardon?'

'Neither of you went out with anybody else?'

'Well, I didn't.'

'What about Joanna?'

'Not as far as I know.'

'As far as he knows!' snorted Jim. 'That's blown it.'

He was right. The inarticulate youth had no chance against Beaumont. The prosecuting barrister rose to his feet and smiled. I was reminded of the wolf in *The Three Little Pigs*.

'How old are you, son?' he began.

'Twenty-one,' Toff mumbled.

49

'Please speak up, the court can't hear you.'

'Twenty-one.'

Beaumont changed his tone to one of quiet admiration. 'Twenty-one, eh? The world at your feet. Tell me, you look like a man who's been around a bit, a man of the world.'

Toff blushed and said he wouldn't have said that.

'Come now, you're too modest. You've had a few girlfriends in your time, I'm sure.'

The young lad stood a little straighter and preened himself. 'I wouldn't say that,' he repeated but with less conviction.

'And with your undoubted experience of women, you will know that a lady does not always say what she means, does she?'

Toff looked puzzled. He wasn't sure where this was leading. 'In what way?'

'Well, let us say one of your girlfriends has met another young man who asks her out. She's flattered and intrigued. She'd like to go but, at the same time, she doesn't want to upset you. On the other hand, maybe she feels it would do no harm to go for a drink with him. So she agrees to meet him one evening when she knows she is not seeing you, just for an innocent drink, nothing more. And then, you ring up to say you have tickets for a film. She panics and says she can't go, she is washing her hair. That's what women always say, isn't it?' He smiled sympathetically as if this was something that often happened to men of the world like them. 'You can see that happening, can't you, Mr Melia?'

Toff looked bemused at this long speech. 'I suppose so,' he faltered.

'Of course, it doesn't mean she's done anything improper, far from it. In fact, once she's with him, she probably realises her mistake and can't wait to get back to you.'

He paused. Everyone in the court except Toff sat waiting for the punch line. They didn't have to wait long.

'So if Miss Smithson told you she couldn't see you one evening, she was washing her hair, it would not be beyond the bounds of possibility that she had a casual date with another man? *Would it?'* He barked the last two words.

'I suppose not.'

Beaumont smiled triumphantly. 'I put it to you, Mr Melia, that on the day in question, Miss Smithson had arranged to meet the unfortunate Mr Dewhurst, for whatever reason,' his lowered tones suggested it was for more than the odd gin and tonic, 'and had decided not to apprise you of the fact. As you yourself have just said, you do suppose such a thing could happen.'

And before Toff could reply, Beaumont rapidly turned to the bench. 'That's all the questions for this witness, m'lord.'

'Just as I predicted,' Jim Burroughs whispered to me. 'Shit all over him and he's supposed to be a bloody defence witness!'

'What amazes me is how an intelligent, good-looking girl like Joanna could go out with a dickhead like that but it always happens, doesn't it? It's the ugly fellas what get the babes.'

'They should never have put him in the box,' Jim said gloomily. 'I hope Smithson does better than that.'

But he didn't. He was all right when Jones led him into all the correct answers but when Beaumont cross-examined him and cast doubt on the veracity of his statements, he lost his cool. He raved on about Mottram trying to swindle him out of Nirvana and kept referring to the threatening phone calls. All things he was unable to prove.

This fiasco lasted until one o'clock when the judge decided to knock off for the day.

'He'll be due on the squash court at three,' guessed Jim, who was used to the vagaries of the Crown Court. 'Let's have some lunch.'

'We'll pick up the dog first,' I said. We'd left Roly at the office. 'Then we'll go to Margie's.'

We went over to Cavern Walks and took an outside table at Lucy in the Sky. Roly sat on the floor beside us looking across at the statue of The Beatles which he probably regarded as an improved version of a lamp-post.

'Hi, Johnny. You know, that baby of yours is looking more like you every day,' said Margie, coming out to take our order. 'Hello, Jim.'

'When did you see her?'

'Maria was in with her last week.'

'She didn't mention it.'

Margie leaned forward conspiratorially. 'And Hilary was in yesterday.'

'Oh.'

'Said she was going with you to this rock'n'roll show at the Kings Dock.'

'That's right, tomorrow night.'

'I take it Maria doesn't know?' I said nothing but Margie is good at reading faces. 'I thought not. Be careful, Johnny.'

'Don't worry, Margie, I know what I'm doing,' I said hopefully.

Jim looked skywards and rolled his eyes. He's always tried not to get involved in my complicated love-life but it's not that easy for him, with Maria and Hilary both quite likely to call the office at any time. Jim's motto has always been to say, 'He's out, I don't know where, who with or when he'll be back,' and hope for the best.

I settled on a curried chicken baked potato and Jim went for the soup and a sandwich. 'Any chance of a bowl of water for Roly?' I asked.

'You should have told me you were bringing him,' smiled Margie. 'I'd have brought him some Pedigree Chum.'

'Just as well you didn't. He'll only touch Chappie.'

In the end, Margie produced the water and a large plate of scraps. 'Maria was telling me about her new hobby,' she said, 'now she's only working part-time.'

'I've not heard about this,' said Jim. 'What does she do?'

'Makes greetings cards,' I told him.

She'd first started when she was pregnant. Using various

materials such as fabrics, feathers, photographs and dried flowers, she made up the cards and inscribed them with the appropriate messages.

She found she was rather good at it and a friend of hers who had a small craft and gift shop had taken a few to try and sell. They'd proved very popular and she sold some more to other, similar shops until she now had enough orders to almost start a business.

'It's not as hard as it looks,' she said, when she proudly showed me her first finished attempts. 'I buy the cards and packaging ready done and use stamps for the various inscriptions like Happy Birthday. All I do is sew on the material, stick on the photo or whatever and paint the design.'

I was no expert but it didn't look easy to me. I wouldn't have had the patience.

'Good for her,' said Margie. 'She's a bright girl, that.'

'I might as well go back to the office,' said Jim, when we'd finished eating. 'Catch up on some paperwork. What about you?'

'I think I'll take a trip to Garston to see this Wally Tennant fellow, the ex-Wavertree Corinthian that Nobby Wharton told me about. He used to have a plumbing business there and apparently it's still going strong.'

'Good idea.'

'Well, it is the only case we've got at the moment.'

'And we've been on it for nearly three weeks now too. I thought this would have been an easy one, Johnny.'

But finding David Blease was to prove anything but easy. Worse still, it was going to turn out to be highly dangerous.

Chapter Nine

'I'll take the train to Garston,' I said. Like everywhere else, driving in the city had become almost impossible. Apart from the exorbitant parking costs, one-way streets were forever being changed round and most days it was fume-laden queues in every direction. Why did other drivers never turn their engines off when they were stuck for long periods in traffic?

I'd toyed with the idea of buying a scooter but the twin disadvantages of cumbersome helmets and inclement weather dissuaded me.

Jim pointed at Roly, dozing quietly under the table, replete with food. 'That dog needs exercise. You'd better take it with you.'

'Walk,' I called and Roly leapt up like a demented ballet dancer, furiously wagging his brown stump. I put on his lead and, leaving Jim some money to pay the bill, we made our way to Moorfields Station to pick up the Underground to Garston.

The train journey took only fifteen minutes. We walked from the station towards the centre and it wasn't long before I located Tennant & Son, plumbers. The lady at the Post Office directed me to a cobbled entry in one of the side streets off St Mary Road.

A notice *Trade* hung over the office door. I knocked and went in. A man in a brown overall and with a battered trilby perched on the back of his head was leaning across the counter.

He looked about fifty. He was reading a copy of the *Mirror* and drawing on a hand-rolled cigarette through a gap in his teeth. Behind him, rows of pipes and fittings were piled haphazardly on crowded wooden shelves.

'I'm looking for Wally Tennant,' I said.

'You've found him, son. Who's asking?' He spoke with a Yorkshire accent which somewhat threw me. When I queried it he told me he'd come to Liverpool from Huddersfield when he was an apprentice and he'd stayed. 'It's a city you get sucked into,' he said by way of explanation.

'You used to play football for Wavertree Corinthians?'

'Might have done.'

'I'm trying to trace a man called David Blease, known as Digger – used to play in goal. I was told he was a friend of yours.'

'Might have been.' I handed him one of the Ace Investigations business cards. He studied it for a minute then looked up interestedly. 'Are you the fellow on the wireless?'

I admitted I was.

'When are you going to play some Eddie Cochran records?' Another old rocker. I wondered if he'd ever been to the Masquerade of a Saturday night.

'There's a new CD due out on Rockstar of his old Saturday Club shows with Joe Brown playing guitar. I've got a demo copy so I'll play a track for you tonight.'

That seemed to loosen his tongue. 'Digger Blease, you say. Yes, of course I remember him. We knocked around together for a bit.'

'Do you know where he is now?'

'You're the second person to ask me that in six months.'

'Norris Pond being the other?'

'That's right. Yon said he were writing a book on the team, though who in hell's name'd want to read it beats me.'

'What did you tell him?'

'Same as I'll tell thee. I've not seen Digger since 1979.

I went on holiday for a week and when I came back he'd upped and gone.'

'Do you know why?'

'Not a clue.'

'I heard a story about some jealous husband chasing him.'

Wally Tennant gave a throaty laugh. 'Shouldn't be surprised. He liked a bit of skirt, did Digger.'

'But you'd not heard the story?'

'Which one? Digger was always chasing married women. They were less demanding, he said. They didn't want fancy dinners, they daren't be seen out in public for a start, and they weren't expecting to move in with you after the second date. No, they were there after the same thing as Digger, a bit of nooky on the side, and that suited him fine.'

Until the husband caught up with him, I thought. 'This one was supposed to be from Childwall. Apparently, her husband found out and Digger left town pretty smartish.'

'Sounds about right.' Only he pronounced it reet.

'Without a word to his best mate? Didn't you think it was odd? Surely he'd have confided in you about this woman?'

'Why? Like I say, he had women all over. We were fancy free, out for a good time, come day go day and all that.'

'How long were you mates?' I asked.

'I knocked around with him for about eighteen months. We'd do the clubs in town. The Chequers, the Four Winds and the Pyramid were favourite. We'd get blathered most nights, pull a few birds, like you do.'

I nodded understandingly. It was pretty well the same as today. Birds and booze still seemed to be the staple diet of a footballer's life. Nothing had changed other than the names of the clubs and the price of the beer, except today's lucky players now made as much in a week as their predecessors did in a year.

Looking at Tennant now, with his dated headgear, gloomy

countenance and bad teeth, it was hard to imagine he'd once been a playboy.

'Had he no relatives? What about his wife?'

'She'd already left him when I knew him and his folks were dead although I believe he had an uncle living in Ormskirk.'

'Was his name Blease as well?'

'Could have been.' He threw the dog end of his cigarette on to the floor and swivelled his foot over it to extinguish the burning ashes. 'Digger just referred to him as Uncle Arthur.'

'Did you tell Norris Pond about him?'

'I don't believe it came up.'

'You'd no idea where his wife was?'

'Not a clue. He never spoke about her other than to say he'd once been wed. He were on his own when he joined the Corinthians.'

'Did he have any children?'

'If he had he didn't tell me.'

'Had he always lived in Liverpool?'

'As far as I know he had. He spoke wi' a Liverpool accent.'

'And you never heard from him again? No letters or phone calls?'

'Nope.' He looked hard at me. 'What's he done to have all these people after him?'

'Only one person,' I said. 'Norris Pond hired me to find him to complete his book.'

'I don't believe it,' said Wally Tennant. 'No one'd go to all this trouble just for a book, especially one that no bugger'll read anyhow.'

'You don't reckon?'

'Nay, lad. Yon's got some ulterior motive, you mark my words.'

He had nothing much else to tell me. I thanked him and wandered back towards the station. There were still a couple of hours to go before I was due to present the show so I walked over the bridge to Long Lane and let Roly have a run on the field before calling in for a cup of tea at Ann's Café.

'It's a while since you've been in these parts, Johnny,' said the waitress. 'What's on?'

'I've been looking for a plumber, Paula, and I found him.'

'Oh yeah?' She put a saucer of milk down for Roly. 'Still as ugly as ever, isn't he?' she said, but she stroked him anyway.

I thought about what Wally Tennant had said. Norris Pond had paid me £250 to look for David Blease. Was it feasible that he would fork out that sort of money just to add what must be only a brief paragraph in his book? After all, Blease had only stayed at the club a few months.

I began to wonder if Wally Tennant was right. Did Norris Pond have a secret agenda? Could there be a more sinister reason why he was so anxious to get hold of David Blease? And what did he intend doing if I managed to find him?

The trains ran every fifteen minutes so I didn't have a long wait on the platform. I got off at Central and walked over to the radio station.

'Do you have to bring that mutt into the studio?' complained Ken. 'What if it barks when you're on air?'

'I see what you mean, Ken. He'll be entitled to a perform-ance fee. Good thinking. I'll put in a chit.'

I played a track from Hank Williams III's great new album. He's the grandson of *the* Hank Williams and he started out as a punk rocker but is now trying to put the country back into country music. Very anti-establishment. I also played a couple of the Eddie Cochran tracks that I'd promised Wally Tennant.

After the show, I went straight round to Maria's.

'How'd it go today?' she asked. She'd cooked salmon fillets in tarragon sauce with sauté potatoes. A bottle of Muscadet was on the table.

'Pretty awful again.' I outlined the events in court. 'Tomorrow's the big day,' I told her. 'Jim and I are due to give our evidence.'

'Oh, what a shame. I'm at the Library all day otherwise I'd have come and sat in the public gallery and given you my support.'

I smiled. 'I don't think Victoria would be so keen.'

'You'll have to tell me all about it when you get home.'

The words hit me. 'It's Wednesday tomorrow,' I reminded her. 'I'm at this rock'n'roll concert at night, remember, but I'll ring you before I do the show.'

I couldn't think of a way of mentioning Hilary without precipitating what the politicians describe as a 'meaningful discussion' so I said nothing.

'How do you think it'll go?' she asked. 'The trial, I mean.'

'I can't believe she won't get off, whatever Jim Burroughs fears. I think this time element will save her, the fact that we already knew about the kidnapping before Dewhurst was dead. They might not have taken Smithson's word for that but they'd have to take ours. Apart from our professional integrity and all that, we've no ulterior motive to lie.'

'Money? A payoff from Smithson?'

I shook my head. 'It would never stand up.' I couldn't believe it would even be considered, although everything else in the trial seemed to be going the prosecution's way.

We watched a re-run of *The Royle Family* on Sky and a couple of old episodes of *The Bill*, disturbed only once by Victoria crying. Just as we were thinking of going to bed at eleven, Maria's phone rang.

'For you, Johnny.' She handed me the receiver. It was Geoffrey.

'I thought I might catch you there, boss.' Geoffrey Molloy is the property manager who looks after the day-to-day running of my flats. 'Why do you never switch your bloody mobile on?'

I'd reluctantly bought myself a mobile phone when I realised that the job necessitated me being contactable at all times, not to mention its importance in emergencies.

'Sorry, Geoff. I left it in the car. What's up?'

'The police have just been on the phone. It's Miss Patel from the house in Kirkdale. She's been attacked. She's in intensive care. The house has been smashed up.'

Chapter Ten

Shani Patel lived in a terraced house that I'd come across a while ago during a case involving a tenant who was found hanged in one of my flats. The old lady who lived in the house, Violet Parker, died and, shortly afterwards, the empty house became the site of a violent gun battle.

Some time later, when the dust had cleared, I'd managed to buy it at a good price and, after suitable renovation, I'd let it to Miss Patel who was nineteen and a trainee nurse at Fazakerley Hospital.

Usually I'd expect someone like her to be sharing, to help with the rent, but I got the feeling her family were subsidising her. Asian families usually look out for each other.

'Where are you now, Geoff?'

'At home, I'm just going over there now.' Geoff lives in Aintree with his mother, only a short drive away.

'I'll meet you there in ten minutes.'

I quickly explained to Maria what had happened then raced over to Kirkdale. On the way, I rang Jim from my mobile and suggested he might like to come down. Geoff had arrived seconds before me and was talking to two police constables.

'Here comes the owner now,' he said.

'Mr Ace?' The taller of the two officers stepped forward.

'Yes. How's the girl?' was my first question.

'She's alive but badly hurt. The paramedics have taken her to hospital. She'd recovered consciousness before she was put

61

in the ambulance. Funny thing is, it doesn't look like anything was taken. Her handbag, with her keys and credit cards and money, was still there on the hall table.'

'It appears to have been a racist attack,' ventured his colleague. 'They've daubed slogans all over the walls.'

The slogans identified the intruders as members of a group calling themselves Auschwitz 101 and were full of execrable references to immigrants and coloured people, 'Pakis' in particular.

'Actually she's from Delhi,' I said, 'not that it would have made any difference. I'm going to have a look round.' Geoff followed me up the stairs.

'I wonder if they'd refuse to let an Indian surgeon save their mother's life?' I mused, as we walked round the vandalised rooms, calculating the cost of the damage. The upstairs toilet was hanging through the kitchen ceiling, the bath had been smashed and the taps left running, creating a flood in the kitchen, which had spread to most of the downstairs rooms.

Shani's television was destroyed and her books and papers lay scattered round the lounge.

'These bastards are sick,' said Geoffrey angrily as he took it all in.

I agreed. 'How can they have that much hate in them for no logical reason? I mean, what does it matter what bloody colour people are?'

I could imagine how James Brown or Little Richard must have felt, growing up in Macon, Georgia after the war. Ku Klux Klan, Southern rednecks, neo-Nazis, where was the difference?

'I'll need to get a loss adjuster in before we start any work and I'll have to find somewhere to put Miss Patel. How long did they say she'd be in hospital?'

'A while, I think, boss. No visitors tomorrow, I was told, apart from her family. The bastards have given her a right battering.'

Jim Burroughs was just arriving as we returned to the hallway.

'So much for a decent night's sleep,' he grumbled, then he saw the state of the building. 'Christ, what a mess! Who the hell's done this?'

'According to the signs painted all around the walls, some lowlifes calling themselves Auschwitz 101.'

'Why this house?'

'Because the girl who lives here is Asian, that's why. Just have a walk round, Jim, and read some of their filth. I take this personally, I can tell you. I'm going to find the gang who've done this and I shall make them sorry.'

Jim shot me a warning look. 'Lynching's not very PC these days, Johnny.'

'I'm not a PC person, Jim.'

'Even so, taking the law into your own hands doesn't help. Look what happened to Joanna Smithson.'

The two police constables came over, having completed their notes of the damage. One of them handed me a piece of paper informing me I'd become a Victim of Crime and was eligible for counselling.

I tore it up in front of him.

'When I find these bastards, they'll need more than counselling,' I informed them. Jim took a white tablet from his pocket and put it under his tongue. He's not been so good at handling stress since his heart attack but at least he's given up smoking.

The policemen didn't reply but shuffled nervously back to their patrol car.

'I'll get Jack started on this in the morning, shall I, boss?' Jack heads my team of workmen.

'Get hold of the insurers first and find out what work we can get on with. Better ring a loss adjuster too, it could be a big job.'

'OK.' Geoff went off to his car leaving Jim and me standing at the door. 'Sorry for bringing you out, Jim, but I know you never go to bed before midnight and I thought you might want to see it for yourself. We've got to find the scum that did this.'

'We will, Johnny. Once this Smithson trial is out of the way, we can concentrate on this.'

Maria was waiting up for me. She was horrified at what had happened to Shani.

'That's terrible, Johnny. She's only a young girl, what harm did she ever do?'

'She's black,' I said. 'Or rather, brown. Harm enough for some people, it seems. Have you ever heard of this Auschwitz 101 outfit?'

She thought for a minute. 'No, can't say I have.'

'I'll look them up on the Internet tomorrow.'

'You'll be in court. I'm in work tomorrow so I'll have a look for you there.'

'Would you? Thanks.' I sighed. 'Here we go again. I can see I'm going to get involved in another case we won't get paid for.'

'Good job you've got the flats. You never seem to make much from the private eye game.'

'Good job Jim's got his pension. You can't say we're not busy at the office though, what with Joanna Smithson and the missing footballer and now this.'

We went up to bed. The baby was fast asleep in her cot in a corner of our room, Roly lying on the floor beside it. Since Victoria arrived, he'd assumed the role of her guardian and he now slept there, proudly, every night instead of on the bed as before.

'Doesn't he look majestic,' said Maria. 'Like those stone lions people in big houses have outside their gates.'

Next morning, I drove first thing to my property office in Aigburth Road where Geoffrey had already set the ball rolling with regards to repairs to the house.

'The insurance people are sending someone down this morning, boss,' he said, 'and I've fixed a meeting with the loss adjuster for tomorrow afternoon, if that's OK?'

I said it was.

'I've told Jack to get round this morning. He's going to type up an estimate for them and they said we can start any necessary work once they've had a look round.'

'Good work.' Geoffrey was indispensable although I'd never tell him so. 'These people last night, Geoff – Auschwitz 101 – you've never heard of them before, have you?'

'Never. I've heard of Combat 18 but I think they're mainly football hooligans.'

'I've got a vague idea, aren't they tied in with the National Front?' It was something I'd have to investigate. 'Either way, it seems to be a racist thing.'

'You'd better warn your friend Shirley in Princes Avenue then.'

'I never thought of that.' Shirley, however, was Afro-Caribbean black, not Asian. Would that protect her? 'Have you heard from her lately?'

'No. Her rent's always been paid on time though.'

'That's on a standing order, it'd go through whatever. I'd better call and see her later.'

But first I had an appointment in court.

'I'll leave Roly with you,' I told him, 'and get a bus into town.'

'Oh, thanks.' He didn't look thrilled at the prospect. He'd had unpleasant experiences with Roly before. I think one of them ended with his mother having to buy a new carpet.

Jim was at the Crown Court before me. 'This is it,' I said, looking around to see if there was anyone I recognised. 'Crunch time. What other defence witnesses are left apart from us?'

'Only Joanna herself.'

'Shit. I hope she's better than her father.'

'Or that pillock of a boyfriend.'

'Like I said, Jim – we've got that one thing Beaumont

can't talk his way out of, the fact we were on the case at six and Dewhurst was not dead until at least an hour later.'

And so it proved. Jim went up to the witness-stand first. Ifor Jones confirmed his identity as a private investigator and an ex-Detective Inspector of Merseyside Police.

'On Saturday March the eleventh, you were contacted by Mr Leonard Smithson in your professional capacity to investigate the disappearance of his daughter?'

'That's correct.'

'At what time was this?'

'He rang me just before six o'clock.' Jim said he was sure of the time because he was listening to the second reading of the football results on Radio Five Live's *Sports Report*. 'I agreed to meet him at my office in Dale Street.'

'And Mr Smithson arrived at your office at what time?'

'Shortly before seven and my partner, Mr Ace, followed him a minute or two afterwards.'

'And it was then, shortly before seven o'clock, that Mr Smithson showed you the photograph of his daughter with her head shaved?'

'Yes.'

'Up to which time Mr Dewhurst, according to the pathologist's statement, was alive and well. Were you present, Mr Burroughs, when Mr Smithson received a call from his daughter on his mobile phone?'

'Yes.'

'And what time would that have been?'

'The call was logged by the telephone company at 19.02.' Jim had done his homework.

Jim emphasised that Joanna said she'd been seized by two men in the car park at Tesco and taken in a van to this house in Bootle. One of the men had eventually left and she'd managed to overcome the other who was now lying unconscious.

'She gave you the address where she was held?'

'Yes. We drove straight there.'

'And when you arrived, what did you find?'

'We found the girl in a distressed state with her head shaven and, upstairs, the body of a man who was later identified as Anthony Dewhurst. We immediately got her to ring for the police and an ambulance. Their records show the time of her call to be 19.27.'

'A gap of twenty-five minutes since she phoned her father. Why did she not dial 999 in that time?'

'She was obviously in a state of shock and was waiting for her father to deal with everything.'

'Thank you, Mr Burroughs. That will be all.'

We waited for Quentin Beaumont to take his turn but, when he stood up, all he said was, 'I've no questions for this witness.'

'There's nothing he can contradict,' whispered Jim, 'and he's got nothing to gain.'

I went on the stand next and repeated pretty much the same story as Jim. Once again, Beaumont declined to cross-examine.

'That just leaves the girl,' murmured Jim. But to our surprise, Joanna Smithson did not appear. Ifor Jones announced that his client would be reserving her right to remain silent.

Being informed that no more witnesses were to be called, the judge promptly adjourned for an early lunch.

'That's a turn up,' I said, 'Joanna not giving evidence. Do you think that's wise?'

'Hard to say,' said Jim. 'The judge is allowed to speculate on whether, by refusing to be cross-examined, she is deliberately concealing evidence but you saw what a mess Smithson was in the box. Beaumont tore holes in nearly everything he said because Lennie couldn't prove any of it. The wilder his accusations got – Mottram, the threats, and so on – the more he played into Beaumont's hands. It'd be the same with Joanna. Like I said before, in the end it's all down to whether or not the jury think she killed Dewhurst out of self-defence or anger. Whatever went before will prove to be irrelevant at the final countdown.'

'"Final Countdown",' I said quickly. 'Europe, 1986.'

'I preferred "Rock the Night",' retorted Jim, 'although I was never that keen on the band. In fact, the whole of the 1980s was crap to my mind.'

His words didn't surprise me. Jim still lived in the 1960s in his head. If you asked him what he knew about Britney Spears he'd probably think they were medieval weapons.

We went to Richie's again for lunch, after which I rang the hospital from a call box outside the bus station. Shani Patel, they said, was comfortable, out of intensive care, and I could visit her tomorrow. She had concussion, a couple of broken ribs, cuts and bruises but was otherwise OK.

We were back in court at two and all Jim's predictions proved to be correct. Quentin Beaumont delivered his final speech for the prosecution and admitted there was a cloud of mystery surrounding the events of 11 March.

'We shall probably never know what really happened that afternoon in that house. We can only speculate. Maybe the defendant was abducted as she claimed,' he conceded, 'although no charges have been brought against any person in connection with this crime and not a scrap of evidence such as a ransom note has been produced. All we have had from the defence are Mr Smithson's wild and unsubstantiated claims against a man of previously good character, and much talk of a supposed "second man" – who has never been traced despite weeks of effort by the police.

'So, let us consider the alternatives. If Miss Smithson was *not* abducted, then did she perhaps indeed go happily along with Mr Dewhurst to his house, in anticipation of an afternoon's sexual pleasure, which later got out of hand with such tragic results?

'Miss Smithson, as is her right, declined to give evidence. However, both of the partners at the detective agency Ace Investigations were able to confirm the two things which ultimately matter in this case, namely that Miss Smithson and Mr Dewhurst were alone in that house and that Miss Smithson admitted to killing him.

'Those are *the irrefutable facts*. And, for whatever reason she committed this terrible crime, could that reason really justify taking this young man's life?'

He managed to rephrase these sentiments several more times before concluding with the recommendation that Joanna Smithson be found guilty of murder.

Ifor Jones's speech was much more low-key. His delivery was hesitant and almost apologetic in contrast to Beaumont's belligerent tone.

He was careful not to mention Mottram's name again but he emphasised that Leonard Smithson had sought the services of a detective agency because he believed his daughter to be in danger and events had proved him sadly right. He reiterated the significance of the time factor, that Smithson had called Jim Burroughs *an hour before* Dewhurst was killed, and wisely concentrated on the most important issue, the question of intent to kill.

'The defendant's only concern was to escape alive. Here was a young girl who was terrified. All her hair had been cut off and her head had been shaved.' He made no mention of the second antagonist. 'Who knows what would have been done to her next?' Only fear for her life, he asserted, had made her pick up the first weapon that came to hand, and hers was a desperate blow which had a fatal conclusion she had never sought.

He quoted from two recent cases that had ended in verdicts of not guilty on grounds of self-defence and pleaded with the jury to treat Joanna in the same way.

After he sat down, the judge declared he would be giving his summing up the following morning and the court rose at 3.30 p.m.

'Unless the jury procrastinate, we should have a verdict tomorrow,' said Jim.

'Do you think she'll get off?'

'I bloody hope so, but you can't tell with juries. I bet Lester Piggott never thought he'd go down.'

I wondered what the consequences would be if Joanna Smithson was found guilty.

Chapter Eleven

I took an 82 bus to the Aigburth Road office. Geoff had been to Kirkdale and sorted the insurance people and Jack had got the work under way.

'I'll be there for the loss adjuster tomorrow,' he promised.

Taking Roly with me, I drove over to my Princes Avenue house, let myself in through the front door, walked up to Shirley's flat and rang her bell.

'Who is it?' Her voice sounded sleepy.

'Your friendly landlord.'

'Johnny!' A squeal, then footsteps running to the door which was flung open. Shirley threw her arms round me. She was wearing a tiny white nightie over her ample black figure. 'I knew you'd come back for me one day. You're taking me home with you, right?'

For a moment, I was startled then she threw her head back and laughed. 'Only joking. Come on in, lover. How's the new baby – Victoria, isn't it? Geoff's told me all about her.'

'Fine.'

'And how's things with Maria?'

'Fine.'

She looked carefully at me then. 'And Hilary?'

'Haven't seen too much of her.'

'And does that upset you?'

'Sometimes. When I think about it. I try not to.'

'Funny, I was thinking about you last night. I was playing

that John Lennon tape you did for me. It's brilliant – and to think it's the only copy in the world.' She smoothed down her nightdress and went into the kitchen. 'So, Johnny, you didn't come over to seduce me and the rent's up to date so I'll make us both a cup of tea and you can tell me why you're really here.'

I settled into one of the huge armchairs. An Etta James album was playing in the bedroom and a heavy scent of patchouli hung in the air. Shirley had decorated the flat with a red and gold wallpaper so the whole effect was that of a bordello in the French Quarter of New Orleans rather than an apartment in Liverpool.

She brought in the tea and settled herself in the other armchair. She had put on a black and gold kimono over the nightdress. 'All right,' she said. 'Shoot.'

I told her about the attack on Shani Patel.

'That's terrible, Johnny, really awful. But why did you think it would affect me?'

'Because it seems to be a race thing.'

'I've had no trouble before and I've lived in this area for over twenty years.'

'Maybe that's why.' Toxteth's more multi-racial than Kirkdale or perhaps it was just because Shani Patel was Asian rather than black. Much of the graffiti scrawled on the walls had referred to 'Paki-bashing'. 'Have you ever heard of an organisation called Auschwitz 101?'

'Never. Who are they?'

'I don't know but they were the people who did this, according to the messages they left behind them.'

'Your friend Badger at Livingstone Drive might know.' Badger, alias Neville Mountbatten, lived in another of my flats and could accurately be described as being very streetwise. 'He's black too, isn't he? Maybe you ought to warn him as well.'

'Good idea.'

'I'll ask at the club tonight,' Shirley said. 'See if anyone there's heard of them.' Most of the punters at the Bamalama Club were black too.

My next stop was Livingstone Drive where Badger lived in the top-floor flat, but he too was unable to shed any light on Auschwitz 101.

'There's lots of gangs with weird names that follow the football clubs, man, most of them racist and tied in with the National Front, but I ain't heard of that one.' Badger wore a lime-green shirt and black leather trousers. The shirt blended nicely with the foliage around the flat, which was beginning to resemble a fernery. 'I tell you, man, these neo-Nazis are a growing force on the Continent and they're bad news.'

'Who would have thought it after the war?'

'Man's propensity for evil remains as strong as ever,' declared Badger, 'despite all the recent technological advances. Have you read any Colin Wilson?'

'*The Outsider.*'

'I was thinking more of his *Introduction to the New Existentialism.*' I knew that Badger had a degree in English Literature – I wasn't aware that he was a Philosophy Major as well. 'That puts forward his "peak experience" theory more fully.'

'You mean the one where people experience moments of great joy and insight?'

'That's it. They're usually attained through music, nature, religion, even sex. Wilson believes that man's survival depends on his ability to permanently raise his consciousness to that higher level. Otherwise we're doomed to continue on this animal level of violence and conflict.'

'Like Auschwitz 101,' I said, in an effort to get Badger off his soapbox. 'Odd that nobody's ever heard of them, isn't it? I thought people like that thrived on publicity.'

'Not necessarily. Perhaps they want to keep a low profile.'

'Yet they spray their name all over my property.'

Badger grinned. 'See what you mean, man.' He regrouped

his ideas. 'Perhaps they're new then, and looking to make a name for themselves. I'll ask around, if you like. Someone may know something.'

'Do that,' I told him.

'Hey, and play some decent dance music on that show of yours.'

I just had time to drop Roly off at my flat before I did the show. I put on a couple of Fatboy Slim tracks and did a trailer for the rock'n'roll concert due to start in one hour's time.

I was meeting Hilary there at a quarter to eight, which gave me just enough time to grab a sandwich in the station canteen and ring Maria.

'Nothing on Auschwitz 101,' she informed me. 'I spent half an hour searching the Net but I couldn't find any mention.'

'That's odd, isn't it?'

'They could have just formed,' said Maria. 'Or be a bunch of crazy local headbangers who are computer illiterate.'

'Could be. Thanks anyway,' I said. I felt guilty just talking to her.

'What happened in court?'

'It's nearly all over. Jim and I gave our evidence, Joanna elected not to speak for some reason, probably just as well, so it's a case of waiting for the judge's summing up and holding our breath to see what the jury decide.'

'And that'll be tomorrow?'

'Unless they take their time.'

'When will I see you?'

'Tomorrow night after the show.'

'Enjoy your concert tonight then.' Did I detect a note of sarcasm? Was she suspicious, or maybe forlorn? Or was I just imagining everything?

''Bye. Love to Victoria. See you tomorrow.' I put down the phone and wondered if my life had always been this complicated. I guessed it had.

Hilary was waiting when I got to the Kings Dock. I was ten

minutes late but the show hadn't started. The place was packed for what was billed as *The Last Ever British Appearance by the Legends of Rock'n'Roll*, as if the advertisers knew something we didn't.

Tomorrow night Elton John was performing and all the tickets for that were long gone.

'Sorry I'm late,' I said. 'Have you been here long?' She wore a kingfisher-blue top, black trousers and black wedges. Her blonde hair had been cut to shoulder length and she looked gorgeous.

'Just arrived.' My foreboding about the evening disappeared. It was a month since I'd seen Hilary, probably the longest gap in twenty years, but we carried on as if we'd never been apart. 'Come on, we'd better find our seats.'

Jerry Lee did ten songs, bang bang, one after the other, and was off and away. Little Richard shuffled on stage, resplendent in a gold lamé shirt and Barbara Cartland make-up. He looked like a cross between Liberace and Max Miller. Two men helped him to clamber arthritically on top of the piano where he stood blowing kisses to the audience for a full five minutes.

'I'm so glad to be in Liverpool,' he cried. 'At sixty-eight, I'm glad to be anywhere.' When he sang, backed by a fantastic tight New Orleans-style band, he was brilliant but, for me, he camped it up too much. If I'd wanted to see drag queens, I'd have gone to Funny Ladies in Blackpool.

Chuck Berry, at seventy-three, looked fittest of all but he stopped abruptly halfway through 'Havana Moon', confessing he'd forgotten the words. 'But at my age,' he smiled wickedly, 'I'm allowed to,' whereupon a Scouse voice bawled out from the audience, 'Not at sixty quid a fucking ticket you're not, pal.'

However, most of the people we spoke to afterwards seemed to have enjoyed it. Ed Jones from the Phil proclaimed it a great success and Spencer Leigh, who was seeing Chuck Berry for the first time, eulogised over the performances.

It just made me think that Buddy Holly had given up at the right time.

I'd seen Willie Nelson at the Phil the month before, I told them, and he'd sung thirty-seven songs, many of which he'd written himself, was on stage for a full two and a half hours and never felt the need to mention that he was sixty-seven.

'He's not inspired you to make a comeback, has he?' asked Ed, who had once played in The Tamsads, a group who in their glory days were billed above Cast and The Verve.

'Funnily enough, Jim Burroughs has asked me to stand in with The Chocolate Lavatory on Sunday,' I said and Spencer groaned at the thought.

'Ooh, I want to come,' cried Hilary. 'I've never seen you play in a band. That was before my time.'

'Take her,' urged Spencer. 'Why shouldn't she suffer too?'

I couldn't think up a suitable objection and I suppose I didn't want to.

'Let's go to the Masquerade,' suggested Hilary, after we left the others. She blinked her eyelids coquettishly. 'They're having a Christmas Party night tonight.'

'In July?'

'They say everyone has their parties in December and they all coincide with one another so Tommy thought he'd get his in early.'

Tommy seemed to have made the right decision. The place was heaving. Dolly, at the door, was dressed as a fairy godmother with glitter in her white hair and a sprig of mistletoe pinned to her silver tutu. Thankfully, I couldn't see her varicosed legs beneath the counter.

I asked Tommy if he'd heard of Auschwitz 101 but he hadn't. I told him about the attack on Shani Patel. 'Bastards,' he said. 'Let me know if you want any help when you find them.'

'If I find them.'

'I'll put the word out though,' he promised.

Behind the bar, Vince was struggling to cope. He was dressed in a red Father Christmas hat, with a bell over each ear and a white bobble on the top, a red eye-mask and a pair of red satin shorts with white fur round the legs. Nothing else.

A huge Christmas tree adorned with flashing coloured lights stood in the middle of the action and the DJ, sporting full Santa gear, was playing Gary Glitter's 'Rock'n'Roll Christmas' at full volume to a packed dance floor.

'It's ages since we were out together,' said Hilary, throwing her arms around me. 'Give me a kiss.'

We stayed until two, by which time both of us had consumed large quantities of Tommy's notorious punch which sceptics claimed was the accumulation of all the unfinished drinks drained from glasses collected during the evening, with the liberal addition of low-grade imported vodka smuggled in by Tommy from Eastern Europe.

'Can we go back to yours?' whispered Hilary in my ear. 'Only I'm on earlies tomorrow and it hardly seems worthwhile crossing the river.' Hilary lives in Heswall. 'We don't have to sleep together,' she added, seeing my hesitation.

I thought of Maria and Victoria and my promise. 'I don't know, Hil. It's a bit different now.'

'Oh, come on, Johnny. We've known each other for over twenty years. We'll always be the same, you and me. Best friends.'

But when we arrived at the flat, Hilary went straight into the bedroom and started undressing. 'I'll take the settee,' I said.

'Don't go for a minute.' She took off her bra and leaned forward, squeezing her elbows together, projecting her boobs forward. 'What song is this?'

Hilary and I have this game we've played for years where we do mimes and the other has to guess the song title. '"Temptation",' I said, with feeling.

She reached for me and started to gently lick my earlobe, teasing me with her tongue. I caught my breath. I tried to think of a good reason to make her stop but my eyes were glazing over and my mind was somehow out of synch.

'Well?' she whispered, pausing for a moment.

'I don't know. I give up.'

Slowly, she lay back, and pulled me on top of her.

'"I'm Yours",' she said. 'And I always will be, Johnny.'

Chapter Twelve

When I awoke, I was alone in the bed. I sat up sleepily and groped for my watch. It was eight o'clock. She'd left a note on the next pillow. *See you Sunday. My place??? Love, Hil xxxxxxxxxx.*

I forced myself up and staggered unsteadily to the bathroom. I felt a hundred years old and vowed never again to drink anything at the Masquerade that didn't come in a sealed bottle.

The hot water from the shower bit into my skin like liquid acupuncture. I turned up the pressure, as if to clean my soul as well as my body.

I was furious with myself for what had happened. Over the past decades, I'd had sex with Hilary hundreds of times, so what did one more time matter? But I knew it did. And it was too late to do anything about it.

There's a Willie Nelson/David Allen Coe song about a man who promises to be faithful, then allows himself to be seduced by a strange woman he spies across a bar. He says she was only a face in the crowd, but before he could tell her that he meant to be true, it was too late, he'd already cheated on her.'

I'd already cheated on Maria. Nothing could change that.

I towelled myself vigorously and went back into the bedroom to dress. Roly slunk across from his basket at the side of the bed. He knew better than to sleep on the bed when Hilary was in it. His eyes looked at me reproachfully and they say dogs aren't intelligent.

'You can have a morning in bed,' I told him. 'Make up for last night. I've got work to do.'

I couldn't face breakfast and I still wasn't fully compos mentis when I met Jim at the Crown Court.

'Christ, what's the matter with you?' he said.

'Don't ask.'

We went inside to hear the judge's summing up. In view of the enormous amount of public feeling for Joanna, I was expecting him to err on the side of sympathy to her but that was not the case.

He pointed out that although the defendant's claim that she was kidnapped could well account for the fact she was at the house with Dewhurst, in a distressed state with her hair cut off, there was only her word for this. There was no conclusive evidence to support it and the only witness was dead. And, by her admittance, at her own hand.

The police inspector had admitted that they had not been able to trace the so-called second man, and it was significant that the police were bringing no charges against Mr Harry Mottram despite the accusations made against him by the girl's father.

Similarly, the other reason offered by the prosecution for Joanna's presence at the house – that she was there for consensual sex with Dewhurst – was pure speculation, with again no tangible evidence to back it up.

The jury, therefore, could only come to a correct verdict by considering which was the *more likely* event to have taken place, because that would influence the defendant's intention at the moment she struck Dewhurst and it was that intention that was the essence of the case.

'You have four choices to make, members of the jury,' he concluded, 'when you consider your verdict. Guilty of murder; not guilty of murder but guilty of manslaughter; not guilty of murder but guilty of manslaughter by reason of provocation; or not guilty.'

He then reminded them that people were allowed to use

reasonable force to protect and defend themselves, if they believed themselves to be under attack.

'The crux of this matter here is, what was in the defendant's mind at the moment when she used the weapon? If you believe that she struck the deceased with the paperweight because she honestly thought it was necessary to save her own life, then you should deliver a verdict of not guilty.' He paused.

'However, if you believe it was used in retaliation or as part of a continuing struggle, and not in the total belief it was necessary to safeguard her life, then that use is unlawful. Even if the blow was an instinctive one and the defendant did not intend to inflict serious injury but merely to ward off attack, it was still unlawful as the risk of injury was there. In both of these circumstances, a verdict of manslaughter should be returned.'

The jury were then sent out to consider their verdict.

'We might as well go back to the office,' said Jim, as the court rose. 'They could be out for days.'

'Not the best summing-up,' I said. 'I thought he'd have been a lot more sympathetic to Joanna.'

'A man died,' Jim reminded me. 'They don't take that lightly.'

'What do you reckon her chances then? I must say, I never thought it would ever get to court, never mind this.'

'Lap of the gods,' said Jim. 'Could go either way.'

It was busy as we crossed Lord Street and walked up Castle Street. The *QE2* was making a rare trip to the Mersey and that had brought a lot of people into town. Crowds were something I could do without in my delicate state.

Back at the office, I took a glass of Andrews and wondered, as always, why they made the bubbles so noisy.

I then dug out the file on Wavertree Corinthians and went through Norris Pond's list again. Missing goalkeeper David Blease was our only official case and I was still miles away from solving it.

'Did you find anything on Auschwitz 101?' asked Jim.

'Maria had a look on the Internet at work but she couldn't find anything.' Mentioning Maria's name made me feel ill again. 'How about you?'

'Nobody at HQ's heard of them and there haven't been any other attacks reported. They could be a new outfit.'

'Or just a band of local hooligans.'

'I had a word with my old mate DI Mike Bennett, told him to put a few feelers out and see if anyone's heard anything.'

'I can't see them being national, although I suppose they could be a local branch of this Combat 18 that Geoff mentioned.'

Jim looked at me slyly. 'Probably disgruntled Everton supporters.'

'Any more of that and you can stick your gig on Sunday.'

'Forget I spoke.'

I carried on searching through Pond's list of names. 'I think I'll try this chap here, Mickey Coleman,' I said to Jim, picking one out at random. 'He played for the Corinthians at the same time as Digger Blease and he was about the same age.'

'Where's he live?'

'The phone number's St Helens. I'll give him a bell.'

Coleman's wife answered the phone. Mickey, she said, was at work. He was a fitter with British Gas. He'd been on an early shift and she was expecting him home at four. I was welcome to call round. She gave me an address near Thatto Heath. I remembered the area. I'd played Thatto Heath Labour Club with The Cruzads a lifetime ago.

'I'm going to call in at Kirkdale on the way,' I told Jim. 'See if any of the neighbours spotted anything when the house got smashed.'

I walked back to the flat to pick up Roly and took him for a walk along the Pier Head as far as the Maritime Museum and back, hoping the fresh air would clear my head. It helped. I made myself a tuna sandwich for lunch then spent an hour at the computer trying to find Auschwitz 101 for myself on the Net. There were references to Combat 18 and another outfit called White Wolves but I could find nothing at all alluding to the people who'd wrecked my house and beaten up Shani Patel.

Who were they? Where were they from? And why Shani?

I decided to drive over to Kirkdale on my way through to St Helens. A bunch of kids were playing in the street when I pulled up outside the house. I got out of the car and called one of them over. The rest followed.

'Have any of you lot heard of a gang called Auschwitz 101?'

They looked at one another and shook their heads. 'Are they supposed to be from round here?'

'Not sure. They could be.'

'Hey,' broke in an older boy. He looked about thirteen and wore the street uniform of cropped hair, combats, T-shirt and earring. 'Isn't that Roly?'

I'd forgotten that this was where I'd rescued Roly after his elderly owner had been taken into a nursing home. The old man's family had locked up the empty house and left his dog to fend for itself on the streets. The lad ran over to the car window from where Roly was peering. Roly licked his hand.

'Yeah, that's right.' They all crowded round to pay their respects to their former canine neighbour.

'You took him away, I remember. After that fella beat you up. Hiya, Roly.' He stroked the dog's head. Roly smiled with pleasure at the unexpected adulation. If he'd been a cat he would have purred.

'So what about Auschwitz 101 then?' I asked at last.

'Are they anything to do with the people what trashed that house?' asked one of the urchins who wore a last season replica Liverpool FC shirt.

'Probably. Did you see them?'

'No. It happened in the night.'

'But we heard about it,' said his friend. 'They killed some girl, didn't they?'

'They didn't actually kill her,' I said.

'It was no one from round here 'cos we'd've known if it was.' The others agreed.

'It wasn't kids,' ventured one of the lads. 'My dad said he'd heard it was a couple of heavies what done it.'

'Is that right?' I hadn't thought of the members of Auschwitz 101 as being anything but youths.

'What's happened to the girl then, mister?'

'She's in hospital.'

'Is she coming back?'

I hadn't considered that Shani Patel might not want to move back there but I realised now it must be a possibility.

'Maybe,' I said. I thanked the kids for their help and distributed a pocketful of coins for which they were excessively grateful.

'Thanks, mister, hope you catch the men. We'll watch out for them for you.' They ran off.

A couple of Jack's workmen were inside the house, making a start on the basic repairs. I went in and had a quick word with them. They were expecting Geoffrey shortly with the loss adjuster so I didn't hang around. My next stop was at Fazakerley Hospital.

Shani Patel was well enough to see visitors. Her face was swollen and bruised but she managed a smile.

'She was lucky,' said the nurse who took me up. 'One of the broken ribs just missed puncturing her lung.'

Shani had no idea who her attackers were. It seemed they'd worn balaclavas. They'd rung the front door bell and, when she answered it, forced her into the house, knocked her unconscious and proceeded to smash up the property.

I asked her if she'd heard of Auschwitz 101.

'That's what they painted on the walls, isn't it? The police asked me about them but it didn't mean anything to me.'

'Have you had any trouble of that sort before?' I asked cautiously. 'Race problems?'

'Is that what they think this is about? Because I'm Indian?'

'It's a possibility.'

'They didn't stop to look what colour I was, they just hit me.'

'Nobody's ever shouted racist things at you or anything like that? Kids playing around outside the house?'

'No.'

'The police tell me they didn't steal anything from you.'

'Nothing that I know of. All my credit cards are still in my bag with my money. It's weird, isn't it?' She looked at me and said, straight out, 'Have you thought that perhaps it's *you* they wanted to get at and not me?'

'Me? Why?'

'I don't know, but they didn't take anything of mine and it was your house they smashed up.'

'Then why attack you?'

'I was in the way. Perhaps they thought the house would be empty.'

I couldn't think of anyone that I'd recently crossed, which made the suggestion all the more disquieting.

'So you think all the racist stuff was a blind and I was the real target? In which case, why didn't the message say *Sod off Johnny Ace*?'

'I don't know, it was just a thought. Look, forget it. You're right, it probably is a racist thing. What's happening with the house?' she asked.

'My men are in there now repairing the damage but it's going to take a week or so. When do you expect to be out of here?'

'In a couple of days, but I can stay with my uncle for a little while until it's ready.'

'I didn't know you had any relatives over here.'

'Only my uncle. He has a newsagents in Smithdown Road.'

Shani gave me his phone number and I promised to let her

know when the house would be ready for her to return to. 'That is, if you still want to go back? I could always move you somewhere else if you're frightened of being on your own. Maybe a flat where there are other people around?'

'No, I'm OK there, really. You get used to trouble when you're a nurse. You should try working on a Casualty ward on a Saturday night.' It was the last thing I'd want. I'd already heard all the horror stories from Hilary. 'Anyway, I like it in my little house.'

'If you're sure. Do you need anything fetching?' I offered.

'Thanks all the same but I've still got my key. My uncle will run me over to pick up some clothes and things when I come out.'

'When do they say you'll be fit to go back to work?'

Shani laughed. 'This is the ward I usually work on, and it's very short-staffed. The sooner I get back, the better.'

'Too many pen-pushers in the NHS,' I said, 'and not enough nurses.'

'Tell that to the NHS Trust,' she smiled. 'We nurses already know.'

I gave her all my phone numbers and made her promise to ring me if she had any problems. Then I set off for Thatto Heath.

Mickey Coleman had been home five minutes when I arrived and was still wearing his blue work overalls. He turned out to be a fit-looking forty-six. Incredibly, he still played football but only for a local Sunday League side.

'I remember the Corinthians,' he said. 'I was only with them a few months but we had some good laughs. Crap team but nice fellas.'

'Do you remember David Blease?' I asked.

'The goalie? Yes, of course.' He smiled. 'A bugger for the women, he was. We were about the same age but I was already wed. He liked to go out boozing on the town, usually with Wally Tennant, another of the team.'

'But Blease was married himself, wasn't he?'

'So they say, and he might have been once, but he certainly wasn't when he played for the Corinthians.'

'What happened to him, do you know?'

'Ah, I knew it, there's a bit of a mystery there, isn't there? I've already had one bugger round asking about Bleasy.'

'It wasn't Norris Pond, by any chance?'

'That was him – Pondy, our old player-manager. A right gobshite he was and no mistake. Thought he was Bobby bleedin' Moore. He told me he was writing a book about the Corinthians but I didn't believe a word of it.'

'Why not?'

He seemed surprised that I should ask the question. 'Who'd be bothered, that's why not? I mean, all they were was a glorified pub team.'

'Even so, local history is very popular these days.'

Mickey Coleman snorted. 'He didn't seem very interested in hearing about any of *my* history. It was all Bleasy, or Digger as they used to call him. If you ask me, the book business was just a ploy to pump me about him.'

'He disappeared mid-season, didn't he? Did you hear any rumours about why or where he went?'

'Everyone knew where he'd gone. He pissed off with this married bird.'

'What happened to the husband?'

'No idea. He had a butcher's shop in Wavertree and when Bleasy ran off with his wife, the shop shut down. Perhaps the husband followed them.' He laughed at the thought. 'Digger could have ended up in one of his pork pies.'

I didn't laugh. Stranger things had happened.

'You say the shop was in Wavertree but someone told me he'd been seeing a married woman in Childwall. Do you reckon he had two of them on the go?'

'It wouldn't have surprised me, not with Digger, but no, I think the shop was a lock-up. They didn't live on the premises.'

'So the butcher and his wife could have lived in Childwall.

You don't know what road the shop was in, by any chance?'

'Picton Road, but I don't know the number. Westcotts, it was called though. They used to make bloody good black puddings.'

'So it must have been Mrs Westcott that Digger ran off with.'

'Reckon so.'

It didn't follow, of course. They could have bought an established business and continued trading under the existing name but it was the closest thing to a clue I'd had so far.

'Did you tell Norris Pond about the shop?'

'Did I heck as like, the nosy bastard. Pretended he wanted to know all about my career when all he was really interested in was bloody Blease. I soon got rid of him.'

Coleman's take on all this was interesting. If Pond's story about the book *was* true, he should have been just as interested in Mickey Coleman as he was in David Blease.

Meanwhile, I finally had some information that Norris Pond, through his own ineptitude, had been unable to discover.

But would it be enough to help me find David Blease?

Chapter Thirteen

I rang Jim from the car. 'I'm running late,' I said, 'so I'm going straight to the radio station. Is there any news from the court?'

'The jury's still out. They're being put up at a hotel for the night so we won't know anything till tomorrow.'

'Taking their time, aren't they?'

'I told you it'd be close. How did you get on with the St Helens Corinthian?'

'I think I might have discovered who the wife is that Blease is supposed to have run off with.' I told him about the butcher's shop. 'I've not had a chance to check it out yet, but there's also an Uncle Arthur in Ormskirk, if he's still alive.'

'What about Blease's ex-wife?'

'Not a clue. Could be anywhere. She's probably reverted to her maiden name or changed it altogether.'

'That's more likely, especially if she's acquired a new partner.' He sighed. 'This is the trouble with nobody getting married any more. There are no proper records.'

He was right. I didn't envy the kids of the future trying to trace their family trees.

After I'd done the show, I went straight round to Maria's.

'Well?' she greeted me. 'What was the verdict then?'

'Verdict?'

'Joanna Smithson. I thought today was D-Day.'

'Oh, sorry, of course.' With Shani Patel and then Mickey Coleman, I'd almost forgotten the morning in court. 'The

judge did his summing up but the jury's still out so we won't
know anything until tomorrow, if then. It could take days, of
course.' Although I couldn't bring myself to believe it would
be that long.

'She'll get off, surely?'

'Jim isn't certain she will.'

'There'll be a public outcry if she doesn't.'

I agreed, although I didn't expect that would be much
comfort to Joanna in jail.

'I've done tuna steaks for dinner,' she said, 'in water-
cress and broccoli sauce. And I've opened a bottle of Casal
Mendes.'

'Great.' I poured us both a glass and sat down at the kitchen
table whilst Maria prepared the meal.

'It'll be ready in ten minutes.'

I picked up the *Echo* and glanced through the headlines. It
was all about the *QE2* and Elton John, but didn't feature the
obvious headline *Two Old Queens in Town*.

'Has Victoria been good?' I asked.

'Screamed when the window-cleaner came this afternoon.'

'That's you out of a job then,' I said to Roly, who was sitting
expectantly by his bowl. 'We don't need two guard dogs.'

And then, out of the blue, Maria said, 'How was your concert
last night?'

My stomach turned over. I tried to speak casually. 'So so,' I
replied. 'On a par with The Chocolate Lavatory. I've decided
that most singers should be like footballers and give up when
they reach forty.'

'Oh dear, that bad, eh? Are you still doing the booking on
Sunday?'

'Unless I can think of a way out of it.' I wondered if she
would ask to come. Babysitters were never a problem with her
sister in Formby.

But she just laughed and I breathed again. 'Listen,' she
continued, 'I had another go at the Internet for you last
night but couldn't find a thing on Auschwitz 101. I must

say, there's some very weird stuff on some of those sites, Johnny.'

I took another sip of wine. I could well believe it. They say you can build a nuclear bomb from instructions on the Net.

'I'll have to have a word with John At The Garage,' I said. John was a fanatical Blues supporter and regular contributor to the *When Skies Are Grey* fanzine under various aliases. He could tell you the name of everyone who'd ever played for Everton since Dixie Dean hung up his boots. 'He'll know about racist groups if anyone will. He used to be a football hooligan himself.' The two hobbies seemed to go together like pigeons and disease.

'Used to be?'

'In his younger days. He's getting on a bit now.' Weren't we all?

'Talking of football, have you found your missing goal-keeper yet?' I was relieved the conversation had moved away from the concert.

'No, but I'm getting closer. I might have found his mysterious married lady. In fact, you can help me, Maria. Have you still got the old business directories in the Library?'

'Some of them. Why?'

'I want you to look up a butcher's shop called Westcotts in Picton Road in 1979. It's possible that it was Mrs W. who did the runner with Digger Blease. I need the number of the shop. It's closed now but some of the neighbours might know what happened to the husband. He could still be around, even. Oh, and if you could find out where they lived as well, that would be a bonus.'

'Didn't you say there was an uncle somewhere, too?'

'That's right, Uncle Arthur from Ormskirk. Don't know his second name though and he's probably dead by now.'

'Maybe not. Be optimistic, Johnny. There's a fifty-fifty chance he's called Blease and I can find him, and what about the ex-wife?'

91

'She was called Brocken – Iris Brocken was her maiden name.'

'You think she could have gone back to that?'

'Or she could have married again and be called anything at all.'

'I'll see what I can find.'

'You should be on the payroll,' I told her. Norris Pond was certainly getting his money's worth. Maybe it was time to send him another bill. At least, for the first time, I felt I was making progress in the case.

Jim Burroughs, in the office the next morning, was less encouraging.

'Even if you do find the husband, so what? Blease himself could be in China so we'd be no nearer finding him.'

'I'm banking on him being with Mrs Westcott, so if I find her, I find him. Either way, at least we'll have something to report to Pond, and justify hitting him with another bill. What about you? Have you had any joy with Auschwitz 101 yet with your lot?' His lot being his ex-employers, Merseyside Police.

''Fraid not. Mike Bennett's been through the files but he's come up with a complete blank. Nothing on record at all. I'm beginning to wonder if this crew really exist or was it just a prank by local yobbos to put us off the scent, make us think it was a racist attack.'

'That's all very well but they didn't steal anything, Jim, so what other reason could there have been for all that damage?'

'Sheer vandalism, I suppose. A change from smashing up phone boxes.'

I told him what Shani Patel had said, that I might have been the real target.

'Possible, I suppose. Who've you been upsetting?'

'No one I can think of. But, if that was the case, why go for that particular house? Why not my own flat?'

'Perhaps the security on Waterloo Dock put them off, I don't know. Have you not found anything yourself?' he asked.

'Not a thing. I spent an hour on the Net yesterday but there was no mention of them and I told you Maria's had a go. She said she came across some very dubious sites though.'

'She wants to be careful. Special Branch will be watching her if she logs on to too many of those.'

It didn't surprise me. Big Brother is well and truly entrenched in our society in a million different ways.

'I'm going to have a chat with John At The Garage,' I said. 'He'll know if anybody does.'

'Who the hell's John At The Garage?'

'You don't know him, he's one of my snouts.' I smiled mysteriously. Like all policemen, Jim set great store by his informers whose identities he guards religiously. 'He might know something.'

I found John at his garage out at Aintree. A huge Great Dane that dwarfed Roly growled as we walked up. Luckily, it was attached to a clanking chain and though it leapt at us, snarling, as we came closer, we stayed outside biting distance.

John looked up from the car he was repairing. A pair of oil-stained navy overalls encompassed his twenty-stone bulk and, standing as he was with a large spanner clasped in his hand, he made a frightening sight. I tried to imagine what it would have been like being confronted by him at a football match. His long greasy hair was tied in a pony tail and hung over one shoulder.

'All right, Johnny lad?' He waved the spanner in greeting and his dog barked. 'Quiet, Gerard,' he ordered. Roly tried to hide his stump between his legs as he edged away from the guard dog. I'd seen smaller ponies.

'You look busy,' I said.

'Business is sound. I'm opening a car wash next week.'

'Aren't there enough car washes? Every petrol station you drive into seems to have one.'

'Not a mechanical one, a hand wash. Bunch of schoolkids and dolies out there with buckets and sponges, cash-in-your-hand job, can't beat it. I've got my eye on a site for another if this goes well.'

'Will that make it a second-hand car wash?'

He grinned. 'Harry Enfield has nothing to worry about then. Stick to being a private eye, Johnny – which is why you're here, I take it. I can't see a broken-down car anywhere and you haven't come all this way to tell me your crappy jokes.'

'I need your help, John. What do you know about an outfit calling itself Auschwitz 101?'

He scratched his head under his Everton FC baseball cap. 'Who?'

I repeated the question but he seemed no wiser. 'Never heard of them. Who are they?'

I told him about the wrecking of Shani Patel's house. 'I thought there might be a connection with some of the football crowd, your old hooligan friends.'

John didn't take offence. I think he regarded his days as a thug as akin to being in the services. It was a wonder he didn't wear medals.

'There's Combat 18,' he said, 'and the White Wolves but I don't know anyone called Auschwitz 101. I'll ask around for you though, Johnny, best I can do.' He moved on to a more important topic. 'So how do you reckon the Blues'll do this year?'

The other matter was closed. We chatted for a while about Everton's prospects for the forthcoming season. John was incandescent with rage about Nick Barmby joining Liverpool.

'You can't expect loyalty in football nowadays,' I said. 'It's all about money.' Not much of the Wavertree Corinthians spirit in the Premiership.

'Yes, but joining The Red Shite,' he stormed. 'Anybody but those bastards. Just wait until the derby at Goodison.'

I didn't hang around to hear his threats, but if the other 35,000 fans felt as vehement as he, I didn't envy Barmby when Liverpool visited Everton.

At lunchtime, I met Maria in the Walker Art Gallery.

'I haven't much time,' she said, 'we're short-staffed so I've got to get back, but I think I've got what you wanted.' She handed me a sheet of paper. 'Peter and Patti Westcott – that will be them, won't it? I checked out who's got the premises now and it's a hardware shop run by a Harry Stone.'

'What about their home address? Did you manage to find anything?'

'It's all written down.'

I glanced at the paper. It had the number of the shop and the Westcotts' Childwall address. 'Oh, it's just down the road from where they film *Brookside*,' I said.

'That's right. A Mr and Mrs Bachelor live there now. It's near the Childwall Abbey pub, isn't it? We went for lunch there once, remember?'

I did. 'You've been wonderful, Maria,' I told her.

'The Westcotts will have left years ago, surely?'

'Not necessarily. If Mrs Westcott ran off with Blease, Mr Westcott could have stayed and moved a replacement in, a new Mrs Westcott.'

'Probably one young enough to be his daughter.'

'That's a thought. I wonder if the Westcotts had children? Anyway, it could be the Bachelors will remember them.'

'Are you going there this afternoon?'

'I might. I've got plenty of time before I do the show.'

'I'll expect you about eight then, as usual.'

Sleeping at Maria's was becoming a habit, I could see. Part of me wanted it, part of me felt trapped. Happily, at the moment, I had enough to do not to have to think about it too much. I figured the best thing to do for now was go with the flow, see how things developed, and hope they didn't all blow up in my face.

I made to go but Maria waved me down. 'Hang on, I've not finished yet. Don't you want to know about Arthur Blease?'

'You've not found him?'

'I've found *an* Arthur Blease living in a council house in Ormskirk. Could be the same one.'

'It's got to be. It's not that common a name. You've done wonders.' I kissed her. 'What would I do without you?'

It was a question I had often asked myself.

I walked into town, picked up a chargrilled chicken sandwich from Tesco Metro and took it back to the office.

'I'll leave Roly with you for the afternoon,' I told Jim. 'I'm off to Childwall on the Digger Blease trail.'

The house where the Westcotts had lived was a smart semi-detached with adjoining garage. The front garden boasted a proliferation of roses of all colours and a clematis plant was spreading across a trellis beside the front door. The lady who opened the door was in her mid-sixties. I took her to be Mrs Bachelor. She had wavy silver hair and wore an expensive gold necklace round her neck. I explained I was looking for a family called Westcott.

'We've been here eight years,' she said, 'and we bought the house from a family called Ramsey.' She hadn't heard of the Westcotts. 'Mrs Bromage at number 44 might know,' she volunteered. 'She's seventy-seven and she's lived here donkeys' years. She's probably out though, she often plays bridge in the afternoons.'

'Thanks.'

It was my lucky day. Mrs Bromage not only was in, but also remembered the Westcotts.

'It was very strange,' she declared in cut-glass tones, her age betrayed only by a slight wobble in her voice. She wore a brightly coloured silk dress and her grey hair was tied in a bun at the back. We sat in her front lounge eyed by two large Burmese cats.

'They left ever so suddenly. There was talk after they'd gone of some scandal between Mrs Westcott and a young man, but the Westcotts certainly left together. I was in the front room as the taxi collected them. The odd thing was, I never saw a removal van but a few days after they'd gone, some people turned up in a big estate car and took a lot of small items away. A week or so after that, one of the local auctioneers arrived for the rest of their furniture.'

'They didn't tell you where they were going then?'

'They never said a word. My husband was alive then, of course, but the Westcotts kept themselves to themselves. Mr Westcott had something wrong with his ears. I forget what it was although he didn't appear to me to be deaf.'

'Perhaps it was tinnitus,' I suggested. 'Does that ring a bell?'

She looked puzzled and I carried on quickly.

'How old would you say they were?'

'Oh, not old. Late thirties, or thereabouts.'

Digger Blease would have been twenty-five. 'They had no children?'

'Goodness me, no. With their lifestyle? What an encumbrance children would have been.'

I had not envisaged the Westcotts as having anything as exotic as a lifestyle, which conjured up pictures of yachts in Monte Carlo Harbour, not something normally associated with Picton Road shopkeepers.

'He only had a butcher's shop, Mrs Bromage,' I said.

She gave me a piercing glance. 'Precisely.'

My next call was on my old friend Leslie Lomax, the auctioneer. There aren't too many auction houses left in Liverpool so there was a fair chance the Westcotts' furniture had ended up in his saleroom.

'Dear me, Mr Ace, you're talking about twenty years ago,' he protested when I explained what I wanted.

'I know, Leslie, but I also know you keep company records going back a hundred years.'

'Why not? People like tradition in the professions. It makes them feel safe.' He went over to a cupboard and stretched up to the top shelf. He was only a small man. He could have done with one of Digger Blease's boxes to stand on.

'Here we are.' He dusted a bound A4 book with the sleeve of his Fairisle pullover. 'The year 1979, you said?'

'Probably April or May.'

Lomax squinted through the pages until he came to the entry

I wanted. 'Here we are. Westcott.' He read out the correct address. 'We collected their furniture on the sixteenth of June and put it straight into the saleroom. It fetched a fair price, too. They had a couple of choice antique items amongst the dross. No mention of doing their removal though so I can't tell you where they went to.'

'Of course you can,' I said patiently. 'You'll have to have had their address to send the cheque to.' Sometimes, Leslie Lomax acted like he was a sheep's ball short of a haggis.

'Silly me, of course.' He consulted an index at the back and turned to a fresh page of his ledger. 'And here it is. Well, well. Is this what you expected, Mr Ace?'

'I don't know till you tell me.'

It certainly was *not* what I'd expected. I'd assumed Patti and Digger had run away together, leaving her husband behind – but not according to Leslie Lomax's records. In July 1979, the cheque for the sale of their furniture had been posted as instructed to Pete and Patti Westcott in Limehouse, in London's East End. So Mrs Bromage had been right – the pair had left together, with no sign of Digger Blease in the picture.

Chapter Fourteen

'The East End, eh? Alf Garnett and Ronnie Kray country,' commented Jim Burroughs.

'It won't be easy to trace them, not after twenty odd years.'

'Impossible, I'd say. Most of that old area's been razed to the ground – Limehouse, Wapping, Isle of Dogs. It's all called Docklands nowadays and you can't buy a studio flat for under a hundred and fifty grand.'

'Maybe not, but what I want to know is, if the Westcotts are nice and cosy in London, where the hell is Blease?'

'I don't know, Johnny. If Mr Westcott did find out about the affair, as everybody seems to think, he could have taken his wife off to the Smoke to get her away from Digger's clutches.'

'I'll go along with that, except where does that leave Blease? Remember, nobody round here ever saw him again.'

'Perhaps Westcott warned him off and he left town before they did.'

'In which case, why did they bother going? More likely Westcott buried him under the patio then fled the scene of the crime.'

'Many a true word, Johnny.'

'Or how about this? We're only assuming the Westcotts left town because of the affair. Maybe they had other reasons for leaving and Blease followed them down south. He'd no ties here, no regular employer. What was to stop him moving to London and continuing to see Mrs Westcott on the side?'

'Mr Westcott for one. If he didn't know anything was going on before, he would then. For Christ's sake, Johnny, he'd think it a bit odd if the same window-cleaner turned up two hundred miles away.'

'Blease could have been more discreet this time round.'

'He doesn't sound the discreet type. Most people in Wavertree knew what was going on between him and Patti Westcott.'

'We don't know that,' I said, 'and London's a lot bigger place than Wavertree.'

'So, what's the next move?'

'You check out Limehouse, Jim. You must have contacts in the police down there.'

'There's a bloke called Walter Glass at Scotland Yard that I used to share a bottle with at the odd police convention. Detective Inspector he was. Southern Comfort was his tipple – and boy, could he put it away! I could try him, if he hasn't retired.'

'All he has to do is check back through the files and dig out anything he can about the Westcotts. They could still be around. You never know, they might have got form of some description.'

'What about you? What are you going to be doing?'

'I've got another lead to follow up.'

'What's that?'

'Maria's found an address in Ormskirk that could turn out to be Blease's Uncle Arthur. I'm going to go round in the morning.'

'Is Maria on wages now? She seems to do better than you at finding people.'

'She's better at computers than I am. Listen, what about Joanna Smithson? Has there been any news?'

'No. The jury's still out.'

'That's ominous, isn't it? I'd have thought it would all have been over on Wednesday and Joanna would be free.'

'I told you it wasn't cut and dried,' said Jim. 'The jurors are being locked up for the weekend in the Adelphi, incommunicado.'

'If that TV documentary was anything to go by, I think I'd rather sleep in the courtroom. Seriously though, I bet the Smithsons are worried sick. They must have thought their daughter would be free by now.'

'Changing the subject,' said Jim, 'I take it you're still OK for the gig on Sunday?'

'I suppose so. Which reminds me, I must ring Hilary. She wants to come.' Jim looked at me but said nothing. I managed to reach Hil at home and arranged to pick her up at her place at seven on Sunday.

'Cutting it fine, aren't you?' Jim worried. What if the Tunnel's busy?'

'Not with my driving,' I assured him. 'We don't have to be there till half past.'

I advertised the gig on the show later but I didn't expect a big response. The Chocolate Lavatory topping the bill wouldn't tempt too many people away from their armchairs and repeats of *Heartbeat* on a Sunday night.

'How did you get on in Childwall?' Maria asked me later.

Victoria was in her cot, Roly lay in his basket and we were sitting on the settee in the lounge watching the lights of the Mersey Estuary and listening to a Dinah Washington CD. It was all very comfortable and reassuring. Except that on Sunday night I'd be out with Hilary.

'Brilliant. I found out that the Westcotts ended up in London in the East End.'

'And what about Blease?'

'Nothing on him, I'm afraid. It all rests on Uncle Arthur now. You did well finding him.'

'If he's the right one.'

He was. I drove over to Ormskirk soon after breakfast. Being market day the traffic was heavy in the town centre. I parked at the bottom end of Aughton Street and walked through the lines of stalls.

Years ago, the market traders were local farmers selling their home-grown produce, and Lancashire traders who worked Chorley, Preston and Wigan. But that was when steam trains ran from Southport and the old Wheatsheaf stood in Burscough Street. Now, many of the stallholders come from Liverpool and are likely to be found on other days at the Great Homer Street and Stanley markets.

I found the little terraced house off the Wigan Road. Arthur Blease answered the door, a bent old man with a grey moustache and a modern deaf aid inside his left ear. There was no hallway. The front door opened into the living room and a cottage staircase at the side of the room led to the two bedrooms.

'I've come about your nephew,' I said, after I'd shown him my Ace Investigations business card. 'David.'

He shuffled across the room and sank into a worn leather armchair, indicating a matching chair for me at the opposite side of the fireplace. A coal fire smouldered in the grate even though it was July. No chance of Uncle Arthur going down with hypothermia.

The room was dark and gloomy, not helped by the brown-painted skirting boards and walls. On the mantelpiece I noticed a couple of photographs in matching darkwood frames featuring a young lad in football kit.

He saw me looking. 'That was him up there. Soccer mad he was, even as a lad.'

Was! 'What happened to him?' I asked quietly, picking up on the past tense.

Arthur Blease shook his head. 'Tragic. He was no age.' I waited as he gathered his thoughts. 'A fire. He was in a lodging-house. They say he must have fallen asleep in bed smoking a cigarette. Furniture burnt like blazes in those days and the whole place went up. David was unrecognisable. Burnt to a cinder. They only identified him by his signet ring.'

'Were there many others killed?'

'No, just David. The owners were out that night. He was the only guest. They said afterwards that they thought the house was empty. It was only eight o'clock at night but he must have gone up to his room early.'

'I've been trying to find David for weeks now,' I said, 'but everyone I've spoken to has said he disappeared virtually overnight.' And no wonder. 'Nobody's mentioned the fire or that he might be dead. When did it happen?'

'Oh, over twenty years ago, not long after he left Liverpool.'

'He didn't die in Liverpool then?'

'Oh no, it was down south. David died somewhere in the East End of London.'

Chapter Fifteen

The fire had occurred in September 1979, six months after David Blease was last seen in Wavertree. Someone had sent Uncle Arthur a letter enclosing a clipping from the local newspaper giving brief details of the fire and his nephew's demise. He never found out who the sender was.

He rang the local police but nobody there knew much about it and he was already too infirm to go down and investigate himself so he did nothing. I asked him who identified the body but he didn't know.

'We were never that close but he was the only family I had left. His mum and dad, that's my brother, they'd both passed on and he was an only child. Now there's just me and I'm eighty-three next birthday so I don't suppose I'll be here myself much longer.' He gave a guttural cough to substantiate his prediction.

'But you did see him when he lived round here?'

'Once a year if I was lucky and then only to cadge money. He never had a proper job, did David. He did a bit of decorating, drove a van for a while, had a window-cleaning round, nothing steady. I told him, "If you spent as much time looking for a job as you do chasing the lassies, you'd be a rich man."'

'I believe he liked the girls.'

'If they'd had humping in the Olympics, David would have won a gold medal.'

'What about his wife?'

'Poor bugger. She soon left him when she found out what he was like.'

'Do you ever see her now?'

'I've never seen her. Ever. He never once brought her up here. I wouldn't know her from Mrs Thatcher, and God knows where she is now. She could be anywhere.'

'Why do you think he went to London?' As if I didn't know.

'Probably running away from someone or something. It wouldn't have been the first time people were after him.'

'Jealous boyfriends, you mean?'

'Those as well. He had a habit of getting mixed up with some funny people from time to time.'

'He hadn't got a police record.'

'Well, he wouldn't, would he? He was too smart for them.'

There was not much more to say. It looked like the case was closed. I'd achieved what Norris Pond had asked of me. I'd traced the whereabouts of Digger Blease so I could send in my bill and that would be it. End of story.

Except . . . I was curious. I couldn't accept that his death had been an accident. I knew exactly why Digger Blease had been in London and I knew someone who had a very good motive for killing him.

I wondered where the Westcotts were now.

'Why are you looking for David anyway?' asked Uncle Arthur.

I explained about Norris Pond and the Wavertree Corinthians history. 'I'm surprised Mr Pond didn't track you down.'

'Never heard of the man. I don't remember Wavertree Corinthians either. David played for a lot of clubs after he left school but he never stayed with any of them for long. Liked to keep moving.'

It didn't surprise me. 'You've been a great help,' I said. 'Before I go, I don't suppose you've still got that newspaper cutting about the fire, have you?'

He rose unsteadily to his feet and opened the door of the

built-in cupboard in the alcove beside the fireplace. 'It's in here somewhere.' He rummaged through a pile of yellowing papers and pulled one out. 'I think this is it.'

The article was headed *Man Dies in Blaze* and it added little to the account Uncle Arthur had given me. It said that the body of a man recovered from the burnt-out wreckage of a guest-house near the Isle of Dogs was that of David Ian George Blease, twenty-five, a salesman from the North of England. The fire was believed to have been started by a lighted cigarette. The paper had obviously gone to press before more details were known.

I handed the paper back to the old man.

'If you find out anything, you will let me know, won't you?' he said as he showed me to the door. 'Not that there's anything to find. He's still going to be dead whichever way you look at it.'

You couldn't argue with that.

I drove back to Maria's to pick up Roly.

'How did you get on?' she asked. 'Was he the right one?'

'He was, thanks to you. And I've found our Missing Goalkeeper too, or what's left of him.' I recounted the tale Arthur Blease had told me. 'So it looks like it's all over,' I said. 'Except . . .'

'Except you don't think the fire was an accident.'

'I'd put money on it, wouldn't you?'

'I'm not sure. What did you say caused it – a lighted cigarette?'

'Yes. But who lit the match in the first place? It's too much of a coincidence that Blease just happened to be in the same part of London as the Westcotts.'

'Maybe so, but it's not up to you to investigate any more, Johnny. You've done your bit in tracing him. It's this Norris Pond's problem now.'

'I suppose so.'

I knew Maria was not deceived by my reluctant tone but

she chose to ignore it. 'Can you drop Victoria off at Kaye's?' she asked. 'I'm running a bit late. Sorry – I know it's not on your way home.'

'That's all right.' Maria was working the afternoon shift at the Library, and Kaye, her sister, was babyminding.

'Don't forget we're going out tonight,' she reminded me. Victoria was staying at her sister's overnight whilst we went for an Italian at Quo Vadis in Formby Village. 'I thought we might go to the Plaza afterwards, if we're not too late,' she added.

'What's on?'

'I don't know. We'll have to take pot luck.'

'As long as it's not *Godzilla*.' My worst film of all time.

When I eventually got back home, I opened a tin of Spam for lunch and did some oven-ready chips and peas. Roly liked Spam almost as much as he liked Chappie but I wasn't keen on Chappie so Spam it was, washed down with a can of Scrumpy Jack or, in Roly's case, water.

After we'd eaten, I rang Norris Pond to tell him the news. I kept it to the basics, namely that David Blease had died in a house fire just a month after he'd left Wavertree Corinthians. I assumed that the simple fact Blease had died would satisfy him for the purposes of his book but he seemed strangely anxious for details of his former goalkeeper's demise.

'Were many other people killed in this fire?'

'Apparently not. It was a boarding-house. The owners had gone out, not realising Blease was up in his room. It was early evening so I guess they presumed he was out too.'

'I don't like the smell of this. What about the other guests? Any of them dead?'

'As far as I know, he was the only one staying there at the time and that's all I can tell you. Anyway, none of this will affect your book, will it? All you need to know is that Blease is dead.' I recalled Wally Tennant's words with some unease. *He's got some ulterior motive.* And Mickey Coleman had not believed that Pond was writing a book at all. *It was just a ploy to pump me about Blease.*

What wasn't he telling me?

Norris Pond didn't answer for a moment then, 'No, of course not,' he said at last. 'It's just that I like to see loose ends tied up properly. Whereabouts did this inferno take place?'

'Limehouse in London's East End.'

'What was he doing down there?'

It would have been natural at that point for me to tell him about Blease's affair with Mrs Westcott. I don't know why I didn't. Instinct maybe. I had the distinct feeling now that Norris Pond was hiding something, so I decided to remain a bit cagey myself.

'Perhaps he'd had an offer to play for West Ham United,' I said.

He ignored me. 'Do you know the name of the people who ran this hotel?'

'Guest-house. No, the paper didn't give it.'

'Only they might still be there.'

'It's twenty years ago, Mr Pond.'

'You could make enquiries.'

'Do I take it that you want to hire me to investigate Mr Blease's death now?'

'If it's the money you're worried about . . .'

'Look, Mr Pond, I was about to send you my account for tracing Mr Blease. It comes to three hundred and thirty pounds including expenses. I can't see that the sales of this book of yours are ever going to justify any further outlay.'

'That's my problem, Mr Ace. Send your bill in and I'll settle it and I'll pay you a further five hundred on account to follow up Blease's m . . .' He stopped.

'Murder?' I supplied him with the missing word.

'Death.' He was quick to correct himself. 'Thanks for calling, Mr Ace. I'll look forward to an early report from you.' And the line went dead.

It was three o'clock. I figured Jim would be at home so I drove over to his house. His wife Rosemary answered the door.

'I believe you're playing with his group tomorrow night,' she said in an accusing voice, as she led me though to the living room. 'I wish you'd get him to give up this music lark, Johnny. It's too much for him with his heart.'

'Nonsense, Rosie,' I said. 'Keeps him young and, besides, it gets him out from under your feet.'

'Since he started in that agency with you, he's been at home less than he was when he was in the Force.' She didn't like being called Rosie, coming as she did from West Kirby. 'Rosie' was common. 'And I do wish you wouldn't bring that dog in the house, it's got muddy feet.'

'Blame the rain,' I apologised. 'I couldn't find any Wellingtons to fit him.' Roly merely smiled at her beatifically.

'You're not pulling out of the gig, are you?' asked Jim anxiously as I entered the room. He was sitting in an armchair by the window, a glass of Newcastle Brown by his side, his tie loose and the top button of his shirt undone.

'No, I've been out there bringing in the income while you sit on your fat ass, boozing.'

'I'm saving my strength for tomorrow. What's this about income?'

'I've found the Missing Goalkeeper.'

'Blease? No! Where was he?' Jim sat up in his chair.

'Was is the operative word.' I filled him in about the fire and Blease's unfortunate demise.

'London, eh? But that's where the Westcotts went.'

'Exactly. The East End. Looking decidedly dodgy, isn't it? But guess what – Pond's paying us to carry on with the investigation. I reckon he thinks Blease was murdered and wants us to prove it.'

'I'd say there's a good chance he was, with Peter Westcott the obvious suspect.'

'It won't be easy to prove though, Jim. Digger was already ashes so even if they'd saved his remains, there wouldn't be much of him left.'

'What do you reckon then?'

'Finding the Westcotts has got to be favourite but God knows where they could have moved to since then. Have you been on to that bloke Glass at the Yard yet?'

'Not yet, give us a chance. I'll do it first thing Monday morning.' Jim took a sip of his beer. 'Sorry, I never asked. Do you want one?'

'No, thanks.'

'What puzzles me,' said Jim, 'is why Pond is so anxious to bother with all this.'

I agreed. 'The Wavertree Corinthians book business is obviously a blind, but I can't for the life of me see what's in it for him.'

We were very soon to find out what Norris Pond's motive was, but that knowledge would put our lives in grave danger.

Chapter Sixteen

Gladiator was the film showing at Crosby's Plaza Cinema. Maria and I were a bit late arriving after our meal at Quo Vadis but Jan in the paybox assured us we hadn't missed anything. 'Only the odd gored Christian,' she said.

Maria wasn't so keen on Roman epics. I enjoyed the film although I kept expecting Kirk Douglas and Charlton Heston to pop up at any moment. Mind you, once digital photography technology has advanced sufficiently, all the old stars will be reincarnated on screen to appear in new films. Cheaper to hire than real people. Imagine a remake of *Dr No* with Humphrey Bogart as James Bond.

'Isn't it wonderful to have a night on our own,' whispered Maria, as we cuddled up in bed later, 'without worrying about waking the baby.' Roly lay still at the bottom of the bed, one eye open.

'Wonderful,' I said, and I meant it.

We had a lie-in the next morning. Maria brought breakfast to bed, I read the *Sunday Times* then we put on an Ella Fitzgerald CD and made love again.

'We'll have to get up,' Maria said at last. 'Kaye and Alex are expecting us at one for lunch. We don't want to be late and Victoria might be missing us.'

Kaye had now become Auntie Kaye and was loving every minute of it. I wondered why she and Alex had no children. Perhaps they couldn't have them. They'd recently acquired a West Highland White Terrier called Haggis which I suppose

111

was a substitute. Kaye took it to the pinewoods every morning before work and doted on the creature.

Kaye had made a roast lunch after which we spent a pleasant afternoon chatting, most of the conversation centring on Victoria.

At five o'clock, I stood up to go. Alex was driving Maria, Victoria and Roly home later.

'He's got a gig to go to,' explained Maria.

Alex said, 'I thought you didn't do your show on a Sunday.'

'No, this is a drumming gig, with a group called The Chocolate Lavatory. I'm doing a friend a favour. It's the first time I've played for nearly twenty years.' Almost going back to when Digger Blease last played football.

'His arms'll ache in the morning.' Maria hugged me affectionately. 'See you tomorrow night,' she said.

I needed to leave early to pick up Hilary over on the Wirral. I didn't feel too proud about it.

Fairfield Police Club was already packed when we arrived. I hadn't realised The Chocolate Lavatory had such a big following but the doorman explained it was always full on a Sunday and he put it down to the attractive prize money in the Bingo, a theory that left Jim Burroughs somewhat deflated.

'God, I thought I'd finished with all this,' I said, hauling Pete's bass drum across the dance floor to the small stage.

'It'll keep you fit,' panted Jim who, at two stones overweight, was hardly a good advert for healthy living.

'Have you not had a rehearsal?' asked Hilary as she followed behind me carrying the cymbals.

Jim shook his head. 'Don't need one. They're mostly the same songs we all did thirty odd years ago.'

They were too. We performed passable versions of 'Smokestack Lightning' (Howling Wolf), 'Turn On Your Lovelight' (Bobby Blue Bland), 'Leave My Kitten Alone' (Little Willie John) and other American hits that never made it over here but were in the repertoire of most Liverpool groups in the early 1960s.

Once the Bingo was out of the way, the second set went down even better, mainly because the audience were now replete with alcohol. We did a couple of country numbers, 'Crazy' and 'Achy Breaky Heart', always popular with Liverpool audiences, and soon everyone was dancing. Some of Jim's retired colleagues waved across the floor to him, all of them tall men, some grey-haired, some bald, and every one still looking like a policeman.

'You're sure you don't want a permanent job?' Jim asked as we dismantled the gear at the end of the show. Sweat was pouring down his neck and his tattered *Reservoir Mogs* T-shirt was sticking to his body.

Maria had been right. I had cramp in my hands and my upper torso felt like it had been through a mangle. I'd be quite happy to wait another twenty years before picking up the sticks again.

'I'll do your hundredth birthday party and that's it.'

By the time I'd helped pack all the gear away it was one o'clock. The rest of the group drove off in their borrowed Transit whilst Hilary and I headed for the Tunnel.

'Why don't you stay the night?' she suggested when we pulled up outside her cottage. 'I'm off in the morning so we don't have to be up early.'

I knew Maria wasn't expecting to hear from me till the following evening.

'It's ages since you stayed,' she continued, and ran her fingers along my thigh. My pulse raced a little faster and I slid lower in the driving seat. 'Maria won't miss you for one night,' she added mischievously, her fingers reaching higher. 'Tonight, you're mine.'

'Completely,' I sang, echoing The Shirelles hit. 'But will you still love me tomorrow?'

'I'll always love you,' smiled Hilary. She kissed me on the lips and dragged me upright. 'Come on, let's get to bed.'

It was after three when we got to sleep and it was ten o'clock before I woke. Hilary was still out to the world so I crept out of bed and went down to let her cat out, fetch the milk and papers in and make myself some tea and toast. My neck and shoulders had stiffened up after the night's drumming. Guitarists don't know what hard work is.

The headline in the *Daily Post* was *Everton Move For Gazza*. I was gobsmacked. They'd be signing Tom Finney next although, being in his eighties, Finney perhaps hadn't the speed any more. Mind you, Gascoigne was class and Everton were The School of Science.

Hilary staggered downstairs just as I finished eating. 'I think I had too much wine last night,' she groaned.

'There's still some tea in the pot, though it might be a bit cold.'

'I couldn't face tea. I need time to wake up. Has Pepper gone out?'

'She's chasing birds at the end of the garden.'

'That's all right then. Listen, why don't we go for a walk up to the shops later? There's a book I want to pick up at Linghams so we can have a drink there.'

We walked through Lower Heswall village, past the Dee View pub and up on to Telegraph Road to Linghams Bookshop, where they have a café at the back of the shop. More and more bookshops are doing this nowadays. I think they got the idea from the Americans.

'When are we going out again?' asked Hil. I'd ordered coriander and carrot soup as I didn't know when I'd get lunch. Hilary settled for a cappuccino and piece of chocolate cake.

'I don't know.'

She looked at me sad-eyed. 'Johnny, you aren't going to finish it now, are you, not after all these years?' I said nothing. I couldn't think of a reply. 'I know we've always said there's no commitment, we're free to do as we want, but Maria's baby has changed all that, hasn't it?'

'I suppose it has.' I knew I should have said 'yes' and 'that's it, it's over' and 'goodbye' but I couldn't.

'Sometimes I think I'd have liked a baby.' I went cold. If Hilary was pregnant too . . . 'But I know I'm not really cut out for motherhood. I've seen what it does to women. It ages them. I prefer to have my own life and have a good time.'

So did I but, then again, I'd grown to appreciate family life with Maria.

'Let's keep it like it is for the time being, shall we?' decided Hilary, before I could suggest an alternative. 'We're still friends and we can still go out occasionally. We're not doing any harm. We're not hurting Maria.'

As long as she doesn't know, I thought, and wondered how many men had said that over the centuries.

We walked back to the cottage and, as I climbed into the car, we left it that I'd ring her. I drove back through the Birkenhead Tunnel and it was gone two when I parked alongside Exchange Flags and ran across Dale Street into the office.

'About time too,' Jim Burroughs greeted me. 'Where've you been? I've been trying to reach you all morning. Don't you ever switch that bloody mobile on?'

'Sorry, I forgot. What's the panic?'

'You haven't heard the news then? The jury came back this morning. Joanna Smithson's been found guilty of manslaughter. They've sent her down for seven years.'

Chapter Seventeen

'I'm going to fight this if it costs me every penny I've got.'

I hadn't noticed Leonard Smithson standing behind the door as I walked into the office. He looked ten years older.

'I don't believe it,' I said. 'How the hell could they?'

'Well, they have.'

I remembered what one of Jim's colleagues had once told me. Liverpool Crown Court had a conviction rate of just over ten per cent. Amazingly low. I'd challenged him about this figure at the time but he confirmed it was correct and, furthermore, he had a theory to explain it. He called it the Sixths Principle.

'A sixth of the jurors, that is two out of twelve,' he added unnecessarily, 'are too thick to know what it's all about; two are scallies themselves; two are scared shitless of possible reprisals if they find the prisoner guilty; two are pissed off at being made to do jury service at all; and two think all policemen are bent anyway. So all of that lot will vote not guilty, which leaves just two who are intelligent, honourable men and women, able to make a reasoned and fair judgement. *Just two*. And by the law of averages, one of them will plump for innocent, which leaves just one juror in twelve voting guilty. Near enough to ten per cent in my book.'

If this were true, then how come Joanna Smithson was one of the ten per cent?

'So much for Andy Fletcher's Sixths Principle theory,' I said. 'It certainly didn't work here.'

116

'Andy talked through his backside sometimes,' said Jim. He looked at Smithson. 'But I must admit I'm shocked at the result, although after that Tony Martin trial, I suppose I shouldn't be.'

'Well, Brenda's taken to her bed – she's on a hundred bloody zombie pills a day now – and I'm totally bloody horrified. I want something done about it.' The man looked close to a breakdown himself.

'Have you spoken to your brief?' Jim asked him.

'Of course I have. We're obviously going to appeal but first of all we've got to decide the right grounds. He's looking at all the legal technicalities we might be able to use to get her off.'

'Like a biased summing up by the judge, you mean?'

'That's one of the things. Interfering with jurors is another.'

'That was one of the grounds in the Martin trial,' I said. 'Have you any reason to suspect it could have happened here?'

'No, but that's where you two come in. As I see it, there are three lines of attack here.' Smithson had obviously been working all this out. 'One is like you just said, to check out the jurors for any suggestion of intimidation and whatever. Two is you've got to find this second man who kidnapped Joanna. We know he exists so he must be out there somewhere.'

'Unless Mottram's disposed of him,' I said.

Smithson grimaced. 'Mottram's number three. We need to dig around for enough evidence to put that bastard in the dock.'

'He'll have covered his tracks well, Lennie,' warned Jim. 'It won't be easy. Inspector Ormesher pulled all the stops out and he came up with nothing.'

'He didn't try hard enough then. I'm offering good money,' said Smithson. 'A retainer of two grand up front plus exes but I'll expect some quick action. I don't want Joanna spending one night more than necessary in a prison cell. She's already been banged up for five months and you should see what it's done to her.'

'Where've they put her?'

'Durham Prison.'

Not the easiest of places to visit from Liverpool. 'Leave it to us,' I said quickly. 'We'll get a result for you.' I was almost as angry as he was. I thought Joanna Smithson was the victim of a grave miscarriage of justice and I wanted to put it right as much as her father did.

'You were a bit optimistic there,' Jim said when Smithson had left. 'We're going to be stretched aren't we, what with the Blease murder and now this?'

'Don't forget the Auschwitz 101 gang too,' I reminded him. That particular problem was personal. It was my house they'd wrecked. 'I daren't let Shani Patel move back into Kirkdale until we get hold of them. I don't want the place wrecked again – and next time they might do her as well. The first time could have just been a warning.'

'You think they might have another go when she moves back?'

'Who knows? They might. We need to find them first to be sure, if only for the girl's sake.'

'It's where to start with all this,' Jim fretted.

'I'll deal with Shani. Have you got hold of that alkie copper in London yet?'

'Detective Inspector Glass, you mean? Did I say he was an alkie?'

'You said he liked a drop of Southern Comfort.'

'Doesn't follow he can't handle it though. Most coppers can hold their liquor.' I could think of a good few who couldn't but I didn't argue the point. 'Anyway, I left a message. He's ringing me back.'

'He's still on the Force then?'

'Apparently so. Same rank too. His face can't have fitted or he'd have made Super by now.'

'Or else he's another of those bolshie buggers who likes to run the show himself.'

'The maverick copper syndrome, you mean? I've come across a few of those in my time,' said Jim.

'When he rings, get him to check on that fire that killed Blease. The newspaper didn't say so but was arson suspected? What was the address of the guest-house and who were the people that ran it? None of that was mentioned in the newspaper report. And don't forget, number one priority is to trace the Westcotts. If Glass can get on with that, we'll have a bit of breathing space to concentrate on Joanna Smithson. Can you have a quiet chat with Clive Ormesher?'

'Why him?'

'He can tell us what leads he followed up when he was looking for Dewhurst's mate. As far as the police are concerned, Joanna Smithson's guilty, end of story, she's history, but Ormesher saw the state of the girl that night and I can't believe he's happy with the outcome. You might be able to get some information out of him.'

'I can try.'

'Leonard Smithson's a friend of yours, Jim. I take it we can accept what he says is kosher – about this Mottram character, I mean.'

'You're not suggesting he made it up?'

'Not the kidnapping, no. I just wanted to make sure he wasn't trying to fit Mottram up for it in order to get his own back for some other business we don't know about.'

'You're too suspicious, that's your trouble.'

'That's why I'm in the job. You're right though, Mottram must be the man. You might find out what Ormesher has on him, if anything, while you're at it.'

'What are you going to do?'

'I'm going to the hospital to see Shani Patel. It's just possible she might have thought of something that would give us a clue as to who this racist mob are.'

But when I reached the hospital, I found that Shani had already been discharged. I'd missed her by an hour.

'Her uncle came to collect her,' the Sister informed me. 'He arrived just after lunch. He's taken her back to his house.' She was reluctant to give me the address, until I

119

explained I was Shani's landlord and needed to get in touch with her.

I left the hospital and drove up to Kirkdale to check on the workmen's progress on Shani's house.

'Should be ready by the end of the week,' Jack informed me. 'The new windows are going in tomorrow. Needed three coats of paint on the walls though. Were they Germans or what?'

'The Auschwitz slogans, you mean? I shouldn't think so but I'd like to know where they came from.'

I drove across town to Smithdown Road and found the newsagents where Shani Patel was staying. It was more of a general store with shelves stocked high with groceries, videos for hire, confectionery and booze as well as newspapers and magazines.

I waited in the self-service queue until I reached the counter where a comely woman in her fifties with large blue-framed glasses was serving.

'I'm looking for Mr Patel,' I said.

'Who shall I say it is?'

'Johnny Ace. Tell him it's his niece's landlord.'

She turned to a telephone on the wall behind her and pressed the extension buzzer. 'A Mr Ace here to see you,' she said into the mouthpiece, then turned back to me. 'He'll be down.'

I stood aside to let the next customer through, a man in a faded grimy anorak. He smelt of stale sweat. The woman ran his purchases through the scanner. With the glasses she reminded me of Dame Edna Everage or maybe Dennis Taylor the snooker player in drag.

A small Indian man emerged from a door behind the counter and came towards me. 'Mr Ace?' He held out his hand in greeting. 'Shakti Patel.'

I shook his hand. 'Pleased to meet you, Mr Patel. I've really called to see Shani.'

'She's upstairs. Do come up.'

I followed him up a flight of narrow wooden stairs into a living room heavily furnished with Indian pictures and ornaments. Shani was sitting on a small couch watching television.

'*Neighbours*,' tutted Mr Patel. 'These soaps are like a drug with the young people.'

'A safer drug than Ecstasy,' I replied.

'Indeed, you are right.' He sighed heavily and sat down, waving for me to do the same. Shani made a place for me beside her and turned the TV off with the remote.

'I must apologise for the trouble at Shani's house . . .' I began, but he cut me short.

'Don't be foolish. It is not for you to apologise. It was not your fault.'

'Maybe it was. It's possible these people, whoever they were, were trying to get at me, it being my house. Although the slogans . . .' I stopped. 'I take it you saw the slogans?'

'Yes.'

'They suggest that Auschwitz 101 are a racist outfit but I've not been able to find any reference to them anywhere. Have you heard of them before?'

He shook his head. 'Forget Auschwitz 101, Mr Ace. This business has nothing to do with Shani's colour or, indeed, with you.' He stood up again and paced the room. 'I am the one for whom this was intended.'

'You?' I turned to look at Shani in bewilderment and she nodded.

'My uncle has just told me,' she said.

'Last week, Mr Ace, you gave evidence for the defence at Liverpool Crown Court in the trial of a young lady who was accused of murder.'

'That's correct, Joanna Smithson. But what has that got to do with the attack on Shani?'

'I was a member of the jury at that trial, Mr Ace.'

Suddenly, it all began to make sense. 'You're telling me that someone tried to get at you?'

'I thought Miss Smithson was innocent, Mr Ace, yet in the end I voted her guilty. I am ashamed of this.'

'Then why did you do it, Mr Patel?' I knew it was a stupid question.

Shakti Patel gesticulated to his young niece, her face still showing signs of the bruising from the attack. 'Why do you think, Mr Ace? Is it not obvious?'

Chapter Eighteen

It was after the second day of the trial that Shakti Patel was handed a note. It said just four words: *Make sure she's guilty.*

'I didn't see the man who handed me this note – he disappeared very quickly – but the next morning in the vestibule another man walked alongside me and whispered to me, had I received the note? I told him I had and I would vote how I believed, not how he told me. He advised me that I should change my mind if I knew what was good for me. That night, my Shani was attacked. I didn't need any more warnings. My niece's life is the most important thing to me.'

'Were any other jurors approached that you know of?'

'Who can tell but, yes, I think so.'

'They didn't confide in you?'

'No, but two people looked uncomfortable with the verdict.'

'Which two?'

'There was a Mrs Ridgeway, a middle-aged lady. She cried a lot when we were debating the issue in the hotel.'

'And the other?'

'A man called, I think, Mr Duxfield. He was a young man with long hair in a pony tail. He was strongly in favour of releasing the girl at first but then he changed his mind suddenly over the weekend.'

'Sounds like intimidation to me. What about the foreman on the jury?'

'A man called Murphy. He was strongly in favour of a guilty verdict from the start.'

'Even before he'd heard all the evidence?'

'On the first day, as we came away, he asked me what I thought and I said I believed the girl was innocent. I could tell he was displeased.'

'And the next day you got the warning?'

'Yes.'

'What about the other jurors?'

'Most of them were ambivalent and he was able to convince them to go along with him. Except for Mrs Ridgeway and Mr Duxfield, that is, but they eventually capitulated.'

'Mr Patel, this could be the very thing we need to get Joanna released. As you will know from the trial, my partner and I are actually working for the girl's father. If I arrange an appointment with Joanna's solicitor, would you be prepared to make a statement detailing what you've just told me? She'll be able to use it in her appeal.'

He looked doubtful. 'And what about my niece? These people have nearly killed her once and they wrecked your property.'

'We'll be on our guard this time. They wouldn't dare try it again.'

Shani spoke up for the first time. 'I think you should, Uncle. I hate to think of that girl being locked up in prison.'

'I'll fix everything up,' I said. 'Would tomorrow morning be OK?'

The two exchanged glances then Shakti Patel said, 'I suppose so.'

'Come to my office at eleven then.' I gave him the address. 'Shani's house won't be ready till the weekend, but I take it she can stay with you for the time being?'

'Of course.'

'I'll see you tomorrow then and, don't worry, everything will be fine.'

*   *   *

Jim Burroughs was delighted when I told him the news. 'Looks like we've cracked it,' he said. 'I'll get on to Leonard Smithson's lawyer straight away.'

'Find out the addresses of the other two jurors, and I'll go round and see them. If we can get them to testify as well, we're laughing.'

'Smithson'll be pleased when I tell him. They won't be able to keep Joanna locked up for much longer after this. It's still only half the job done though, Johnny,' he cautioned.

'Mottram, you mean?'

'You can bet your life he'll have covered his tracks this time just as he did with the kidnapping.'

'Which means Smithson's still got him on his back.'

'I reckon we've got to carry on with the investigation into Harry Mottram as a separate issue. If nothing else, it'll keep the fees coming in. Doesn't do to solve cases too quickly.'

'God, you're a cynical bugger, Jim. How did you get on with Ormesher? Did he tell you anything about Mottram?'

'He's on leave till tomorrow but I did speak to Walter Glass at Scotland Yard about the Blease murder.'

'And?'

'He's on the case. Your observation was spot on – Glass is a maverick copper all right, likes to do things his own way. Now I've given him his own little mystery to investigate, he's as happy as a pig in shit. If anyone will find the Westcotts, he will.'

'A good day's work, Jim, and the Auschwitz puzzle solved too, don't forget. No wonder no one had ever heard of it.'

I went off to do the show in good humour. Maria would have a meal ready afterwards and I was glad to be going back to what I realised I'd come to regard as home.

My night at Hilary's I'd wiped from my mind.

'There's been loads of phone calls about this Joanna Smithson case,' Ken said when I reached the radio station. 'People are saying she ought to be released and that she should never have been brought to trial in the first place. Do you want to do a phone-in?'

'Good idea,' I said. The response was amazing. I played 'I Want To Break Free' by Queen and, by the time it finished, all the phone lines were lit up. A hastily conducted TV poll had revealed at teatime that ninety-one per cent of people who voted thought Joanna should be released immediately. Little did they know there was now every chance she would be.

'How did the gig go last night?' asked Maria when I arrived at hers. 'Were The Chocolate Lavatory the stars of the show?'

'Put it this way, I won't be doing a Frank Sinatra and making an annual comeback. That's it for me and drumming. My shoulders feel like I've rowed the Channel single-handed.'

'Just when I've told Victoria her daddy's going to be another Ringo Starr. That'll teach you to try being a teenager at your age.' Maria laughed. 'Sit at the table and I'll bring the dinner through.'

'I take it you've heard about Joanna Smithson,' I said as she sat down to eat. She'd made curried chicken with sultanas and there was peach chutney to go with it.

'It was on the news at lunchtime. Oh, Johnny, it's terrible. That poor girl, still stuck in prison.'

'It might not be for much longer.' I related the story of Shani's uncle.

'No wonder we could never find Auschwitz 101. They didn't exist. So all that searching we did was a waste of time?'

'Seems like it, but at least we've got to the bottom of it in the end.'

'So her uncle is going to testify, is he?'

'Jim's arranging for him to see Joanna's solicitor tomorrow morning. Furthermore, there's two other members of the jury that he thinks may have been got at.'

'Does he know which ones?'

'I've got their names and Jim's trying to find out where they live. With a bit of luck, we'll be able to persuade them to give evidence as well.'

'So that'll be all your cases solved in one weekend?'

'Not quite. There's still the Missing Goalkeeper.'

'I thought that was finished. Burnt to death in a house fire, you said, and you thought it was murder only it wasn't up to you to prove it.'

'It is now. Norris Pond wants me to investigate Digger Blease's death.'

'So you're back on the case. Does this mean you'll be going to London?'

'Maybe, but not yet. Jim Burroughs has got some old police buddy of his down there trying to trace the Westcotts for us.'

'You do think it's them who killed him then?'

'Not them, him – Peter Westcott. Who else? The cuckolded husband. He had the perfect motive.'

'There is another possibility, Johnny. It could be that Mrs Westcott had got tired of him and wanted rid.'

'I never thought of that. Blease wouldn't leave her alone, you mean?'

'She could have persuaded her husband to move to London without telling him the real reason, to get away from Blease. Maybe he never even knew about him. Imagine her horror, though, when he turns up again on her doorstep in London.'

'So she kills him, is that what you're saying?'

'It must be a possibility. Or they did it together. She tells her husband Blease has been bothering her. It won't have been difficult for them to find out where he was staying.'

'Mmmm.' I knew Maria was right. But I was still left with the same problem, finding the Westcotts.

'What are you doing in the morning?' she asked.

'It's Tuesday, isn't it? I usually go to Aigburth Road to check out the flats with Geoffrey then at eleven I've got a meeting at the office with Mr Patel and Smithson's solicitor. Why?'

'No reason. I just thought we might take Victoria for a walk into Crosby Village. There's a book I want to pick up at Pritchards Bookshop and I've a few things I need from Sainsbury's then I thought we could have a cup of tea at the Copper Kettle. It'd be nice to go out as a family for once and Roly could do with the exercise.'

'Yes, all right. I'll ring Geoff and tell him I won't be in till the afternoon. But I'll have to be at the office at eleven.'

'I'll make sure we get up early.'

We were in Pritchards by nine-thirty. Maria had ordered a copy of the new Lyn Andrews novel. She was a big fan of Liverpool sagas. I thought of the morning before when I'd been in a similar shop in Heswall. With Hilary. It seemed like I was living two parallel lives.

We never got to the Copper Kettle. As we came out of Pritchards, my mobile rang.

'At last you've switched it on,' came Jim Burroughs's voice. 'You'd better get down here quick.'

'What's up?'

'It's Mr Patel. He's been murdered.'

Chapter Nineteen

It was a classic execution. Two bullets in the forehead. Instant death. He was shot down a few hundred yards from his shop towards the top of Smithdown Road by a man on a motor cycle. Witnesses saw nothing.

'They wouldn't do in Smithdown Road,' I said. 'It would be more than their lives were worth.'

'It happened late last night. According to his niece, he had a phone call from someone asking him to meet them down the road.'

I was in the Dale Street office along with Jim Burroughs, Detective Inspector Clive Ormesher, Leonard Smithson and his solicitor. The solicitor was a small Jewish man in his late forties with a thin black moustache and John Lennon glasses.

'We'll need these other two jurors from the trial to come forward and testify,' said Ormesher, 'if Patel's claims are to be substantiated.' Jim had already apprised him of Shakti Patel's revelations.

'If they're not dead already,' I said.

'What we should be doing is finding Harry Mottram,' said Jim Burroughs angrily.

'There's nothing to connect Mottram to the case,' pointed out Ormesher. 'We suspect him of being involved in various nefarious activities but officially he's clean. You find me something concrete and we'll bring him in.'

Leonard Smithson spoke up. 'Does this mean my daughter's appeal can't go ahead?'

'We've already lodged the appeal,' his solicitor said. 'I'm waiting for a date.'

'With a bit of luck, you'll have the other two jurors by then,' said Jim.

The solicitor looked doubtful. 'Provided they're not too frightened to talk.'

'We'll give them protection,' said Ormesher, but nobody was impressed by that.

The meeting broke up shortly afterwards. 'What do you reckon then?' I asked Jim when everybody had left.

'Mottram's efficient and ruthless. What's more, I tend to think that the second man in the kidnapping, whoever he was, has been killed as well so there'll be no witnesses left there either.'

'What was the point of making sure Joanna was convicted, that's what I don't understand. There'd be no monetary gain in it for him.'

'Nastiness, I guess. His kidnap attempt was foiled so he was going to make her pay for it.'

'In which case, it's time I started doing a little digging.'

'Be careful, Johnny. He's not a man to be crossed and he knows we're working for Smithson. Someone must have seen you at Patel's yesterday afternoon and that's why he was killed.'

'No, Jim. Patel's fate was decided before he left the court-room, take my word for it.'

I needed to know more about Mottram and who his associates were, and the man to tell me was Tommy McKale. I found him at his Marina Health and Leisure Club.

'He's working out in the gym,' the receptionist informed me. 'He says to wait in the juice bar upstairs and he'll be with you in a few minutes.'

The juice bar was newly fitted out in stainless steel and black leather furnishings. A West Indian bartender in a tuxedo served me with a freshly squeezed orange juice and I flicked through a copy of *Men's Health* until Tommy appeared, a few minutes later, dressed in a purple tracksuit and towelling his hair.

He fetched himself a bottle of isometric Lucozade from behind the bar and led me to a table.

'A contract killing, eh?' he mused, when I told him of Shakti Patel's shooting. 'It's a good game to be in, all right, although it's getting a bit overcrowded of late. You can book a hit for just a couple of ton these days although there's no guarantee of success, of course. A lot of these so-called hit-men are just looking for their next fix. They'll do anything for money. No way are they pros. You still think Harry Mottram's behind it all?'

'If Smithson is to be believed, and I can't see why he'd lie.'

'Mottram wants Smithson's club, doesn't he?'

'I don't think he's pursuing that after what's happened.'

'I wouldn't assume that, Johnny. He may lie low for a bit but I wouldn't bank on him giving up.'

'You know Joanna Smithson's been found guilty of killing this Dewhurst, Mottram's henchman, don't you? It was in all the papers yesterday. She's pulled seven years for manslaughter and we believe Mottram was nobbling two other members of the jury besides Patel to make sure she got sent down.'

'Of course he would be. He'd owe one to Dewhurst's family.'

'Honour among thieves?'

'That's bollocks. No, to stop them talking. He wouldn't be able to risk Dewhurst having mentioned his name somewhere along the line and the relatives would be looking for revenge. They'd want to see the girl go down, and I expect he'll be bankrolling them as well to keep them sweet. Mottram will be an angry man right now. This little lot will have cost him.'

'The thing is, the day before he was killed, Patel gave me the name of two other jurors who might be willing to admit they were intimidated, so if they testify, the girl's sentence could be quashed.'

'If they've any sense they'll be on their way to Australia by now.'

'The police are going to see them today.'

'Today? They'd have been too late yesterday. The minute Mottram got the verdict he wanted, those jurors' cards would have been marked. They'd served their purpose. Mottram's man would have been primed for the job the second the verdict was read out.'

It wasn't what I wanted to hear.

'There's also the other kidnapper, Tommy. Nobody's ever traced him. Jim Burroughs reckons he might have been stiffed.'

'Burroughs could be right. He'd be a loose cannon and nobody wants that. On the other hand . . .'

'What?'

'He could be Mottram's first lieutenant. He could be the one who did for Patel.'

'How much do you know about Mottram himself, Tommy?'

'He's behind an outfit called Conqueror who've got the security sewn up in ninety per cent of the clubs in town.'

Why, when anyone mentions security firms, does one always think ex-cons?

'But not yours?' I said.

Tommy gave a chilling laugh. 'I do my own security.' I didn't press the point.

'How did he manage to get that percentage?'

'The usual way – strong-arm stuff. He took out a couple of important faces early on. That won him the respect.'

'The Law has nothing on him.'

'They won't have. He's careful.' Tommy smiled. 'Either that or he must be on the Square. Did I tell you, by the way, that I'm to be the next Grand Master at our Lodge?'

It didn't surprise me. 'I remember when Big Alec had the honour. How is he, by the way?'

'Alec? He's sound. He'll be on hand if you have any trouble with Mottram.'

'Mottram's not an easy man to be up against. He covers his tracks well.'

'Delegation, Johnny, that's the secret. All the best generals knew it. The trick is not to let the troops know who's doing the delegating, then they can't cough if they're caught.'

'Can you nose around for me?'

'Sure. Tell the truth, I'm getting a bit fidgety about Mottram myself. He's moving too close to some of my own operations. He may need a gentle reminder.'

'Won't that be risky?'

Tommy McKale spat on his newly polished pine floor. 'If he tries anything with me, my boys will have him melted down for glue, the old Dr Mengele trick – which reminds me, what happened about that Auschwitz business?'

'There was no Auschwitz 101. It turned out to be Mottram. My tenant that got beaten up was Patel's niece. Trashing my house and putting the frighteners on her was Mottram's way of making sure Patel helped persuade the other jurors to go for the guilty verdict.'

'Pretty much his style. He owes you for the damage and the inconvenience, Johnny. It's personal. And as you are a friend of mine, he owes me.' He spoke the words as if he was pronouncing a capital sentence on Harry Mottram and, knowing Tommy McKale, he might well have been.

'I've never even met the man and I think it's time I saw what he looks like. Where does he hang out?'

'Different places. All upmarket. He's into the charity circuit, sportsman's evenings, golf club dinners, you know the sort of thing, where the rich and respectable are allowed to mingle with gangsters, footballers and showbusiness personalities and give their money away. All in a good cause, of course, and it gives them a vicarious thrill.'

'A bit like this place really.' I'd noticed a couple of Liverpool players come in earlier.

'Exactly.' He thought for a moment. 'There's a fashion show on tonight at Formby Hall Golf Club, big charity do. Local dress designers showing off their wares, slap-up meal followed by an auction. I bet Mottram will be attending that.'

'Where do I get a ticket?'

'Fifty quid at the door but I'm sure you'll be able to blag your way in, Johnny.'

'I'll let you know how I get on,' I said, rising to leave.

'Just take care, that's all. My funeral suit's at the cleaners.'

I stopped off to buy fish and chips in Park Road on my way to the Aigburth Road office.

'I've heard the news, boss,' Geoffrey said, 'about Mr Patel.'

'Terrible, isn't it?' I spread the fish and chips out on the table. They taste better from the paper although not as good as in the days when they used to wrap them in out-of-date copies of the *Sun*. 'Help yourself to chips,' I added, seeing Geoffrey's eyes staring hungrily at the cod. I went over to the fridge and found myself a can of Scrumpy Jack.

'Thanks.' He managed to cram three in his mouth. 'So it wasn't a racist attack at Kirkdale after all?'

'That doesn't make the damage any less.'

'No, but it means it's unlikely to happen again,' pointed out Geoffrey, who was forever practical.

'True.'

'Will Shani Patel be going back there, do you think?'

'Too soon to say. I must go round and see her. I've not been in touch since her uncle was killed.' Things had got so busy. 'Have there been any messages for me?'

'Hilary rang. Said she's finishing early and wondered if you were free for a drink.' That stopped me dead. I knew I'd left it on Sunday that I'd ring her, but Hilary wasn't stupid. She wasn't going to let me go without a fight. As things were with Maria at the moment, I might have not returned Hilary's call, but taking her with me to the Golf Club would be good cover. Or so I told myself. Maybe I needed the excuse.

'Anyone else?'

'Only Shirley. She rang to see if everything was OK with you.' I smiled. I knew she'd be referring to the Hilary and Maria situation.

'Tell her I'm fine,' I said. 'No, wait a minute; tell her I'm a walking time bomb, that'd be nearer the truth. She'll know what I mean.'

'We all know what you mean, boss,' grinned Geoffrey, helping himself to more chips. He'd had years of experience of my turbulent love-life.

'Oh, and tell her she's nothing to worry about any more with the Auschwitz business. I'd been warning her to watch out for attacks herself. Say it was a false alarm.'

I rang Maria to apologise for abandoning her in Crosby Village but I got the answerphone and remembered it was her afternoon shift at the Library. I left a message saying I'd be out late and would probably spend the night at the flat and that I'd ring her in the morning. Roly wouldn't be pleased at spending an enforced afternoon in his basket. He was used to being out with me. Sometimes, it was a dog's life.

I phoned Hilary at the hospital, had the usual problems with the switchboard, but they finally put me through to her ward and I told her I'd pick her up at nine. She was delighted we were going out again so soon.

'Good job I keep a change of clothes here,' she said when I told her about the Golf Club.

Finally, I rang Jim to find out if Clive Ormesher had managed to get in touch with the two jurors yet but he'd heard nothing.

'Have you got their addresses there?' I asked.

He had, but I wasn't going to be allowed to visit them. 'Leave this one to the police, Johnny. Clive knows what he's doing. You concentrate on Mottram. Have you had any luck so far?'

'Give me a chance. I've got Tommy McKale looking out for me.' Jim didn't reply. He's never been keen on

Tommy, possibly because he'd never managed to put him away during his thirty years on the Force and, now he'd retired, he never would. Obviously, it still rankled. 'I'll see you in the morning,' I said.

I wasn't due at the radio station till half-past five so I drove over to Livingstone Drive. Badger was somebody else I ought to bring up to date on the Auschwitz situation.

He was in his living room recording some dance tracks on his massive hi-fi system. The sound shook the walls, vying with the thumping of Bon Jovi coming from Pat Lake's flat on the floor below. As the landlord, I felt I ought to say something but Badger spoke first, almost shouting over the booming music.

'I've dug up nothing about your neo-Nazi mob, if that's what you've come for, man.'

'That's because they don't exist, Badger.'

I walked into the room. He shut the door, turned the volume down and I briefly explained the new developments to him.

'You're telling me I spent all those valuable man hours on a wild-goose chase?'

'I'll see you right,' I said.

'See me right? You should take me on your staff.'

'Maybe I will, but for now what I'm after is information on a man called Harry Mottram who runs a security outfit called Conqueror. He's a killer.' I corrected myself. 'Maybe not literally but he's pulling the strings and it wouldn't do to cross him.'

'What's your interest?'

'A client of mine,' I said guardedly. 'He's had a run-in with Mottram and asked me to check him out, but don't ever mention my name. Mottram knows I'm involved with this client.'

'Wouldn't be a Mr Smithson, by any chance?' And, when I looked surprised, 'I read the papers too, you know.'

I'd forgotten the trial had been fully reported in the press. 'You'll know then that Smithson believes Mottram kidnapped his daughter.'

'In order to get his hands on Nirvana. Nice place. I go there myself.'

'Is there anywhere you don't go?'

'What's the deal then?'

'Fifty upfront to cover the Auschwitz débâcle and a ton on top when you find anything useful.'

'Make it two-fifty, man. This is skilled work.'

'For two-fifty, Badger, I could have Mottram shot and buried and save us all a lot of trouble. A ton it is.'

He sighed. 'Worth a try.'

I handed over a fifty-pound note. 'I want to know where Mottram comes from, how he got his money, what's the next job he's pulling, who works for him, that sort of thing.'

'You don't ask much but, as a matter of fact, you might have struck lucky here.'

'Why's that?'

'I happen to know your Mr Mottram.'

'How come?'

'In fact, I've been doing a little work for him.'

'What sort of work?' Despite his academic background, Badger could turn his hand to most things.

'Just a bit of driving.'

'In all the years I've known you, Badger, I'd never have had you down for a cabbie.'

'Not quite like that, man. Mottram hangs around at a few of the places I go to. One night his chauffeur didn't turn up and he offered me a ton to drive him home in his Ferrari.'

'To Cheshire?'

'That's right. Hunt balls and stables country.'

'How'd you get home?'

'He put me up for the night and I ran him back into town the next morning.'

'Was his wife with him?'

'I'll say. A tasty piece too. Half his age, of course.'

'And you've done this more than once?'

'Three or four times. Nice motor.'

'I can imagine. And has he said anything about what he does?'

'No, but he's certainly one of the top players in town, that's for sure.'

'Tell me, have you ever seen anyone else in his house apart from his wife?'

'No, never – wait a minute, one morning there *was* a guy in the kitchen. I thought he must be a gardener or something.'

'What did he look like?'

'Mean. In his twenties, thin, about your height, very short hair.'

I was excited. It was only vague but it fitted the description of the second man who had helped kidnap Joanna Smithson.

'And you only saw him the once?' Badger nodded. 'Did he speak at all?'

'Just "all right, pal" or something like that.'

A Liverpool expression and Joanna had said the man had a Scouse accent. I felt we could be on to something. I made my way to the door and Badger followed me on to the landing. 'See if you can find out who he is,' I said, 'but be careful. Mottram's dangerous.'

'Before you go, *Mr Landlord*,' he emphasised the word, 'I wish you'd tell that woman downstairs to stop playing that heavy-metal crap.' Bon Jovi was echoing up from the first-floor landing. 'It does my ears in.'

I drove straight to the radio station to do the show. I played a couple of tracks from the soon-to-be-released album by Southport band Gomez; the Beatles' composition, 'Getting Better', and 'Cowboy Song'. Gomez were the latest Merseyside group to hit the big time and I noticed their record company was cleverly marketing them as a roots band, thus extending their shelf-life beyond the normal boy-band span and giving them a chance to be recognised as individual musicians.

I was still in the studio, putting the last track up on the screen, when the door opened and Jim Burroughs marched in, followed by my anxious producer.

'I told him you were on air,' protested Ken, 'but he insisted.'

'It's OK, Ken,' I said and, gesturing to Jim, hissed, 'Sit down and shut up a minute.' I turned to the mike. 'That was "Cowboy Song" for David and Jill, and for our last track tonight, we've got one from the new David Allen Coe album, just in from the States.' Ken winced. He remembered what had happened when I last played a David Allen Coe track, the wrong one, and got banned off the air. 'It's the old George Jones classic, the ultimate weepy song, "He Stopped Loving Her Today". That's all from me tonight, folks. This is Johnny Ace saying, Have fun, be good, see you the same time tomorrow.'

I clicked on the mouse, switched off the mike and turned to face Jim. 'Now what's so bloody important?'

'Mrs Ridgeway, the juror Ormesher went to see. She's topped herself.'

Chapter Twenty

'Genuine suicide,' I asked, 'or murder in disguise?'

'She left a note saying *I can't live with my conscience.*'

'That's not much use. She might at least have given us the full lowdown on the jury rigging before she went, made her death worthwhile. How did she do it?'

'Tablets. Enough to put a dinosaur to sleep.'

'Saved Mottram two hundred pounds then.' Jim looked at me queryingly. 'That's what Tommy McKale reckons you can get a hit-man for these days.'

'Does he? Well, he'd know, wouldn't he? I don't think it's a good idea getting him involved with the agency, Johnny. We'll get a bad reputation using people like McKale.'

'You know what they say, Jim. Set a thief to catch a thief and all that.'

'McKale's more than just a simple thief. You should see the dossier we had on him at HQ.'

'Same principle applies down the line. Set a gangster et cetera. And it's the dossier *they've* got on him, Jim, not we. You're not with the Old Bill any more.'

Ken was watching this exchange with obvious enjoyment. 'You two don't half see life when you're outside this studio, don't you?'

'Not only see it, Ken, but live it as well.' I clapped him on the shoulder. 'See you tomorrow if we haven't been assassinated.' I waited until we'd walked out into the car park before I asked Jim, 'What about the other juror, the lad with the pony tail?'

'Graham Duxfield his name is. He's missing from home. Ormesher's men went round to his flat off Sefton Park but there was no sign of him.'

'He's probably dead behind the door.'

'No, they went in. By the looks of it, he hadn't been back since the trial ended. The weekend newspapers were still in his letterbox. Ormesher left a man outside his door in case he comes back.'

'They should have collared him as soon as he came out of the court. He'll be floating in the Huskisson Dock by now.'

'That's where they found your pal Matt Scrufford, isn't it, in the Huskisson?'

'My first case. A popular spot for dumping corpses, I'm told.'

'There could be any number of reasons he didn't go home. He could have gone on holiday, be staying with a friend . . .'

'Come on, Jim. You know it and I know it. Mottram's got to him.'

'Not definitely,' objected Jim, reluctant to give up hope.

I remembered what Tommy McKale had said about delegation. 'The annoying thing is that, even if we had got Duxfield on the witness-stand and he'd admitted to being threatened in some way, he wouldn't have known it was Mottram behind it all.'

'Maybe not, but at least he'd have confirmed the jury was rigged which would help Joanna in her appeal.'

'I wonder how she's coping in prison?'

'I don't expect she's loving it.'

'Durham's where Rosemary West is, isn't it? It doesn't seem right that a young girl like that should be closeted with mass murderers.'

'In the eyes of the Law, Johnny, she's a killer herself.'

'I wonder what hold they had over Mrs Ridgeway to make her vote the way they wanted. Did she have family?'

'No, she was a widow. Lived alone with her Yorkshire Terrier.'

'Oh, that would be it then. They probably threatened to kidnap the pooch. How about Duxfield?'

'He lived on his own as well.'

So many people do nowadays. No wonder we're short of houses. 'What about family?' I asked.

'His mother's still alive. Clive Ormesher was going there next.'

'I'm going to Formby Hall Golf Club tonight in the hope I can spot Mottram. I like to put a face to my enemies. Are you off home?'

Jim nodded. 'I'm already late for dinner. Rosemary will be having kittens.'

We got into our respective cars. I drove back to the flat and threw a chicken tikka masala into the microwave. I knew that by the time we reached Formby, the dinner would be as good as over.

Meal finished, I took a hot shower and put on a dark charcoal suit for the occasion, with a purple shirt and tie and was pleased to see, when I picked her up, that Hilary had thought the same. She wore a black trouser suit with a cornflower-blue blouse and black platform shoes.

'I'm starving,' were her first words, followed by, 'Did you say it was dinner?'

'It was, but I think we're going to be a bit late for it. We should be able to get something though,' I added hopefully.

As we drove along the bypass, we stopped at the traffic lights at Tesco. I pointed it out to Hilary. 'That's where Joanna Smithson was adbucted.'

'I bet she wished she'd gone to Safeways instead.'

'I don't think it would have made any difference. It was carefully planned. They were following her car.' And now I was about to meet the man who'd masterminded it all.

There was no problem getting into the function. The dinner had just finished and most of the diners were taking a break whilst staff cleared the tables and set up rows of chairs in preparation for the fashion show. We mingled with the crowd.

I stopped a waiter and enquired about the chances of some food, explaining we had arrived late.

'I could fix you a plate of sandwiches, sir,' he said helpfully, and he didn't ask to see my ticket, which was a bonus. 'Would poached salmon be acceptable?'

Hilary said it would be and she waited by the bar whilst I ordered drinks.

'Doesn't Kenny Dalglish own this place?' she asked.

'I don't think he owns it but he certainly plays here from time to time, along with Kevin Keegan, Jimmy Tarbuck and all the other celebrity golfers.'

We were making conversation. I knew Hilary was annoyed about missing the meal but the underlying reason was undoubtedly The Situation.

When the sandwiches arrived, we found seats at the back of the room. The fashion show was just starting. A procession of girls with skeletal figures marched on stage, demonstrating the latest in designer wear as stocked by Charis, Southport's answer to Yves St Laurent. As if to prove that they didn't cater just for bulimics, an army of plumper, more matronly women were brought on next, all dressed as if on their way to a Buckingham Palace garden party.

Finally, the Kate Moss brigade returned in revealing swimwear followed by a belly dancer called Fatima. This brought forth a few whistles from some inebriated members of the audience, egged on by bawdy infantile banter from the compère, a portly man with bushy hairs sprouting from his nostrils and damp patches under the arms of his gaudy Hawaiian shirt.

'He's embarrassing,' said Hilary. 'What made them hire a man to compère a women's fashion show? They should have had proper radio presenters like Erica Hughes or Debi Jones, people who know what they're doing.'

'I agree.'

'I tell you what, I love that bikini,' she said, indicating a bright yellow creation that barely covered the girl modelling it. 'I wonder how much it is?'

'If the amount of material is any guide, I'd say not more than 50p.' Hilary would have looked sensational in it.

More fashion houses followed and it was eleven o'clock when the final part of the evening, the charity auction, began.

It was the usual stuff. A Liverpool shirt signed by Michael Owen, a free hairdo at Headlines, a meal for two at the Red Squirrel and so on – all expected to fetch prices far beyond their value.

As a selling pitch it was perfect, exploiting the punter's one-upmanship at being seen to outbid their colleagues and taking advantage of their guilt at being rich enough to attend the event in the first place.

Business was brisk. Fuelled by alcohol, the audience fought to give their money away. It didn't take long for me to pick out Harry Mottram.

'Four hundred.' He was in the bidding for one of the football shirts. He wore a red cummerbund with his dinner suit and the hand that was raised was adorned with two large gold rings. Flashy and trashy.

The compère was careful to identify each bidder by name. 'Mr Mottram's bid,' he emphasised. 'Four hundred pounds. It's up to you now, Mr Donaldson, can I say five hundred?'

All heads turned to an affluent-looking man, also in evening dress, who had previously bid £350. He hesitated for a moment then, conscious of the eyes of the room upon him, he nodded.

'Five hundred, Mr Donaldson. Mr Mottram?' The auctioneer turned his gaze across the room. 'Your bid. Can I say six hundred?'

No hesitation here. 'Why not?' boomed the alleged kidnapper of Joanna Smithson.

'Six hundred to Mr Mottram.'

There the bidding stopped. To a round of applause, Mottram was ceremoniously handed the shirt as he wrote out a cheque in full view of the room.

'I bet that shirt cost less than a tenner to manufacture,' I whispered to Hilary, 'yet just because some millionaire footballer has scrawled some indecipherable message on it, it sells for an inflated price like that.'

'Didn't you ever collect autographs when you were a boy?' she asked.

'Never. Of course,' I admitted, 'if I'd known what they'd be worth later, I'd have been right in there.'

The auction continued but I was paying more attention to Harry Mottram. The blonde girl next to him, at least fifteen years his junior, I took to be his wife. Sitting down, she was slightly taller than he. His skin was sallow with a noticeable five o'clock shadow. He was too old for designer stubble. His brown hair hung an inch too long over the collar of his light grey mohair suit.

Despite the surface geniality, I found his a menacing face, the face of a man you wouldn't care to cross.

And I had a strange feeling I'd seen him before.

Or maybe I was subconsciously projecting what I knew of the man's character on to his features. Either way, I wouldn't have bought a second-hand car from him, as they used to say of President Richard Nixon, another of the great unshaven.

We got away a touch after midnight. Hilary snuggled up to me in the car as I drove out of the car park and along the winding road to the bypass.

'Twice in three days,' she whispered. 'Aren't I the lucky one?' She slipped her hand under my seat belt.

'I'm not sure this is allowed in the Highway Code,' I said, but I didn't move her hand away. By the time we reached the flat, we were both in a state of some agitation.

'Your eyes have gone glazed again,' she giggled. 'They always do that.'

'No wonder. The windows are steamed up too.' I staggered out of the car. 'Let's get inside before we're arrested.'

'Where's the dog?' she asked as we walked into the flat. 'I was expecting to be knocked over.'

'He's at Geoff's.' The lie came quickly and, for a split second, before Hilary resumed her ministrations, I remembered where I should have been. But I didn't get any time to worry about it.

I was awake at seven. Hilary was sleeping peacefully so I didn't wake her. I had a shower, put on a clean T-shirt and jeans and went to make myself my usual breakfast – 'mush' as Hilary calls my mixture of Force wheat flakes, Bemax, All Bran, honey, nutmeg, sultanas and boiling milk, followed by tea and toast.

On the morning local news, the Mrs Ridgeway suicide was top billing amid speculation that Joanna Smithson might get a re-trial. I thought it unlikely. Nothing was mentioned about the missing juror, Graham Duxfield.

Hilary yawned her way into the kitchen an hour later, wearing my dressing gown. 'God, is that the time? I'm supposed to be on duty at nine.'

'You'll make it. I'll give you a lift. The tea's still hot and I'll put some toast in for you.'

She looked fondly at me. 'This could have been us, you know, Johnny.' She put her arms around my neck and nuzzled my ear. 'Still could be if you want it.'

'No, it couldn't, Hil. "Us" was freedom, able to do what we wanted but still having each other. Free spirits. No ties.'

'And what are you and Maria? Is she a free spirit too?'

'Hil, it's eight in the morning, you're late for work, I'm in the middle of a case, I've no time for philosophical discussions.'

Her lips tightened. 'That's a "no" then?'

'It's not anything. It's just not the time to discuss it.' I didn't know when the right time would be.

I dropped Hilary off at the hospital. 'It was good last night, wasn't it?' she said.

'It was,' I replied and I meant it. 'I'll ring you before the weekend. Promise.'

'I'll hold you to that.' She smiled, kissed me on the lips and jumped out of the car.

Who said bigamy was all bad?

*   *   *

For once, I was in the office before Jim, just in time to take a phone call from London. It was Jim's Scotland Yard contact, DI Glass.

'I'm his partner,' I explained. 'How are your enquiries going?'

'As if we haven't enough cases of our own without you digging up new ones,' he grumbled.

'It is a case then?'

'You tell me. It hasn't been up to now, unless you want to make it one. As things stand, the Fire Brigade have it down as an accident. The blaze started in the bedroom. A classic case really. The victim has probably had a skinful, he lights a cigarette then passes out in a drunken stupor. The bedclothes catch fire and within minutes the whole house goes up by which time he's long dead, suffocated by the smoke. End of story.'

'Did you find out the address of the guest-house?'

'I did.' He read it out to me and I knew we were on the right trail.

'I think we have a case,' I told him.

The address was the one to which Leslie Lomax had sent the Westcotts' cheque.

Chapter Twenty-one

But Detective Chief Inspector Glass, as he now was, already knew this.

'The house had been bought two months before by Peter and Patricia Westcott. I presume this is the couple your colleague asked me to trace?'

'Yes, and the time-scale fits in with when they left Liverpool.'

'From what I can gather, it doesn't appear to have been registered as a hotel with the local authority. It seems as if they just took in the odd lodger.'

'You don't have to register if you let three rooms or less.' At least you didn't before the advent of Mr Blair and all the European regulations. Now you need government permission to have your mother-in-law to stay for a week.

Blease was the only person lodging there on that fateful night.

'According to the evidence the Westcotts gave at the inquest, Blease arrived about five o'clock and Mrs Westcott showed him to his room. He told her he would be going out for a meal later whereupon she gave him a front door key, explaining that she and her husband were attending the theatre and might not be back in time to let him in.'

'Seems plausible.'

'And when they came back . . .'

'A remake of *The Towering Inferno*.'

'With Mr Blease burnt to a crisp save for a signet ring which Mrs Westcott later identified as the one she'd seen on his finger when he signed the register.'

'It was Mrs Westcott who identified the body?'

'That's right.'

'And what was the coroner's verdict?'

'Accidental death, of course.'

'Of course?'

'Nothing else he could give. There was no suggestion of foul play or arson. I've checked the insurance claim. Nothing untoward there. The Westcotts had nothing to gain by torching the place.'

'They may have had debts.'

'I don't think so.'

'What makes you say that?'

'They owned the house outright, no mortgage.'

I remembered the comments their neighbour at Childwall had made about the Westcotts' lifestyle. Perhaps they'd had money stashed away. 'Our theory is that Blease was murdered,' I said.

'By the Westcotts?'

'By Mr Westcott. Blease had been having it away with Mrs W. when they all lived in Liverpool.'

'That never came out at the inquest.'

'Was anyone at the inquest from Blease's family?'

'The report doesn't say.'

'Like his ex-wife?'

'No mention of anyone.'

'What about a will?'

'I haven't checked with Somerset House. Do you want me to?'

'It can't do any harm.'

'I'll get back to you.'

'Before you go, I take it you haven't found out yet what happened to the Westcotts?'

'Give me a chance. We do have other crimes down here, you know. I've had three murders, a jewel robbery and two armed raids so far this week and it's only Wednesday. Who is it behind this enquiry, anyway?'

'Believe it or not, a man writing a football club history.'

'It's all right, you don't have to tell me.' He sounded aggrieved.

'No, really. Blease was their goalkeeper.' I had to admit it did sound far-fetched. Why had I believed it? And what was Norris Pond's real reason for hiring me?

'I'll be in touch.' Glass rang off. Less than a minute later, Jim came in.

'You've just missed your DCI Glass on the phone,' I said.

'Has he found anything?'

'He certainly has. The Westcotts owned the guest-house Blease died in.'

'Well, well, so it looks like foul play for certain. Revenge of the wronged husband, eh? I don't suppose he's had any joy finding the Westcotts?'

'Not yet, but he knows now that he's looking for a possible murderer. I'm afraid I might have upset him, though.' I explained about my football club remark. 'I think he thought I was taking the piss.'

'I'll give him a ring later and smooth him over,' promised Jim.

'You know, we need to try and track down Blease's ex-wife. There was no mention of her at the inquest, strangely enough.'

'Who identified the body then?'

'Patti Westcott.'

'Well, she'd recognise it if anyone would. She'd seen it often enough.'

'Not in that state. If you remember, Jim, he was cinders by the time she saw him. Ready for his new career as an egg-timer.'

Jim sat down behind his desk. 'Let's get this straight then. We both agree, do we, that Westcott somehow knocked Blease out and set fire to the bed before creeping away to the theatre with Mrs W. to establish his alibi?'

'Or just got him legless and then perhaps smothered him.

Wouldn't have been too difficult. There is the other possibility, of course, that it was Mrs Westcott who did it.'

'I'd go for Mr personally, but I take your point. Certainly it's one or other of them.'

'Or maybe both?' I suggested. 'A joint effort.'

'Wherever they are, they'll hardly be on their guard any more. They must think they've got away with it after twenty years.'

'They certainly won't be expecting to have their collars felt, that's for sure. It's just finding them that'll be the hard bit.'

'Going back to Blease's missus, Jim, surely someone would have informed her at the time?'

'If they knew she existed. His next-of-kin would have been notified and presumably that would have been his ex-wife with both his parents dead.'

'It would help if we knew where he was buried. Was it in London or was he brought back to Liverpool to be buried with his parents?'

'Or cremated.'

'Second time round on the toaster, the poor bugger.'

'If it was in London, the Westcotts must have been holding their breath. If they did kill Blease, they wouldn't want too many relatives arriving for the funeral, poking their noses in, asking questions.'

'Maria couldn't find any trace of the ex-Mrs Blease in the phone book or the voters' list.'

'She's probably got married again and changed her name, or left the area altogether.'

'Whichever it is, she won't be easy to find either. She certainly never came forward when I asked for information about Blease on the radio.'

'I'll mention her name to Glass when I ring him,' said Jim.

'I asked Glass to find out for us if Blease made a will. We might get some more names from that – distant relatives perhaps.'

'You know, Johnny, perhaps we're barking up the wrong tree here. We ought to be looking for relatives and friends of the Westcotts instead. It's the Westcotts we need to find. We know where Blease is.'

'True.'

'In the meantime, let's move on,' said Jim. 'Joanna Smithson. How did you get on last night at the Golf Club? Did you see Harry Mottram?'

'Yes, and I didn't like him. I'm sure I've seen him somewhere else, too. Do you think he'll make another move for Smithson's place?'

'He'd be mad to try.'

'Tommy McKale thinks he won't give in that easy.'

'What does he know?'

I didn't pursue the point. 'I take it there's no news on Duxfield?'

'Not yet.'

'I told you, Jim, he'll be ten fathoms deep by now.'

But there I was wrong.

The call came later that morning, seconds after I'd put the phone down on Maria, telling her I'd be round tonight after my show. 'Is that Johnny Ace?' said a trembling voice. 'My name's Graham Duxfield.'

Chapter Twenty-two

'Where are you speaking from?'

Hesitation, then, 'I'm in a mate's flat in West Kirby. I've been staying here since Monday.' He gave me the address and I told him I'd be there within the hour.

'This could be our big break,' I told Jim. 'If we can get him on the stand, we've cracked it. Joanna will be out in hours.'

One half of the Wallasey Tunnel was closed for repair, par for the course, but I still got through to West Kirby in twenty minutes, taking the Moreton–Hoylake road. Apart from the new Safeways down the road from the Promenade, West Kirby has hardly changed since Victorian times. It wouldn't have surprised me to see horses and carriages trotting down the streets. As I drove along the Promenade, a light rain was falling, obscuring the view of the Welsh mountains across the River Dee.

The house was a semi-detached close to the park. I rang the bell and saw the front-room curtains twitch before the door was opened a few inches.

'Johnny Ace?'

'Mr Duxfield?' but I knew it was he by Mr Patel's description. His long blond hair was scraped back from his forehead into a pony tail which hung down over his back. He wore a Grateful Dead T-shirt, faded denims and a pair of scuffed Adidas trainers that could have stunk for England.

He peered round the porch to make sure I was alone then stepped back to allow me entrance into the hallway.

'Can't be too careful,' he whispered nervously. 'They're after me.'

I followed him into the front room where he indicated two bean bags for us to sit on. The walls were lined with concert posters featuring acts like Jimi Hendrix, King Crimson, Captain Beefheart and other progressive rock bands of the 1970s. Boxes of 45s and LPs took up much of the floorspace.

'My friend has a record shop,' he explained, 'mostly rare vinyl. He keeps a lot of his stock here.'

He began to tell me his account of the Joanna Smithson trial. 'Most of us on the jury were rooting for the girl, but the foreman . . .'

'Murphy?'

'That was his name. He was all for finding her guilty from the start and he tried to persuade the rest of us.'

'All of you?'

'Yes. It wasn't hard. Three or four of them didn't seem to give a toss one way or the other. Two of them looked absolute villains themselves. They seemed to think everyone who appeared in the dock was fitted up by the police but they were quite happy to go along with Murphy. Perhaps he threatened them, I don't know. Mind you, there were some who thought the girl should be put away anyway because, for whatever reason, she had killed the bloke after all.'

I thought of Andy Fletcher's Sixths Principle.

'What about the ones who did go against Murphy?'

'There was an Asian bloke, he was all for letting her go, then he suddenly changed his mind. And this old woman, she switched sides too but she didn't seem too happy about it.'

'And what about you? You found her guilty in the end.'

Duxfield lowered his eyes. In the unlit room with his face unshaven and bags under his eyes, he didn't look so young. I had him down for over thirty. 'Murphy found out where my mam lived.'

'And he threatened her?'

'He told me on Saturday night when we were in the hotel

that if I didn't want to be an orphan I had to help put the girl away.'

'But you did as he said, so why are you hiding?'

But I knew the answer. 'Me and the Paki bloke and the old lady, we could have told on him afterwards, couldn't we? He had to shut us up.'

He'd done that all right except, in Mrs Ridgeway's case, she'd saved him the trouble. The big question was, Who was Murphy? And what connection was there between him and Harry Mottram?

Duxfield was coming out of the court when he was stopped by a shaven-headed man. The one Badger had seen in Mottram's kitchen? The second kidnapper? 'He stuck a knife in my side and told me to walk to this car parked up the road outside the Queens.'

'How did you know it was a knife and not a gun?'

'I didn't. It could have been a fucking banana for all I know. I didn't wait to find out.' What he did do was push the man aside and leg it down the road. He managed to give his attacker the slip and dodged into James Street Underground station where he caught a train to West Kirby. He'd stayed here at his friend's house the last two nights.

'What do you know about this Murphy character?'

'Nothing really. He was about forty-five, big chap, forceful manner. That's all I know.'

'You'd recognise him again?'

'Oh yes.'

'And the man with the knife, would you know him?'

'I think so. I saw you at the trial,' he said, 'and I thought you might be the best person to help me. I'm frightened something's happened to my mam. I've been ringing her and there's no answer but I daren't go round in case they're waiting for me.'

That sounded ominous.

'You could have rung the police anonymously and asked them to check up on her.'

He looked at me scornfully. 'Oh yeah? Do you think they'd take any notice? Anyway, they might find out where I was if I did that.'

I didn't argue. 'Look, what we'll do is this,' I said. 'I'll take you to see DI Ormesher, the detective who's handling this case, and you can make a statement to him. On the way, we'll call at your mother's to make sure she's OK.' I dreaded to think what we'd find when we arrived, but that wasn't something I was going to share with Graham Duxfield.

However, he had other ideas. 'I'm not going anywhere near Mam's. I told you – they could be waiting for me. You go and I'll stay here. I'll come with you to the police when she's rung me and I know she's all right, and not before.'

He was adamant and, in the end, I agreed to go to his mother's alone. Mrs Duxfield lived in Anfield, a stone's throw from Liverpool's ground. I wasn't happy about leaving him but I figured he'd been OK so far.

I rang Jim on my mobile to keep him up to date with things. He sounded worried. 'Two dead already, Johnny. You shouldn't have left him. I don't like it.'

'Another couple of hours won't hurt, Jim. I'd like you to find out what you can about this foreman of the jury, this Murphy character. Could he have been planted, do you think?'

'Impossible. They're picked at random. Mottram could never have fixed that.'

'Well, could he have been got at before the trial? Duxfield said he was all for sending the girl down from the very beginning.'

'Can't see it but leave it with me.'

Mrs Duxfield lived in a terraced house with no front garden and a door opening on to the street. The stand of Liverpool's football ground dominated the skyline, making the surrounding streets look like models in a miniature village. There was no reply when I knocked. I tried the house next door and a wrinkled old woman in a headscarf and apron came out.

'Who's it yer want, darlin'?' she asked, a cigarette burning perilously close to her chapped lips.

'I came to see Mrs Duxfield.'

'Not the son?'

'No. His mother.'

'He's hardly here, that lad. Treats the place like a friggin' 'otel. I don't know why she hasn't slung him out.'

'Has she gone away, do you know?'

She spat the dog-end on to the floor and twisted her slippered foot on it. 'Haven't seen her for a couple of days and I've not clapped eyes on him for over a week. She might have gone to her sister's in Kirkby and taken that apology for a dog with her. You a friend of hers?'

'Her son asked me to pick something up,' I lied.

I needed to get inside the house. Just as I was wondering how I could do this, the woman came to my rescue.

'If you know where it is, I've got the spare key. She left it when they went on holiday last year and she never took it back. Not that I'd ever go in, like.'

'Of course not.' Talk about the burglar's friend. She'd made no attempt to ask me for any identification. Whatever happened to Neighbourhood Watch?

The woman disappeared inside her own house and returned, seconds later, with a Yale key in her hand. 'This is the one, dearie.' Ignoring my outstretched hand, she marched up to Mrs Duxfield's front door and inserted the key in the lock. 'There we go, lovey.' She pushed the door open and stepped inside before I could stop her.

I didn't know what I was expecting to find. Probably Mrs Duxfield's body, I suppose, but if so, I was disappointed.

'No one 'ere, darlin',' said her neighbour unnecessarily.

'I'll try upstairs.' I went into both bedrooms. The back one, with record posters on black-painted walls, had obviously been Graham's. Maybe his mother was hoping he'd come back one day. Her room was at the front. The dressing table was littered with bottles of cheap make-up and perfume. Both rooms had single beds made up and not slept in. The bathroom was empty too.

'Must have gone away,' I admitted, going back downstairs.

'Have you got what you came for, sweetheart?' The old lady gave as near an imitation of a leer as was possible with rotting teeth and cold sores. She took out another cigarette, lit it and blew the smoke out in rings.

'Er, no. It was a CD but he must have forgotten to leave it.'

'If I see them, who shall I say you were, luv?'

'Just say Tony called.'

I made a mental note of the telephone number in the hall on my way out and went back to the car, leaving the old lady to lock up.

It was coming up to lunchtime but I'd no time to stop. I rang Jim at the office. 'She's not there,' I told him. 'The woman next door hasn't seen her since Monday.'

'The day of the verdict,' he pointed out grimly.

'I'm going back for Duxfield,' I said. 'Can you let DI Ormesher know I'm bringing him in? We can't afford to let him go, he's the last witness.'

This time, I went through the Birkenhead Tunnel up to the Arrowe Park Hotel and across to Heswall, the route I usually took when I went to Hilary's. Which made me think of Maria who'd be expecting me back tonight, not to mention Roly. I felt as if I'd been away from them for a week.

I came down into West Kirby past The Column, drove through The Crescent and came to Duxfield's hide-out through a neighbourhood of redbrick houses and stone churches. I knew something was wrong the minute I drew up. The front door was slightly ajar. I ran inside and searched all the rooms. There were no signs of a struggle but the house was empty. Graham Duxfield had vanished without trace.

Chapter Twenty-three

'I told you you shouldn't have left him,' Jim barked angrily, after I'd explained how the front door had been open and I'd searched the house in vain.

'I know, I know, it's my fault. Look, I'm going to get some lunch then I'll come straight back to the office.'

'Where are you now?'

'Still at the house in West Kirby.' I remembered his wife came from there. 'Are there any decent pubs round here I can get a bite to eat?'

'The White Lion does a nice steak sandwich.'

'That'll do me. I'll see you later.'

There was a small beer garden behind the pub and I sat outside with my pint of cider and Steak Canadian. The rain had stopped and the sun was trying to come out. An old man with a Robin Hood hat and a walking stick was surveying a pint of bitter at the opposite table. I thought Robin Hood hats had gone out with corgis and cuckoo clocks but West Kirby is a place where people still wear cravats.

I tried to get my head round the Joanna Smithson case. So far as I saw it, once he'd been thwarted on the kidnap job, when Joanna killed Dewhurst, Mottram had embarked on a pretty effective damage-limitation exercise to cover his tracks.

The second kidnapper had been concealed from sight, possibly murdered and disposed of by now. Alternatively, he could be the man Badger had seen in Mottram's kitchen and the one who had accosted Graham Duxfield outside the

159

court. In which case it was probably he who had shot Shakti Patel.

But we now had another man who was probably in Mottram's employ: Murphy, the jury foreman. Again, Mottram had been clever in never allowing himself to be implicated. The way to get to him, I figured, had to be through one of these two men. But where would I find them?

I finished my meal, nodded to Robin Hood Man, who assured me it looked like brightening up, and set off back through the Tunnel. The toll had recently gone up to £1.20. I seemed to remember reading once that when they built the Tunnel they promised free passage in the future as soon as the costs had been recouped, which was about as likely as 'viewers will never have to pay to watch football on British television'.

Jim was in a brighter mood when I got back to the office, and with every reason. 'I've found out where to get hold of this Murphy character; he lives in Netherley in a highrise council flat.' He handed me the address.

'Great. I'll go round there now and find out what's going on. Did you tell Clive Ormesher about Duxfield?'

'I did. He's put out a call for him.'

'I won't be holding my breath.'

'Do you think Mottram's got to him?'

'Can't see how, Jim. More likely he's holed out somewhere else. My going round scared him. He's afraid of facing the police until he knows his mother's safe. I take it you told Ormesher about Duxfield's mother?'

'He already knew about her. Can't see he can do much though. She could be anywhere.'

'I don't think she'll be dead, though,' I said. 'She's only useful to Mottram as bait to lure her son out of hiding.'

'Take care with Murphy, Johnny. How are you going to make him talk?'

'I'll think of something.'

Netherley was a half hour's drive in the traffic. The tower

blocks where he lived boasted the usual litter and graffiti. 'Mean streets in the sky' as someone once called them.

I parked the car, half-expecting never to see it again, and climbed the stone steps to the sixth floor. The smell of urine vied with the odours of stale cooking and decaying rubbish. I knocked on the thin wooden door to Murphy's flat, noticing the red paint flaking off in patches. The window frames were down to bare wood. Nobody answered. I peered through the letterbox and became aware of a different smell, one I recognised immediately. Decomposing flesh. I didn't hesitate. Nobody was around. I stepped back and took a running kick at the door, adjacent to the Yale lock. It splintered open and I rushed inside.

The corpse wasn't looking at its best. It was swollen, putrefying and discoloured, host to a stream of Michael Winner wannabes of the insect world who were busy feasting on a cornucopia of flesh.

A cursory glance, I didn't intend sticking around too long, told me that the victim had been shot in the head, similar to Mr Patel. I now had a problem here with identity. Murphy had been undoubtedly alive and well on Monday, when he delivered the jury's verdict at the Crown Court, yet this man had been dead at least a week, so he obviously wasn't Murphy.

So, who was he? What was he doing in Murphy's flat? And where was Murphy? He couldn't have been back to his flat during the trial or he'd have found the body. Or maybe he had been back, taken one look at the unwelcome visitor lying on his living-room floor and scarpered. Or had Murphy himself killed the man? I just didn't know.

After one last look round to make sure there were no more dead bodies on the premises, I stepped out of the flat and shut the door after me the best I could. Still nobody was about. I ran down the steps to the RAV4 and phoned Jim Burroughs on the mobile with the latest news.

'I'll get Ormesher down there,' said Jim. 'You'd better stick around till he arrives.'

'No chance, Jim. I've got the show to do at six. Once the police turn up here, I'll never get away.'

'You should stay, Johnny. You're the one who discovered the body. They'll need a statement.' This was the policeman in him talking.

'No way. They'll have plenty of time to talk to me later.'

I could hear the sigh at the other end of the line. 'OK, I'll lock up here and come down myself.'

'You'll need a mask, it's ripe in there.'

'You should have put a dollop of Vick under your nose and you wouldn't have noticed it. An old police trick.'

'No good telling me now. I'll ring you later.'

I started the engine and opened the car windows as I pulled away, hoping the fresh air would take the smell from my nostrils. It didn't. As I drove back through Belle Vale, a police car with its siren blazing passed me going towards Netherley.

Ken was waiting anxiously for me in the studio. 'You're cutting it fine these days,' he said. 'Not another suicide, is it?'

'No, a murder this time,' I told him, and gave him a quick and lurid description of the corpse in Murphy's flat.

'Shut up, I don't want to hear it.' He'd turned pale. 'I think you were better when you were just a simple DJ.'

'Never simple, Ken,' I told him.

I played a track from the *Licence to Kill* soundtrack CD and dedicated it to Billy Murphy. He didn't ring up to complain.

Whoever the dead man was, I thought, somebody must be missing him but I should leave that to the police. That was their speciality more than mine. I'd only had one missing person to find, David Blease, and it had taken me long enough to track him down.

After the show, I went straight to Maria's.

'I kept Victoria up for you,' she said, kissing me at the door. 'She hasn't seen her daddy for two whole days, but she fell asleep anyway.' Roly, standing on his hind legs, pushed her aside and licked my face eagerly. I stroked his head and we all went through to the lounge. A nice family evening.

'Sit down and I'll get you a drink,' said Maria. She poured us each a glass of wine and sat beside me on the sofa. Roly lay at our feet. 'So tell me how you've got on.'

I hardly knew where to begin but I managed to compress the hectic events of the last two days into a ten-minute précis.

Maria looked serious. 'This Mottram man means business, Johnny. You want to be careful.'

I didn't need telling. I was sure Mottram was involved somehow in the death of the man at Netherley. What I didn't know was how or why.

I'd switched my mobile off but Jim Burroughs was wise to that. We'd just finished our meal when he rang on Maria's phone.

'I thought I'd find you there,' he said. 'Ormesher's after you. He isn't happy about you leaving. He wants you at the station first thing in the morning to make a statement.'

'Fair enough. What happened at the flat?'

'You were right about the stench.' He must have forgotten his jar of Vick. 'They reckon he'd been dead a week at least.'

'At least.'

'The SOC boys were giving him a going-over when I left. We should know more tomorrow.'

'No word on Duxfield or his mum?'

'Not a dicky bird.'

'Let's hope we find him before Mottram does.' Meanwhile, Joanna Smithson was still stuck in Durham Jail. 'I'll be in after Ormesher has finished with me in the morning,' I said, 'all being well.'

'Hang on,' said Jim. 'Don't you want to hear the important bit?'

'What's that?'

'Who the dead man was.'

'You know?'

'Oh yes,' said Jim, surprisingly. 'We found a plastic holder in his jacket pocket full of ID of various kinds.

I noticed the *we*. Once a policeman . . .

'The interesting thing was the name on the cards,' he told me.

'Go on.'

'It was William Rufus Murphy.' He paused to let the implication sink in.

'You mean, Murphy . . .'

'Is the deceased. You've got it.'

Suddenly, things took on a new, ominous perspective. If the dead man really *was* William Murphy, then who had taken his place on the jury at Liverpool Crown Court?

Chapter Twenty-four

I didn't have too much to tell DI Ormesher the next morning. He was more interested in why I went round to Murphy's flat than in what I'd found there when I arrived. He'd seen all that for himself.

I explained. 'Murphy was the jury foreman and, according to both Shakti Patel and Graham Duxfield, he was the one pressing for Joanna Smithson's conviction from the start. I wanted to find out why.'

'You mean the man *calling* himself Murphy? The real Murphy had been shot before the trial began.'

'I didn't know that when I went round. I just wanted to confirm my suspicion that Murphy was working for Mottram. Unfortunately, I was a week too late. Mottram beat me to it.'

'Look, Johnny,' the inspector's tone was not unfriendly, 'I'm prepared to go along with Leonard Smithson's story, that Harry Mottram kidnapped his daughter, but I can't do anything until I have the evidence so let me know anything you dig up, because I'm on your side.'

I was a bit taken aback by this. Most policemen I'd met in the past had either warned me not to interfere or told me they didn't believe a word I was telling them. This was a refreshing change.

'It would appear,' declared the inspector, moving on, 'that Mottram somehow got hold of the list of jurors.'

'How could he?'

'Come on, Johnny. Have you never met a nurse, or a

secretary who worked in a bank, or a doctor's receptionist, be they male or female, who hasn't treated you to a bit of confidential gossip about a mutual acquaintance? You know the sort of thing – *I shouldn't really be telling you this but I don't suppose it'll do any harm.*'

'I see what you mean,' I agreed.

'He's obviously picked out Murphy as the one least likely to be missed and replaced him with a ringer. He was lucky in that there was a man like Murphy on the jury panel, seemingly without friends, living alone and not likely to be recognised.'

'What about identification at the court though? Surely the impostor would have to produce some proof that he was William Murphy?'

'No sweat. He had the run of Murphy's house, didn't he? He could have helped himself to any of Murphy's documents and there was no reason for anyone to be suspicious. The courts aren't expecting people to turn up for jury service voluntarily. Most people try their damnedest to get out of it.'

'So that's two men we know are working for Mottram,' I said. 'The fake Murphy and the man who apprehended Duxfield outside the courtroom, who could be the missing second kidnapper.'

'I'm having the security cameras at the court checked. With a bit of luck we might get an ID on the fake Murphy, as you call him, if not the other one.'

'We could do with Duxfield to stand up and say he was threatened. That would win Joanna her appeal, surely.'

Clive Ormesher looked pensive. 'I'm not confident of that,' he said quietly. 'My aim is to go for Mottram. He's involved in a number of things in this city that we can't pin on him so this might be our best chance of banging him up.'

I remembered Badger. 'As a matter of fact, I know someone who's doing a bit of driving for Mottram and he's keeping an eye open for me.'

'So long as he doesn't tread on our toes I've no problem with that. We're short-handed enough, as you can imagine.'

I could. It had been in the paper only the week before about a woman in Southport who dialled 999 early one evening, after a group of yobbos threw stones at her window, and was told by the police operator they'd do their best to send someone round but she was twenty-fourth in the queue.

God knows how far down she'd have been if she'd lived in Toxteth.

'I hope you've warned him,' Ormesher continued, 'about what happens to people who get in Mottram's way.'

'He can look after himself.'

At least I hoped he could.

I arrived at the office at eleven.

'Trouble's back then,' Jim greeted me, indicating Roly who had rushed into the office to make sure his basket was still under the desk. Jim had bought the basket, not as a gift for Roly, he insisted, but as an attempt to preserve the pile on the carpet, which he felt was being worn out by Roly's constant scratching as he sought to make himself comfortable.

'Have you heard anything from Graham Duxfield?'

Jim shook his head. 'I can't see him ringing again.'

'I think he'll be trying to find his mother.'

'He won't know she's not at home.'

'He wouldn't dare go there anyway, but there might be a relative somewhere where she could be staying that he'd know about.'

'Maybe.'

'I'm going to go back there and see the neighbour. She might know. I'll leave Roly with you.'

I drove out to Anfield. I tried Mrs Duxfield first but, as I expected, there was no reply. I didn't need to knock on her neighbour's door because the old crone was watching me through the window and came out.

'She's still not back then?' I asked.

'No, sweetie.' She wore an ankle-length purple dressing gown and a new cigarette burned between her lips.

'You don't know where she might be, by any chance? Her sister's maybe?'

'Perhaps. Or she has a niece she sometimes visits. Her late husband's brother's girl by his first marriage. Sharron she's called. She used to work at Vernons before she had the baby. Little Oliver.'

'Do you know where this Sharron lives?'

'Somewhere in Croxteth, I haven't got the address.'

'What's her second name?'

She almost shrieked. 'Ay, I wouldn't know that, lovey. Why would I know that?'

I gave up. 'Never mind. I'll call back another time.'

'I do have her phone number though, sweetheart.'

'What?'

'Sharron's, darlin'. Hang on, I'll go and get it for you.' She went inside her house and closed the front door after her. I waited a few minutes until she eventually reappeared, clutching a piece of paper. 'Here it is, my love.' She read out the number and I copied it into my notebook.

'You've been most helpful,' I said, thanking her. I pulled out a business card. 'If either of them come back, would you ask them to ring me at my work number?'

'This isn't any relation to that Johnny Ace on the wireless, is it?' she said, screwing her eyes up to read the small print. 'I can't stand him.'

'Neither can I,' I agreed. 'Give me Zoe Ball any day.'

'Who?' she said, but I was already on my way to the car.

I took the ring road, through Toxteth to Sefton Park and Livingstone Drive. I wanted to see if Badger had made any progress. I let myself in through the front door and ran upstairs. It's the only exercise I get most days. There was no reply when I rang Badger's bell but a door opened on the first floor and a thin, middle-aged lady with grey hair called up the stairs, 'I thought it was you, Johnny, I saw the RAV4 through the window.'

'Hi, Pat.' Pat Lake lives in the flat below Badger with her

elderly chair-bound mother. She's a retired schoolteacher who looks like a spinster librarian but she's into heavy-metal music and I've caught her from time to time in the Masquerade Club. Shows you can never go by appearances. Unlike on my last visit, however, the dulcet tones of Perry Como, not Bon Jovi, were coming from her hi-fi. It was obviously her mother's day to pick the playlist. 'Have you seen Badger?'

'Not since yesterday lunchtime. He didn't come home last night.'

'You'd know if he did?' Surely Pat wasn't doing it with Badger.

'The first thing he does when he gets in, no matter what time it is, is put that awful rap music on so, yes, I'd know. You'll really have to do something about his row, Johnny.'

More complaints. Who'd be a landlord? 'Leave it to me. Give my love to your mum,' I said. 'Must dash.'

When I got to the car, I dialled the number Mrs Duxfield's neighbour had given me but there was no reply. I felt helpless. Every avenue of enquiry seemed blocked.

Instead of going back to the office, I went to my flat, microwaved a Sainsbury's vegetable curry, opened a can of Scrumpy Jack and switched on the PC to play some rare recordings I'd recently downloaded from Napster. Etta James's 'Someone To Watch Over Me' was a track I'd never seen on record or CD and it was brilliant. So was Wee Willie Harris's 'Rockin' at the Two I's', which should have been a massive hit back in the 1950s.

I sank into an armchair, eating from the plate on my knee, and tried to make some sense of the Joanna Smithson case. Mottram had it all boxed off. Two out of three of the dissenting jurors dead, one missing, the foreman killed, Joanna Smithson in jail and his two anonymous henchmen totally untraceable.

Maria's phone call interrupted my thoughts. 'Jim's been trying to get you but your mobile's switched off.'

'I left it in the car.'

'What are you doing at the flat?'

'Believe it or not, I've come here for a few minutes' peace and quiet to think.'

'The case, is it?'

'Something like that. To be honest, Maria, I don't know what the next move is.'

'Well, I've got some news for you, Johnny. That policeman from London's been in touch with Jim.'

'Glass, you mean?'

'That's the one. He said he's found David Blease's final resting-place. He's in the East London Cemetery.'

I didn't see the significance. 'So what?' He had to be buried somewhere. A cemetery seemed as good a place as any.

'You'd better speak to Jim,' said Maria. 'Apparently there's more to it than that.'

'A startling development,' confirmed Jim, when I got through to him. 'Glass went along to the cemetery to check out Blease's grave, see what other names might be on it.'

'And were there any?'

'No, but guess who he found buried close by?'

'Lord Lucan?'

'Try Patti Westcott.'

'You're joking?'

'No. Died twentieth of November 1999.'

'She couldn't have been that old.'

'Forty-two.'

'What was it? Cancer?'

'No, Johnny. Glass made some enquiries. It turned out to be an "accident".' He spoke the word in inverted commas. 'Patti Westcott died in a house fire in Shadwell.'

Chapter Twenty-five

'Bit of a coincidence that, Jim.' I'd finished my lunch, given up on the siesta and driven back to the office and now we were sitting contemplating the latest development in the David Blease mystery.

'That's what Glass thought. We could be talking about a double murder here, Johnny. Westcott kills his wife's lover then, twenty years down the line, does away with his wife. But why?'

'Probably traded her in for a younger model.'

'But why kill her?'

'Perhaps no one would take her in part-exchange?'

'Seriously, Johnny.'

I thought about it. 'My guess is, she wouldn't give him a divorce. Maybe she threatened to spill the beans about Blease's murder if he left her.'

'So he pulled the same trick with her.'

'Was it the lighted cigarette again?'

'I don't know. Glass wants one of us to go down to London to see him.'

'What for?'

'Well, he reckons there could be something in this but he hasn't got the resources to start a proper investigation until he has some definite proof that a crime has been committed. On the other hand, if Westcott does turn out to be a double murderer, Glass will be able to set the ball rolling. He's up for this, Johnny. It'll look good on his record so basically it's

171

a case of you setting the bonfire and he'll come in with the matches and . . .'

'And steal all the glory.'

'Not quite like that.'

'You should go, Jim. You're the one that knows him.'

'Can't see Rosemary being so keen,' he said. 'And I don't fancy all that driving. Very stressful.' He tapped his chest. 'Not good for me in my condition.'

As if two hours' sweating on stage with The Chocolate Lavatory in a smoky nightclub was beneficial cardiac exercise.

'OK, I'll go,' I said. It didn't take me too long to think about it. 'I could use a break.' Nothing was happening with the Smithson case and a couple of days away might give me a new perspective. 'Let Glass know I'm coming.'

Jim indicated the brown creature snoring contentedly under the desk. 'Don't forget to take that with you.'

'I'll take him to Maria's.'

'And switch your mobile on. I'll need to ring you with the arrangements in London.'

'OK. Do me a favour, Jim. Book me a room for tonight at the Four Stars in Sussex Gardens.' It was a hotel I'd stayed at before, the last time a couple of years ago with Linda Roberts, whose sister had been murdered in one of my flats. It was cheap, clean and handy with the bonus of an English breakfast and a parking space thrown in. What more can you ask for in Central London where you can pay £400 a night for a cell in a tower block?

As Tommy McKale would say, you could have two men assassinated for that.

As soon as I finished the show, I went straight to my flat. Roly wasn't pleased to be woken but he cheered up when I produced his lead. I stuffed a change of underwear, clothes and shaving tackle into an overnight bag and drove out to Blundellsands. Maria was at the Library so I left her a note saying I'd be back by Saturday. Roly slunk to his basket, disappointed he wasn't getting the trip.

The M6 was pretty clear until Walsall when it became its usual nightmare as the evening rush hour kicked in. Rather than fight it, I stopped at Hilton Services for an overpriced curry (lorry drivers call them 'meals with a mortgage'), and gave Jim a call.

'I was just about to ring you. The inspector wants you to meet him at his home in Chiswick. Here's the address.' I took out my notebook and scribbled it down. 'Can you make it for eight o'clock, only he says he has an assignation at ten?'

'Sounds painful. Tell him not to worry, I'll be there.'

That gave me two hours. I finished the meal and paid a quick visit to the Gents where I couldn't resist stepping on the Health Machine they have that tells you your height, weight, blood pressure, pulse, the time of day and the weather forecast. All for £1.

My blood pressure was 139 over 79, which wasn't bad, I reckoned, for someone of fifty. It was higher than that twenty years ago. Pulse 72. Acceptable. Height 6ft, weight 162lb. Still OK to enjoy a few more Christmas puddings before I needed to worry about diets. My BMI, it said, was 22, whatever that meant. I was happy with that until I noticed that the weather was described as wet when it was sunny. I shrugged it off. I supposed even a machine could be allowed one mistake.

I took the M42 and the M40 which brought me into West London. Roadworks along the A40 end at Uxbridge Road caused the only serious hold-up and I was outside the policeman's house at 7.45 p.m.

Detective Chief Inspector Glass lived in a large redbrick semi on the river side of Chiswick High Road. A silver BMW '5' series was parked in the drive and, behind it, incongruously, a beige Morris Traveller 'woody' circa 1958.

I walked up to the front door and rang the bell. A tall, bulky man in a crumpled tweed jacket and cavalry twill trousers opened the door. 'Johnny Ace? Walter Glass.' His handshake was firm and he led me into a spacious back living room with patio doors leading to a leafy garden. An attractive girl in her twenties was sitting on a settee watching TV. 'This is my daughter, Sue. She's married to a policeman. Two of the buggers to look after. Wouldn't wish it on my worst enemy.'

Sue smiled and offered to make us all a cup of tea. An exceptionally large grey and white cat lay in front of the fire. 'Sailor,' said Glass, noticing my gaze. 'Getting on now like all of us. Thirty-five years I've been in the Force.'

I looked at the Chief Inspector. He must have been in his late fifties, almost old enough to be a TV detective. Wexford, Morse, Frost – they'd all kept at it well into their dotage, long after any real-life Force would have pensioned them off. Glass's sparse hair was greying, he needed a shave and he wouldn't have won prizes at the London Fashion Show.

'Don't you fancy taking an early pension?' I suggested tactfully, thinking even Jim Burroughs could have given him a year or two although I was never good with ages. Perhaps Glass had just had a hard life or he'd been born with the wrong genes. Not everybody could be like Joan Collins.

'Me? Christ, no. I'd be lost if all I had to do was watch daytime television.' He shuddered. 'I'll hang on till they put me out to grass.'

'He wants to die with his boots on,' said Sue, coming back into the room with cups and saucers. 'Like in those old wartime films he watches. Tea won't be a minute.' She returned to the kitchen.

'Nice place to live,' I observed, changing the conversation.

'Chiswick's full of luvvies,' grumbled Glass. 'The TV studios at Shepherds Bush are just down the road. Attracts them like maggots to a rotting corpse. John Thaw's round the corner. Still, it's handy enough for me to go and watch The Rangers of a weekend.'

'I'm an Evertonian myself,' I said, failing to keep the arrogance out of my voice. Queens Park Rangers had long been relegated to the First Division.

'We all have our problems.' He turned to a display cabinet and brought out a bottle of Southern Comfort. 'While she's

174

pissing around making tea, let's have a proper drink and you can tell me all about this Westcott character. Here, grab a seat.' I settled in an armchair and he put a full glass in my hand and raised his own in the air. 'Cheers. To Eddie the Nose.'

'Who?'

'That's my name for snouts. Whatever they say about DNA and that HOLMES thing, we couldn't solve ninety per cent of cases without informers, though my son-in-law wouldn't agree with that. He's one of them college coppers, is Robin. A fancy degree and a fast track to the Chief Constable's chair. Doesn't know what pounding the beat means. Mind you, do any of them nowadays?'

Jim Burroughs would have agreed with him.

Sue appeared again, this time bearing a tray of tea and scones. 'Not lecturing you about the old days, is he?' she said affectionately, then she spied the drinks. 'And you've been at the booze again, Dad. You know what the doctor told you about your liver.' She took the glass from his hand and replaced it with a cup of tea. I clung on to mine just in case.

Glass didn't dare to defy his daughter. He took his cup meekly and turned his attention to the matter in hand. 'Westcott,' he said. 'Looks like you've stumbled on something here.'

'It looks that way.' I helped myself to a scone which appeared to be home-made. 'These look nice.'

'Freshly baked,' declared Sue. 'He insists on it.'

I could imagine. Chauvinism was alive and well in West London.

'I can't see there being any more murders,' I said. 'It's not as if Westcott's an armed robber or a serial killer.'

'No, he just disposes of the odd person who gets in his way,' agreed Glass sarcastically. 'Or perhaps he's on commission from the cemetery.'

'Have you managed to track him down yet?'

'Give me a chance. I only found his wife's grave yesterday. As I told your oppo, I'll give you what I've got so far but it'll be up to you to follow it up. We're very short-staffed these days. Since that McPherson Report came out, officers have been leaving in droves. You can't arrest anyone these days unless they're in Burke's Peerage, and if you stop a black man in the street to ask him the time, you risk losing your pension.' He bit angrily into his scone. 'But, first of all, tell me how you started on all this, right from the top.'

I started at the beginning with Norris Pond coming to me for information on David Blease, otherwise known as Digger, for his incomplete Wavertree Corinthians book. I explained how Blease had had a reputation as a womaniser and this had led me to track him down to Limehouse whence I learned about his unfortunate demise.

'So that story you gave me about the missing goalkeeper was true? Strange way to find out about a murder. Makes me wonder if your Mr Pond didn't know something already and this football angle was just a blind to get you to look into it.'

'You think Pond knew all along that Blease had been murdered? But why not just say so and hire me to find the killer?'

'He must have had his reasons but I'd say the answer to this mystery lies in Liverpool, not London. For a start, why is this bugger Pond looking for Blease now all of a sudden? Something must have set him off and I don't accept this pathetic excuse about a book.'

I had to admit that neither did I any more. If the book *was* the real reason for me tracking down Digger Blease, it would have ended when I found out he was dead.

'It could be he'd only just found out that Blease had died so he concocted the tale about the book as an excuse to have me investigate without letting on about any personal interest.'

Glass sipped his tea and looked pensive. 'I wonder why Blease's death would affect him? If what you say is true, all he did was play football with the bloke and then only for six months. Nobody you spoke to suggested Pond and Blease were friends or anything, did they? Secret lovers maybe?'

'You're joking.'

'You never know. The world's full of brown hatters these days,' said Glass sadly. I wouldn't have gone so far as to say he was homophobic but he didn't look like he'd be a regular reader of *Gay News*. 'I had a case only last year, two old queens frolicking inside a Pantomime Cow. Both got their throats slit.'

'Because they were gay?'

'No,' admitted the inspector, 'because they knew too much, but I was just saying, there's a lot of them about.'

'Dad still lives in the last century,' explained his daughter, who had been listening to the conversation. 'Best to ignore him when he talks like that.'

'So let us say there *is* a connection between Digger Blease and Norris Pond,' I said, trying to keep the inspector on the subject. 'The probability is, then, that Pond suspects Peter Westcott has murdered his friend Blease and wants me to expose him.'

'Or deliver him to Pond to take his own revenge.'

I'd not thought of that possibility. What would that make me? It smacked of the Wild West. Johnny Ace – bounty hunter. 'But you've found no trace of Westcott, Chief Inspector?'

'Not a dicky bird since the fire in 1979 that killed Blease.'

'Yet Patti Westcott is buried in East London Cemetery which suggests they stayed in the area. You say she was found in Shadwell. Is that near Limehouse?'

'One stop along on the Docklands Light Railway,' stated Glass, 'but worlds apart. A lot of Limehouse has been redeveloped – you're talking about Canary Wharf there, City money – but it hasn't reached Shadwell yet. Most of the place is a shithole. You must have heard of Tower Hamlets?' I nodded. 'Well, Tower Hamlets is next door to Shadwell. Urban squalor at its worst.'

'What was Patti Westcott doing in a place like that?'

'Selling her body, Johnny. What else?'

'On the game? But she'd be well over forty in 1999.'

'Probably that's why she was in a tenement in Shadwell and not a posh suite in Mayfair. I've made a few enquiries. She rented the flat under the name of Christina Williams and she'd been there about twelve months, living on her own.'

'Where was Peter Westcott then?'

Glass shrugged. 'That's for you to find out. I've got enough on my plate. I think I told you about the three armed robberies.'

'I thought it was two.'

'That was yesterday. Ram raiders backed a lorry into an off-licence last night and made off with a few grands' worth of booze.'

'But you do think Peter Westcott's behind his wife's murder?'

'The two fires clinches it for me. I've never believed in coincidences, and the fact they lived apart suggests they'd fallen out somewhere along the way. He'd probably found a bit of young and wanted the old bag out of the way, though God knows why. I've always preferred older women myself. They fit round you better, rather like an old glove.'

It wasn't an argument I subscribed to but I didn't pursue it. 'How did you find out that this Christina Williams was really Patti Westcott?'

'Didn't I tell you?' He looked momentarily sheepish. 'Fingerprints.'

'You mean she'd got form?'

'I only got round to checking yesterday. Nothing on Peter Westcott but Patricia Westcott had been convicted twice for shoplifting and three times for soliciting, all since 1996. Each time she had a different address and each time she'd used the alias Christina Williams. Not unusual, of course, that she'd used another name. Most toms do. And then, the final entry. She'd died of suffocation in a house blaze in Shadwell, which naturally got me thinking.'

'I take it the inquest verdict was Accidental Death?'

'What else? Chip pan caught fire, no reason for it to be

anything else.' He glanced at a large chronometer on his left wrist. 'Christ, twenty-five to ten, I must be off,' and he rose clumsily to his feet.

'He goes to Old Tyme Dancing on a Thursday,' explained Sue. 'With his ladyfriend.'

'Mrs Lewthwaite is not my ladyfriend,' protested Glass. 'She is merely a longterm acquaintance.'

'Not what I've heard.' Sue winked at me. 'Nice to meet you, Johnny,' she smiled. 'I hope you find your missing man.'

'I will,' I assured her, thanking her for her hospitality.

'Keep me informed,' Glass commanded me at the door. 'As soon as you've got something concrete on Peter Westcott, I'll have the case opened officially.'

But, as I drove along Bayswater Road towards Sussex Gardens and the Four Stars Hotel, I knew that finding Peter Westcott was not going to be easy. I didn't suspect for a moment that it was also going to be highly dangerous, putting me at grave risk of my life.

Chapter Twenty-six

I slept well at the Four Stars, ate a big breakfast and set out the next morning for Shadwell, leaving the RAV4 parked on the service road outside the hotel. A car is no use in London where, most days, it's gridlock on the roads. I bought a one-day travel card at Marble Arch and took the Tube to Bank where I changed to the Docklands Light Railway with its driver-less carriages.

Shadwell was the first stop. I descended the steps from the station and walked up a narrow street till I came to the tenement where Patti Westcott had ended her days.

It wasn't unlike similar buildings in Kirkby and Netherley. Sink estates are pretty much the same whether they're in Bristol, Oxford or Peckham; they just have varying degrees of violence, deprivation and anarchy.

Drugs, crime, poverty, broken families, missing fathers, decline of religion, poor schooling, lack of discipline – everyone has an explanation for the problem but no one, it seems, has the will to solve it.

I knocked on the door of the flat next to Patti's. A woman of about forty answered, dressed in a loose filmy scarlet peignoir. She opened the door a crack and peered through. Tiny red veins had burst on her face and were poorly camouflaged by liberal use of powder.

'Yeah?'

'I don't know if I've got the right house,' I said.

'Are you looking for business, ducks?' Her large breasts

hove into view like helium-filled balloons struggling to escape from Santa Claus's sack.

'Sort of.'

'Well, make up your mind. What is it – a blow job? That'll cost you twenty. Full sex, that's thirty, fifty if you won't use a condom.'

'OK,' I said, and she stepped back as I pushed open the door and edged past her into an ill-lit room. A combined TV and video set stood in the corner, a couple of chairs, a table and a single bed placed alongside the wall.

'What's it to be then?' She had already started to strip off and move towards the bed.

'The girl who used to live next door a couple of years ago, Christina Williams, did you know her?' This made her stop in her tracks and she pulled the garment round her again.

'Here, wot is this? I thought you'd come in here for a shag. What's with the questions? You're not the filth, are you?'

I showed her my card and repeated my original question. 'I want to know everything you can tell me about her and I'll give you the twenty quid.'

Her eyes lit up at the suggestion of payment. She put on a towelling dressing gown she'd obviously been wearing before I knocked and sat at the end of the bed. 'You're lucky, as a matter of fact. Yeah, I did know 'er. Me an' 'er was mates, like. Used to double up with clients sometimes, if you know what I mean?'

I did. She lit a cigarette but didn't offer me one.

'What happened to her husband, did she ever say?'

She shook her head. 'I knew she'd been married but he'd pissed off with some young tart years ago.'

'You don't know where?'

'Not a bloody clue.'

'Did she have any regular clients?'

'We all do, luv. Yeah, Tina had a few.'

'Any in particular that you noticed that might have been unusual in any way?'

181

She thought. 'There was one fella from down Docklands had started to come and see 'er every week. She was very secretive about 'im which wasn't like 'er. Wouldn't tell me 'is name or nuffink.'

I cursed the fact that I'd never seen, much less possessed, a photo of Peter Westcott to show her. 'Did you ever see him?'

'Once I did. He called when I was over in her place and she soon got rid of me, I can tell yer.'

'What did he look like?'

'I'm not good at ages, luv, but I'd say he was about forty, average height but posh-looking, know wot I mean? Nice clothes and jewellery. I noticed, though, that she seemed frightened of him somehow.'

'What about when she died? What happened?'

'That was terrible. Funnily enough, he'd been there that day, in the afternoon. I saw him leave. They say she'd been making chips and the fat caught fire. Place went up in no time.'

'What time was that?'

'Teatime.'

'You didn't go to her funeral?'

'Knew nothing about it. The ambulance took her away and that was the last I heard.'

'She never told you anything about herself?'

'Not about her past, no. Poor Tina, she was well out of it, the poor cow. She never looked happy.'

It was as much as I was going to get. I gave the woman her twenty pounds, which she snatched from me and shoved in her dressing-gown pocket. Then, out of the blue, she whispered, 'I can tell you where he lives though, that client of hers.'

'What?'

'It'll cost yer another twenty quid.'

I took the note from my wallet and watched it follow its predecessor before she spoke.

'I saw him one day, coming out of a flat just by Westferry Station. There's a new block been built, you can't miss it – it's painted bright yellow and blue. He had a young girl with him, young enough to be his daughter. All over her he was.'

'You don't know which flat?'

'No, but it was the block on the main road because I passed by one night and I thought I saw him at the window, he was on the second floor.'

I thanked her and retraced my steps to the station where I travelled a further two stops on the railway to Westferry. Standing on the platform looking across to Canary Wharf tower and the rows of skyscrapers, I might have been in New York.

The yellow and blue building was called Première Place and it was on the road directly outside the station exit.

'All the blocks are named after film stars,' explained a porter. 'This front one's Garland. After Judy,' he added unnecessarily. 'The one behind is Welles.'

'Don't tell me, after Kitty.'

He looked puzzled. 'Orson.'

Obviously he wasn't a country music fan.

'It was Garland I was after,' I said. 'I'm looking for a man who lives in one of the front flats on the second floor. He's either on his own or living with a girl young enough to be his daughter.'

'Oh yes?'

'Do you know him?'

'Was it official business, sir, only we're very big on security here?'

'Of course.' I showed him my business card. 'It's nothing serious,' I assured him. 'A lady client of mine lent him some paintings some time ago and she's leaving the area and is anxious to get them back before she goes. If, of course, it's the same man. Has he lived here long?'

'He doesn't actually live here, sir, at least, not all the time. Just uses it when he's in Town.'

'A pied à terre.'

'Exactly. Perhaps once or twice a month he comes, no more than that, often with a young lady.'

'Is the gentleman around at the moment, do you know?'

'I haven't seen him myself for a couple of weeks but I'll take you up to his flat, if you like.'

He led me into the block and up the stairs to the door of the apartment. I rang the bell a couple of times but nobody answered.

'Looks like they're both out,' said the porter.

'You don't know his other address, by any chance?'

'I'm afraid not. Somewhere up north, that's all I can tell you.'

I knew there'd be no chance of being allowed to look in the apartment, even supposing the porter had a master key.

'Thanks anyway,' I said. 'Look, I'll give you my number and if you do see Mr Westcott, ask him to get in touch with me as soon as possible.'

He looked at me curiously. 'That's his name is it, Westcott?'

'That's the name I know him by – why? You sound surprised.'

'Westcott,' echoed the porter. 'Presumably he's just a tenant then?'

'Why do you say that?'

'Simply because he can't be the owner. The owner of that flat is listed as a Mr Mottram. Harry Mottram.'

Chapter Twenty-seven

I sat with a plate of tapas and a glass of Spanish wine at an outside table at La Tasca, overlooking the waterfront near Canary Wharf. The sun was shining on the cobbled stones and a few office workers were taking time out from their offices, although half of them seemed to be keeping in touch by mobile phone.

Shadwell might have been on another planet as, indeed, might the rest of London. This part of Docklands belonged strictly to the twenty-first century.

I took a sip of wine and tried to work out the implications of my discovery.

What could possibly be the connection between Peter Westcott, arsonist and murderer, and Harry Mottram, gangster and racketeer, who was behind the Joanna Smithson kidnapping? It seemed an incredible proposition yet it was almost too much of a lucky chance to be otherwise and what had Chief Inspector Glass said about coincidences?

Yet, if it was *not* a coincidence, then the inescapable conclusion was that my involvement in the Smithson case was the reason Norris Pond had hired me in the first place. The cock and bull story about his football team was just an excuse to steer me towards Peter Westcott and Harry Mottram.

But why?

Glass had been right. The solution to this case belonged back in Liverpool with Norris Pond. He was the person I needed to speak to.

I took out my mobile and dialled Jim at the office to tell him what I'd discovered.

'I'll get hold of Lennie Smithson and find out if he knows Pond,' he said. 'This is a real turn up. Something's going on behind the scenes that we know nothing about.'

And all the time, I thought, people are getting killed. Which reminded me of our missing juror. 'No word, I take it, from Duxfield?'

'Not a whisper.'

I remembered I still had his Cousin Sharron's number. The sooner I got back to Liverpool the better.

I managed to get in touch with DCI Glass and apprise him of my findings. 'It all seems to be connected with another case we've been working on,' I told him. 'If I'm right, Peter Westcott could be involved in the kidnapping of a local businessman's daughter.'

'Do you think he's still in London? If so, perhaps I'd better try and find him immediately and bring him in for questioning about the fires and maybe the kidnapping as well.'

'It wouldn't do any good at this stage. You've no evidence and he'd deny everything. Besides, I think it's much more likely he's back in Liverpool now or even Cheshire. Don't worry, as soon as I get anything on him, I'll let you know. Meanwhile, out of curiosity, you could check out if you've got Harry Mottram on your files – that's the man we have down as the kidnapper.'

The waiter brought my bill and I made my way through the shopping mall to the impressive new Canary Wharf Jubilee Line station where I took a Tube directly to Bond Street.

There seems to be an increasing trend for underground shops. It reminds me of Atlanta, Georgia where the climate is either too hot or too cold so most of the shops are in a temperature-controlled mall below ground.

I walked along Oxford Street and up the Edgware Road to pick up the RAV4 at the hotel. The journey back up the M1 and M6 took five hours, courtesy of the Birmingham rush-hour traffic. I rang Maria from the car to tell her I was on my way and it was eight o'clock when I pulled up outside her flat.

'I've missed you,' she said, kissing me at the door. 'So has Victoria.' The baby was asleep but Roly wasn't. He barked a greeting as he stood on his back legs and licked my face.

'I smell worse than he does,' I said. Driving in summer is no fun, even with air conditioning. 'I'm sweating like a pig.'

'Dinner won't be ready for half an hour, so you go ahead and have a shower. I've put a clean T-shirt and jeans out for you.'

'You're wonderful. If you can get a babysitter tomorrow, I'll take you out for a meal.'

'You're on.'

I realised as I stepped in the shower that I'd promised to phone Hilary before the weekend but I knew I'd have no time to see her. On Sunday, Maria and I were taking Victoria out for the day. I'd have to ring Hilary during the week. She wouldn't be happy.

After the meal, I told Maria about my trip.

'What do you know about Norris Pond?' she asked.

'Nothing at all other than he's a large, arthritic pensioner who once ran a pub football team. He seems harmless enough.'

'But there's obviously a lot more to him than that. What job does he do?'

'No idea. Compiling his football book's more of a hobby, I'd guess. He's probably retired but he's got cash, otherwise how would he have paid us £830 so far?'

'If it's his.'

'You mean someone could be bankrolling him? But who?'

'Someone who wants to get at Westcott and Mottram and is using you to do it.'

'Well, the only way to find out is by tackling Pond.'

'Where does he live?'

'Somewhere in Aintree.'

'You're going to see him?'

'First thing in the morning.'

* * *

I had to call at the office first to get Pond's address. Jim was already in. He usually got there early on a Saturday before Rosemary could make him go shopping.

'It's a rum do, this,' he said. 'I spoke to Lennie Smithson and he told me he's never heard of Norris Pond or the Wavertree bloody Corinthians. Are you sure this is the same Harry Mottram?'

'There's a connection somewhere, I'd bet your life on it. Did you ask Smithson if he'd heard of Peter Westcott?'

'Course I did and he hadn't. And, before you ask, he hadn't heard of David Blease either.'

'What exactly have your lot got on file on Mottram?'

'He hasn't a police record if that's what you mean.'

'We need to find out when and where he was born, all his personal details and his known associates including how he came to be mixed up with Westcott. My guess is Westcott could be the man who impersonated Billy Murphy at Jo Smithson's trial.'

'It's possible, I suppose.' Jim didn't look convinced. 'When do you reckon Westcott teamed up with Mottram? In 1979 when he moved to London, after he'd killed Blease?'

'Oh no, I'd say much later than that, Jim, and I don't think it was necessarily in London either. We know Mottram was in Newcastle before he came to Merseyside. There's never been any suggestion he was ever based in London, even if he owned property there.'

'So where do you think they met?'

'Possibly up in Geordieland. Maybe Westcott moved there after he left Patti. We know he was living with her in London until 1996.'

'How do we know that?'

'According to DCI Glass, that's when they first had Patti Westcott on file – for shoplifting and soliciting. The inference being that, until then, she lived happily with her husband.'

'You can't infer anything,' Jim warned me sternly. 'She

could have split with her husband way back in 1979 after the fire and enjoyed seventeen years as a high-class call girl with the odd bit of undetected shoplifting on the side before she was eventually caught.'

It seemed unlikely to me, especially as I'd seen the state of the flats at Shadwell. I didn't see too many rich businessmen or Arab oil sheiks trekking out there for their delights of the flesh but I wasn't going to argue about it.

'No Jim, I'd stick to 1996 and I guess Patti was stinging him for money which is why he turned up at her flat from time to time, when the woman next door mistook him for a client.'

'So he was paying her hush money?'

'Until her demands got too much and he decided to kill her.'

'It's a working hypothesis, I suppose,' he said, 'until we find out anything different. Pond only got in touch with us at the end of June, didn't he?'

'A couple of weeks before the trial.'

'And Joanna was kidnapped in March. So something happened between March and June that set Norris Pond on the trail of Peter Westcott.'

'But what?'

'Presumably that's when Pond discovered Blease had been killed by Westcott. It needn't have anything to do with the Smithson case at all. Just coincidence.'

'No. I still think he hired us because we were involved in Joanna's kidnapping and somehow Pond knew Mottram and Westcott were connected with that.'

'Hold on, Johnny. Pond needn't necessarily have known that Peter Westcott even knew Harry Mottram. He might still not know, come to that. If Peter Westcott had rented the Première Place flat through an agent, he would have no idea who the owner was. Mottram could have bought it under a company name, for instance. In which case, the connection between Mottram and Westcott wouldn't exist.'

'You could be right, Jim, of course, but I prefer to think there's some tie-up.'

'Suit yourself,' he said resignedly. 'Either way, it seems pretty certain that the man Pond really wanted us to find all along was not Digger Blease himself but his killer.'

I agreed. 'And whether Joanna Smithson's kidnapping enters this equation at all,' I said, 'is what I'm about to try and find out.'

The address we had on file for Norris Pond was on a new estate off Higher Lane in Aintree. The houses were detached and most of the drives had more than two cars in them. Norris Pond was obviously not on his uppers.

There was no car in his drive so I drove right up to the front door and, leaving Roly on guard in the front passenger seat, walked over and rang the bell, which chimed a few bars of 'Coronation Scot'. Very tacky. No answer. I rang again. More music. I remembered where I'd heard it before. It used to introduce the Paul Temple series on the radio. I gave a third push on the bell but still nobody came. Not even Paul Temple.

I peered through the small leaded light window beside the door and noticed a bunch of keys on the ledge inside. If Norris Pond was out, why had he left his keys behind? If he was in, why hadn't he answered the door?

The front garden consisted of a lawn with a variety of plants circumnavigating the borders. Some of the plants had thin wooden stakes tied to the stems to prevent them from falling over. I pulled out one of the stakes that was holding up a top-heavy lupin and took it over to the front door.

Nobody was in sight to observe as I pushed the thin stick, about eighteen inches long, through the letterbox and angled it towards the bunch of keys. My arm was inserted almost to my sleeve as I peered through the frosted glass and guided the end of the stick through the inch-wide diameter of the keyring. So far, so good.

Slowly, I lifted the stick and allowed the keys to slide towards my hand. The weight nearly made me drop them but I held on and withdrew my arm and brought out the stick and the keys.

Still nobody was around. There were five keys on the ring. The second one I tried opened the front door. I stepped into the hall and shouted, 'Mr Pond!' No reply. On the wall was a large framed photograph that I recognised. It was the team picture of the Wavertree Corinthians that Nobby Wharton had shown me as a newspaper cutting.

So the Wavertree Corinthians story was true, but when did the hunt for David Blease and Peter Westcott become the raison d'être for Norris Pond's quest? And why?

I peered into the lounge, nobody there. A clock ticked quietly on the mantelpiece. I went from room to room, upstairs and down. The beds were made, the rooms tidy, no sign of anything untoward. I realised I'd half expected to find Norris Pond's body – why else would I have broken into his house? The keys had fooled me. He obviously kept a second set. Now I just wanted to get out as quickly as possible.

Just as I was about to open the front door, I noticed a letter on the mat. I picked it up. It was a quarterly phone bill from BT. Who was Norris Pond in touch with, I wondered? An itemised phone bill would tell me. I put it in my pocket, opened the door, shut it briskly after me and walked confidently down the path to the car. Still not a soul about. No wonder burglary is so profitable in modern times. What with working housewives, crèches for babies and day centres for the elderly, nobody's ever at home in the daytime any more.

I wasn't sure what to do next. I'd no other address for Norris Pond. I sat at the wheel of the RAV4 and pondered. Roly leaned across and licked my hand companionably. Suddenly, I realised I wasn't too far from Croxteth where the niece of Graham Duxfield's mother lived. There'd been no sight nor sound of the missing juror since I'd left him alone at West Kirby. That hadn't been one of my better decisions.

I took out my notebook, found Sharron's number and dialled it on my mobile. I could hear it ringing out but, again, there was no reply. Where was Graham Duxfield hiding? The only living witness who could testify to jury-rigging at Joanna Smithson's trial and I'd let him get away. Was he still alive? If he wasn't, it would be my fault and that wasn't something I wanted to live with.

I drove back to the office.

'Well?' demanded Jim when I walked in, Roly behind me.

'Not in,' I replied.

'Or not answering?'

'Not in.' I explained how I'd been inside and searched the house.

'Oh Christ, breaking and entering now, that's all we need.' Then he looked hard at me. 'Find anything?'

'Only this.' I threw the telephone bill on the desk. 'I thought it might tell us who he's been in touch with.'

'Theft as well.' But he picked up the envelope, opened it and went through the contents. 'Hard luck, Johnny. No itemised bill.' He handed me the invoice sheets. 'I'm afraid we'll never know who Mr Pond has been ringing.'

'Not necessarily.' I went across to the computer and connected to the Internet. I opened the file icon at Open and typed in *www.bt.co.uk.*

Jim came across and peered over my shoulder. 'What are you doing?'

'I've got his home number and his account number. I can go online and check if he's got Family and Friends.'

'And if he has?'

'BT will kindly tell me which are the ten numbers he should be using as his chosen ones instead of the ones he may have picked. In other words, the numbers he dials the most.'

I wondered if Mrs Pond would be interested in seeing that list. Nobody has secrets any more in this technological age. Come to that, was there a Mrs Pond? She had never been mentioned but there had been a double bed in the bedroom, although I didn't recall any family photos or women's touches in the house.

'Go on then.'

I logged in and fed in the information as requested. Sure

enough, up on screen came the numbers I wanted. I handed him my notebook and a pen. 'Write these down, Jim.' I repeated them to him, adding the number of minutes that Norris had spent talking to each one since his last statement.

'What are you going to do with that bill now?' Jim asked when I'd finished.

'Seal it up and post it. What else?'

Jim sighed. 'Sometimes I wonder which side of the law you're on.'

'The winning side – now let's have a look at these numbers.'

I glanced down the list. Most of them were 0151 Liverpool numbers. I didn't recognise any of them.

'We'll have to try ringing them,' Jim said. 'Tell them they've won a television set and where do they want it delivered.'

'It'll never work. They'll know you're really trying to sell them double glazing and tell you to piss off.'

'Have you a better idea?'

'The simple way, Jim. Always best, you'll see.'

I was about to pick up the receiver when the phone rang.

'Is that you, Johnny? It's Badger.' He sounded excited. 'You still interested in that rich Mr Mottram, man? Well, have I got news for you.'

Chapter Twenty-eight

'It had better be good, Badger.'

'It is. I need to meet you. Do you know the Number Seven Café? It's in Falkner Street, opposite Mount Street.' The artist Adrian Henri, one of the Mersey Poets, lived in Mount Street. 'All the university crowd hang out there.'

'I'll find it. What number?'

'Try seven.' His tone was sardonic.

'Oh sorry, of course. I'll be there in twenty minutes.' I turned to Jim. 'This could be the break we're looking for. I'll leave Roly with you, it might be a vegetarian place.'

When I arrived at the café, Badger was sitting in the window seat, resplendent in a vivid red silk shirt and black leather trousers, drinking caffe latte and reading a copy of the *Guardian*.

'I think my information merits lunch,' he said. He rose and followed me to the counter to study the menu blackboard.

'They live well these days, students,' I observed. 'Chicken in lemon, mushroom risotto with spinach and leeks.' Roly would have loved it. 'What happened to Big Macs and fries?'

'You must be joking,' said Badger. 'I'll have the halibut with rice.'

'Make that two,' I said, 'and two glasses of mineral water.' I paid upfront and we returned to our table.

Across the road, I could see the assembly of stone packing cases outside the Liverpool College of Art, the same college where John Lennon met Cynthia in 1962. The cases, inscribed with the names of Liverpoool notables, were supposed to represent some form of modern sculpture but, intermingled with an accumulation of litter, they looked like so much uncleared rubble left over from a building site.

I took a sip of the water and looked across at Badger. 'Well then? What have you got?'

'I've been over at Mobberley the last couple of nights.'

'At Mottram's?'

'Got it in one.'

'And?'

'He's really got it in for your Mr Smithson, hasn't he?'

'How do you mean?'

'I stayed the night and when I woke this morning, he was on the phone to Smithson. I could hear his voice through the wall. That guy's a real bully, you know. He was shouting and threatening—'

I interrupted him. 'How do you know it was Smithson he was talking to?'

'There was an extension in the guest room. I pressed the monitor and listened to the whole conversation.'

'A bit risky, wasn't it?'

'I'm glad you appreciate the fact that I earn my money.'

'Go on.'

'I'm afraid your pure-as-driven-snow Mr Smithson has been a naughty boy.'

With a sinking heart, I knew what must be coming next. 'How naughty?'

'Mind you,' said Badger philosophically, 'it all depends what you call naughty. Put against the massacres of Bosnia or the Holocaust . . .'

'How naughty?' I repeated impatiently.

'Try a three-in-a-bed marathon complete with whips, handcuffs and unusual uses for Coca Cola bottles and starring Liverpool's ex-Businessman of the Year in a leading role?'

It sounded naughty enough to me. Obviously Mottram

thought so and I was sure Leonard Smithson wouldn't argue. 'I take it Mottram has the sole film rights?'

'Quite. Pictures Smithson won't be too keen on his wife and daughter seeing.'

'And the price for the negatives?'

'What do you think? Smithson's club, Nirvana.'

'That's odd.' If Mottram had pictures like these, why hadn't he used them before instead of going to the trouble of kidnapping Joanna? Unless, of course, he'd only just taken them. But surely Smithson wouldn't be that stupid after all that had happened. Would he? 'When were these photos taken, Badger?'

'Last week after a Lodge outing. Smithson stayed overnight at a hotel in Chester, had a skinful before he turned in only to find two sexy young ladies waiting in his room. I believe Mrs Smithson is a bit old-fashioned about such things.'

The food arrived and I thought about the implications of all this as I ate. Four people dead, Joanna's kidnapping, the ordeal of the court case and her subsequent imprisonment, and all for nothing. Lennie was going to lose his precious club anyway.

'Apparently, he was thinking about putting up for Parliament at the next election, too,' went on Badger.

'He'd be well qualified for it,' I replied drily. 'He's already acting like an MP. What was his reaction when Mottram broke the news?'

Badger chortled. 'He was devastated. Realised he'd been set up, swore and cursed for a bit and ended up pleading.'

'And Mottram?'

'Shouting the odds. Not interested in deals or cash. "The contract's in the post," he told him. "I shall expect it back within forty-eight hours of receipt or the photos will be sent to your wife and the *Sun*."'

'Which means we've got until Monday night to get hold of the negatives or Smithson's ruined.'

'Sounds about right.' Badger paused to savour his meal.

'Nice bit of fish, this.' He waved his fork in the air appreciatively.

'Anything else you can tell me?'

'Isn't that enough? What else do you want to know?'

'This other guy, the young shaven-headed one with the Scouse accent, have you seen him again? Or anyone else who might be working for Mottram, in particular a big bloke of about forty-five?'

'The young bloke's been around but I've not had a chance to talk to him properly. Nobody else.'

'I'd like to know his name. I don't suppose you've heard any mention of a Peter Westcott, have you?'

'No. Who's he?'

'We think he's the big fellow, the one who impersonated the foreman of the jury at the Jo Smithson trial.'

'Right.'

We ate the rest of our meal in silence. When we'd finished, I extracted five twenties from my wallet and gave them to Badger.

'When are you next driving Mottram?'

'Tonight. His regular driver's got flu. I'm picking him up at two in the morning from the Casino.'

'In Renshaw Street?'

'That's the one.'

'In his Ferrari?'

'He's using the Lexus at the moment.'

'Let me take your place, Badger.'

'What!'

'You heard. I'll say you're sick and you've sent me instead. He'll have no idea who I am. The guy has been keeping well away from any of the action. He won't know me from Adam.'

Badger looked doubtful. 'You're the one who told me this cat's dangerous.'

'Exactly. So I know what I could be letting myself in for.'

'What's the plan?'

'I haven't got up to that bit.' I had a vague idea of rooting round the house and finding the photos or maybe setting a bug on his phone to tape a blackmail threat.

'Why don't you let me come along in the boot?' offered Badger. 'At least you'll have some back-up.'

'Why would you need to ride in the boot? You've got his address, you could just roll up there.'

'He's got electric gates, opened only by his remote. CCTV cameras record every vehicle and I drive him straight into the garage which has another remote-controlled door.'

'I see. I think, in this case, I'm better going it alone but ring me at the office later and we'll sort out what we're doing then.'

Once in the car, I rang Leonard Smithson on my mobile. 'Johnny Ace,' I said. 'I need to see you urgently.'

'What for?' He sounded wary.

'Mucky photographs, blackmail, Mottram, Nirvana – take your pick.'

There was a stunned silence then, 'How do you know?'

'It's my job to know these things.' I delivered the words as Robert Mitchum might have done. Laconically. 'My office, three o'clock.' And I pressed the cancel button.

Jim Burroughs was horrified when I broke the news to him, back at the office, about his chum. 'The bloody idiot,' he fumed. 'Leonard Smithson's always been a pillar of the community. Mason, Rotarian, school governor . . .'

'You've said it all, Jim. These do-gooders, they all piss in the same pot. Wouldn't trust any of them. Masters of the you-scratch-my-back brigade. Arseholes to a man.'

'Not all of them, Johnny. That's taking it a bit far.' He grinned. 'I must say though, I never thought it of Lennie. A well-respected man, self-made but with the common touch.'

'Pity is, he's been touching more than is good for him. Why do these fellows always keep their brains in their dicks?' Not that I was one to judge.

'By the way, Hilary rang,' said Jim, as if reading my mind.

'She said to phone her at home, she's off work with flu. I think she wants you to go round and minister to her.'

'No chance at the moment, Jim.'

Leonard Smithson arrived on time looking suitably chastened. 'Before you say anything, either of you, I'm signing the club over,' he said. 'I've had enough trouble.'

'Won't work, Lennie,' Jim told him. 'Sorry, but it won't stop there. He'll clean you out. Take it from me, I speak from thirty years' experience in the Force.'

'He's right,' I added. 'And then he'll probably send the pictures to your wife anyway, just for devilment.'

Smithson looked a broken man. 'If Brenda ever sees them, I'm done for. She'll be off and she'll take Jo with her. What can I do?'

'As I see it, you've got four options. You could go to the police, top yourself, kill Mottram, or pay us to get the photos back.' I waited while he took in what I'd said. It didn't cheer him up. 'Here's the deal,' I continued. 'No pics, no fee, but ten grand if we pull it off.' I figured if we didn't get the pictures, knowing Mottram's reputation, we'd be dead anyway. 'On top of the two grand we've had. Plus expenses.'

Jim looked more horrified than Smithson but I was adamant. 'Why not?' I was addressing Jim more than the client. 'It's a big risk and ten grand's nothing compared to him losing his precious Nirvana, not to mention his wife and his business – and I don't suppose Joanna will be too happy either. They do get the papers in prison.'

Smithson threw his hands in the air. 'All right, stop. You've made your point. I'm not going to the police. If Mottram found out I'd contacted them, and he would, the pictures would be all over the papers.'

'And probably the Internet too,' I murmured. I didn't think a *Leonard Smithson Live Show* on the Web would go down well with our client.

Smithson gritted his teeth. 'Ten grand it is. How are you going to do this?'

That was the difficult point. 'Better you don't know,' I said. 'Bring Mottram's letter containing the contact round tomorrow as soon as it arrives and then we can start moving.'

'What price is he offering this time?' asked Jim.

'The same as before when he kidnapped Jo. Half its bloody value.'

'Leave it to us,' I said, 'but whatever you do, *don't* send that contract back to Mottram until you've spoken to us. Right?'

'If you say so.'

'Well?' Jim asked me, after Leonard Smithson had departed.

'I'm thinking,' I replied. The idea of storming Mottram's house was receding as my number one option.

'You'd better think quickly, we've only got another forty-eight hours.'

'Maybe our best chance of nailing Mottram could be through Peter Westcott.' I didn't know why I thought that, except it seemed we had more angles on Peter Westcott, namely Norris Pond and his Friends and Family list, than we did on Mottram. 'I'll have a go at those numbers of Pond's now,' I said. 'See if any of them leads us anywhere.'

'How about Duxfield,' suggested Jim. 'Why don't you give him another try?'

'That's an idea. He could be bait to lure Mottram.'

I dialled the number Mrs Duxfield's neighbour had given me.

This time there was an answer.

Chapter Twenty-nine

'Hello.' The voice that answered had a broad Scouse accent.

'Is that Sharron?'

'Yeah.'

'I'm actually looking for Mrs Duxfield, Graham's mother. I was told she might be with you.'

'Who are yer?'

'Johnny Ace. I was with Graham a couple of days ago.'

'Hang on.' She shouted to someone in the house. 'It's Johnny Ace. He wants to talk to you. Are you here or what?' Frantic whispering in the background then, 'She's not here, sorry.'

'Hang on a minute.' I knew she was ready to hang up. 'When I saw Graham, he was frightened some men were after him. I'm trying to help him but I really need to talk to you.' There was a pause. 'It could save his life,' I added.

There was more whispering and then she said, 'Graham's here and his mam. He says you don't need to bother any more.'

'Can I come and see him? It's really important. I'm not going to tell anyone else the address.'

I could hear shuffling in the room and this time Graham himself came to the phone. 'Look, Mr Ace, I'm not up for trouble. I just want to be left alone.'

'But you were going to testify against Murphy.' I saw no point, at that stage, in telling him that the real Murphy had been murdered. That would have finished him.

'I've changed my mind. Me and my mum are safe now. Nobody knows we're here.'

'Graham,' I said patiently, 'it didn't take much effort for me to find you and if I can do it, then so can your man.' There was a minute's silence whilst he absorbed the information. 'Once you've testified, you won't be in danger, don't you see? As far as they are concerned, the damage will have been done so why would they risk exposing themselves by chasing you any more? You don't even have to leave the building. I can get a solicitor to call on you there and take a sworn affidavit from you.'

'They won't know I've told you, will they, Murphy and his lot?'

He had a point. 'I'll make sure it gets in the papers,' I promised, 'then you'll be safe. Free to go back to your flat.' Marty at the *Daily Post* would welcome the exclusive. I could see the headline: *Juror Confirms Interference in Jo Smithson Trial.*

He said nothing for an agonising minute then, 'OK, Mr Ace, I'll do it. Make it soon, will you?' He gave me his address in Croxteth.

'Thanks, Graham,' I said. 'I'll ring you back as soon as I've sorted out a lawyer.'

'Where will you get one of those at this time?' enquired Jim when I'd put down the phone.

'Alistair Crawford from Goldbergs. I'll ring him at home. He'll come out for me. He gets most of my conveyancing business. He might not be cheap but we can stick it on Smithson's expenses.'

'Or Pond's if the cases are as intertwined as you say.'

I smiled and slapped him on the shoulder. 'Or both, Jim, me old son.'

Alistair Crawford readily agreed to drive down to Croxteth in his Rover 75 to take Graham Duxfield's statement when we phoned him at his Woolton home. 'I was talking to Ifor Jones after that trial,' he said. 'He was always dubious about that jury.'

'Really?' Myself, I hadn't been all that impressed by Ifor Jones's performance but this wasn't the time to say so.

Jim left a message at St Ann Street Police Station for DI Ormesher, telling him we were getting an affidavit from Graham Duxfield. I knew the inspector would want to interview the lad himself but he wasn't due on duty until the next morning.

Jim seemed pleased with the turn of events. 'Once we get that statement, the way's open for the appeal. I just wish Duxfield would be able to finger Mottram.'

'Like we said, Jim, Mottram's clever. He covers his back all along the way; gets others to do his dirty work for him. Anyway, maybe we'll get a clearer picture of the fake Murphy now. I take it none of the court cameras captured him on film?'

'I've not heard so I guess not. You still think it's Peter Westcott, don't you?'

'Seems a fair bet. Come on, let's get over to Croxteth.' Roly followed us out to the car. Saturday traffic was always light round the commercial centre so I'd been able to park in Dale Street without much problem. I realised I hadn't phoned Hilary but that would have to wait. Besides, Maria was expecting me home and tomorrow was supposed to be our day out with Victoria. Case permitting!

Everything went well at Croxteth. The flat itself was in a tower block not unlike Billy Murphy's at Netherley but Sharron had made the best of it. It was cheaply furnished but tidy. A baby, presumably Oliver, crawling inside a plastic playpen, bawled his head off when Roly went over to sniff him but he was unable to outscream the widescreen television set which had Michael Barrymore blasting out at top decibels.

'I'll turn this off,' Sharron said, realising none of us had graduated in Advanced Lip Reading, and she pressed the mute button on the remote, leaving us just the wails of the nine-month-old child to cope with.

The pony-tailed Graham Duxfield was still dressed in his

hippie uniform of faded denims and T-shirt except that Alice Cooper had replaced The Grateful Dead. I wondered if old T-shirts acquired a collectable value like old books and records.

His mother must have been well on her way to seventy but sported a hideous blonde wig that, with her overdone make-up and prominent veins, made her look like a super-annuated tart.

What with Alistair Crawford, as always, in Dickensian mode of dress, and Roly hopping on his hind legs trying to join Oliver in his playpen, the gathering had taken on the aura of a carnival, belying the gravity of the occasion.

However, once Graham Duxfield sat at a table in front of Alistair and started to tell his story, the atmosphere changed. Jim and I sat alongside them and heard Duxfield clearly indict the foreman of the jury as the man who threatened to kill his mother if he didn't find Joanna Smithson guilty.

As the lawyer transcribed his statement, Duxfield went on to describe how a shaven-headed man held a knife to his back as he left the court.

When he had finished, Alistair got him to sign the statement under oath and duly added his signature. Jim and I witnessed it.

'That should do it,' I said. 'I think we should ring Leonard Smithson now, cheer him up a bit, let him know his daughter's on the road to freedom.'

Jim snorted. 'Oh yeah, just in time for her to read about her old man's bedroom adventures in the *Sun*.'

'Look, the bloke has been under a terrible strain, right? With a bit of luck, we can hush it up for him.'

I hadn't decided yet how, but it was Saturday night and I'd had enough for one day. Then a thought struck me. If Mottram *had* posted the contract this morning as Badger had said, Smithson couldn't possibly receive it until Monday at the earliest. There was no postal delivery on a Sunday.

I said as much to Jim.

'That means,' he said carefully, 'that if Mottram keeps

to the forty-eight hours he told Smithson, he won't expect the signed contract back until, let me see,' he counted on his fingers, 'if he posts it on Tuesday night, Wednesday morning. That gives us three days' breathing space to do something.'

'Exactly,' I agreed. But I still didn't know what.

I gave Jim a lift back to his car then drove out to Blundellsands to Maria's. On the way, I stopped at a phone box on the Dock Road to ring Hilary and wished I hadn't. She complained she felt bloody awful, was on her own and asked how soon could I be round.

I tried to explain why I couldn't go. 'It's the Mottram case, Hil, you know, the man we saw at the Golf Club dinner. He's . . .'

But she didn't seem too interested in the latest developments. 'I haven't seen you since then, Johnny, and we only went there because you were working.'

'You enjoyed it,' I protested.

'Oh yes. "I'll take you out for dinner, Hilary" and all I get is a measly sandwich!'

'The rest of the night was good though.'

She changed tactics and started to cry. 'Can't you come over just for an hour?'

'Honestly, I would if I could.' I recalled someone on Radio Four only a week ago declaring that people who begin sentences with 'honestly' are always lying. 'I'll ring you next week, Hil, I promise, as soon as all this is sorted.'

I didn't get the chance to say any more. Hilary put the phone down.

Maria met me at the door as I parked the RAV4 outside her flat and walked up the drive. She held a finger to her mouth. 'Ssssh. I've only just got Victoria off to sleep.' She looked tired.

At that moment, my mobile rang. The caller said, 'You tell me to ring you at the office and you're not there.'

'Badger! Sorry about that. A lot's been happening today.'

Maria went off to the kitchen, followed closely by Roly, whilst I made my way to the lounge and gave Badger my full attention.

'I'm supposed to be picking Harry Mottram up at midnight,' he reminded me. 'Are you coming or what?'

'Not tonight, Badger.' I explained that Mottram's letter wouldn't reach Lennie Smithson until Monday, which gave me time to work out a better plan. 'Sneaking into Mottram's house may not be the best tactic, but if I can't think of anything better we can talk about doing it on Wednesday. In the meantime, see if you can find out if Peter Westcott is one of the men working for Mottram.'

'Leave it to me, man. I'll be in touch.'

I brought Maria up to date with events over dinner, starting with Leonard Smithson's latest plight. Maria was highly scornful about it.

'It beggars belief, being taken in by an old trick like that. How stupid can he get?'

'I don't know. To be fair, I suppose most men might find it difficult to ignore two attractive half-naked girls in their bed, especially if they've had a few drinks.'

Maria's reply was instant and condemning. 'I wouldn't like to think you'd behave like Smithson, Johnny.'

'Just playing devil's advocate,' I said hastily. 'You're right, of course. The guy must have been crazy. He's in a mess now right enough.'

'Serves him right too, though it's his family I feel sorry for, his wife especially. She's been through enough as it is, what with her daughter in prison, and now her husband exposed as a pervert.'

'I don't think quite a pervert, Maria,' I began.

'Any man who takes two girls to bed is a pervert, Johnny,' she said sternly.

Or just plain lucky, I thought but refrained from saying it. I wondered what Hilary's reaction would have been. She'd probably have found it amusing and even arousing. Hilary was easily aroused.

'You reckon he'll lose his club then?' said Maria.

'And his wife, unless I can get to Mottram first.'

'At least his daughter has a good chance of getting out of prison now.'

'Yes, that's something.' Although if Joanna shared Maria's view of the universe, she'd probably never speak to her dad again, which was pretty tragic. 'Even if Mottram's men do get to Graham Duxfield, we've got his affidavit so she should get at least a re-trial.'

'You don't think they'll still try to kill him, do you?'

'They don't know he's signed the statement, do they? But, no, he should be safe with his relatives for the time being.' At least, that's what I'd told him. I could have misjudged the situation. I didn't care to think about the consequences if I had.

'You still haven't found out where Norris Pond stands in all this,' Maria said. 'Why was he so anxious to find his missing goalkeeper?'

'I think it was Peter Westcott I was meant to find, Blease's killer.'

'Fair enough, but why? Surely Pond was after Westcott only because he knew he killed Blease. So what was Blease to Pond that he cared about him so much? That's the real problem you've got to solve.'

'No, Maria. The real problem is the link between Pond and Harry Mottram.'

'If there is one.'

'That's what Jim said.'

'He could be right. It doesn't follow there's a connection. Pond could have got your name out of *Yellow Pages* and it was pure coincidence you happened to be working on the Smithson case.'

'DCI Glass doesn't believe in coincidences and I'm not sure I do. I still think Mottram's involved somewhere. After all, Westcott was living in his house in Docklands.'

'That's the only link between them though, isn't it? Well, like I say, once you know why Pond really hired you, the rest might begin to make sense.'

'True.'

'You never mention Hilary these days,' she said casually, in the next breath. It was so unexpected, I choked on my asparagus. 'Have you not seen her at all?'

'I had a coffee with her on Monday,' I replied truthfully.

'And has she accepted you're not taking her out any more?'

'She's seeing her doctor friend,' I said and was grateful to be saved from further questioning by the phone ringing. Maria went to answer it and I heard her talking to her sister, Kaye. Happily, it looked like being a long conversation.

I carried my wine over to the settee and took out my notebook to study Norris Pond's Friends and Family call list. He didn't make too many calls. Most of the nine numbers listed were for amounts of a pound and less. Our own office number came out the third most called and he hadn't rung us all that often. Second favourite was a Liverpool number I didn't recognise but his most regular contact was somebody with an 01772 number. Preston area.

Was this the clue that we were looking for?

Chapter Thirty

'I'll ring it,' said Maria next morning. 'People are less intimidated by a woman phoning.'

I wasn't going to argue with that. We'd finished breakfast. Victoria was in her high chair slopping food over her face. She looked like an exhibition in the Tate Gallery. Roly stayed within throwing distance, ready to gulp down any stray bits that came his way.

To my relief, Maria had not mentioned Hilary again.

She dialled the Preston number and I waited. Victoria took a handful of food from her dish and jerked it towards Roly, giggling when it splattered on the end of his nose. I went across, picked up the spoon and proceeded to feed her. Roly slunk under the table, licking his chops.

'Hello,' I heard Maria say. 'I'm returning your call. Who is that, please?' A pause then, 'I'm Maria Bowers. Your number came up on my call display, Mrs Fewtrell.' Another pause. 'Maybe someone else rang – your husband perhaps, calling my husband.' A clever move, I thought. Maria wouldn't want Mrs Fewtrell thinking she could be her husband's mistress.

'Oh, I see,' she went on. 'You're in Preston, aren't you? No, I'm in Blundellsands, between Liverpool and Southport. Oh did you? Whereabouts?' She was getting quite chatty now. 'A friend of ours used to live near there, Norris Pond, I don't know if you know him,' then, 'You're joking! What a small world, isn't it? You must send him our regards. We haven't seen him for years. Maria, Maria Bowers and what's your first name? Well, it's been nice talking to you, Iris. I can't think how your number came up but we may find out one day. Bye for now.'

Maria turned round to me, flushed with excitement. 'You'll never believe this, Johnny,' she said. 'Mrs Fewtrell is Norris Pond's sister, Iris.'

'Wait a minute,' I said. 'Iris. Isn't that the name of . . . ?'

'David Blease's ex-wife. I bet you any money it's her. Norris Pond must have been Blease's brother-in-law!'

'But Blease's wife was called Iris Brocken – it can't be her.'

'Now Johnny, remember what you said about coincidences. There can't be that many Irises around.'

'But she'd have been Iris Pond.'

'Not if she'd already been married before when she met Blease.'

Maria was right. 'So this could be the connection between Pond and Blease we've been looking for. What else did she say?'

'She hasn't got a husband so Mr Fewtrell's either dead or she got rid of him along the way.'

'She's going through them, isn't she? That would be three that we know of.'

'Maybe more, who knows? Anyway, she's near enough for you to go round and find out. She's living in Fulwood.'

'Not a bad area. She must have copped for the alimony or Mr Fewtrell left her well heeled. Perhaps it's her money Pond's using.'

'Could be.'

'Is she living on her own?'

'She didn't say.'

'So we don't know if she had any kids?'

'No. Are you going to go and see her? With a name like Fewtrell she shouldn't be hard to track down.'

'Talking of tracking down, you did remember to dial 141 before you phoned her? We don't want her sussing us.'

Maria put her arms round me and kissed me. 'Of course I did, silly. I'm not a private eye for nothing.' She grinned. 'Now go and find Mrs Fewtrell and get to the bottom of this mystery.'

Directory Enquiries gave me a G. Fewtrell and I coaxed an address from them.

'The number's right,' I said, 'so it must be her and the phone's still under her husband's name.'

Sunday morning seemed as good a time as any to visit Iris Fewtrell, formerly Blease, formerly Brocken, née Pond. At least she was unlikely to be at work.

'Are you coming for the ride?' I asked.

Maria shook her head. No, I've got to pop over to Kaye's. She's got some things for the baby. You'll be back for lunch, won't you? We could take Victoria and Roly to the pinewoods at Freshfield for a picnic this afternoon, if you like.'

It took me only forty-five minutes to reach Fulwood and I found Iris Fewtrell's house without difficulty. It was a smart semi-detached, 1930s vintage, with a red Ford Ka parked in the drive. A carved wooden name plaque hanging over the porch announced it was called *Fairview*.

The lady who answered the door was about forty-five. Her hair was golden but styled with tight curls like a pensioner's. She wore a light blue blouse and a navy blue pleated skirt, mid-calf length. Her shoes were navy coloured brogues. Sensible shoes, as my grandmother would have said.

'Yes?' she enquired.

'Johnny Ace,' I said, and handed over my business card. 'I'm working for your brother, Mr Norris Pond.'

She looked startled. 'Oh. Well, you'd better come in.' She led the way into the crowded front room, which contained a three-piece suite, mahogany sideboard and display cabinet. Matching dark wood photograph frames stood on the sideboard and there were more of them on the mantelpiece above a living-flame gas fire.

On the wall was a photograph of the Wavertree Corinthians, identical to the one I'd seen on my illegal excursion round her brother's house.

'How did you find me, Mr Ace?'

'Wasn't I meant to?'

She gave a bitter laugh. 'I suppose it doesn't matter in the long run.' It seemed a strange thing for her to say.

'Why should it?'

'Would you care for a cup of coffee?'

'I'd prefer tea, if that's all right?'

'Tea it is.'

I took advantage of her trip to the kitchen to study some of the photographs. I recognised the young Norris Pond in what looked like Newcastle United's colours, and a later one of him, spectacularly older, in his Wavertree Corinthians strip. There was also one of Digger Blease, in his goalkeeper's jersey. He couldn't have been more than twenty-one or two. Next to them was a reproduction of the Wavertree Corinthians club photograph that Nobby Wharton had given me.

On the mantelpiece were three wedding portraits, each featuring Iris in her capacity as a serial bride. In the first one, she looked scarcely out of school, dressed in a white bridal gown, her hair straight and down to her shoulders, standing alongside an equally callow youth who, I imagined, was Mr Brocken.

She'd grown up a lot in time for the second ceremony. With her hair shorter and her low-cut dress too revealing for the occasion, she almost dwarfed the familiar figure of David Ian George Blease. He had his arm possessively round her shoulders. I had the strange, uneasy feeling I'd seen him before but I couldn't bring the occasion to mind.

Judging by the third photograph, Iris had waited a good while before allowing Mr Fewtrell to escort her on her next trip down the aisle. A good few years had elapsed, she'd put on a lot of weight and her hair was already short and curly as it was in real life now. This time, she was wearing a primrose two-piece suit. Her latest groom was at least twenty years older, grey-haired and bespectacled. She'd obviously opted for security rather than going for broke with a toy-boy.

'You're looking at all my disastrous attempts at matrimony.' She came back into the room and set the crockery on a coffee-table. 'I shouldn't say that. George was very kind, poor lamb.'

'That's Mr Fewtrell, I take it. What happened to him?'

She sighed. 'He died last year. We'd only been married two years when he developed prostate cancer. He was sixty-seven. That's what happens when you marry older men. They peg out on you.'

'So do young ones,' I said gently. 'You can't legislate for death.'

'I suppose not.' She said it with an air of weariness as if she didn't quite believe it. 'I'll fetch the tea. Sit down, Mr Ace. I've a feeling this could take a while.'

And so it proved. I got the whole story.

Norris Pond was already eighteen when his sister, Iris, was born, a surprise both to him and their parents who were well into their forties. Naturally, Norris was very protective of his baby sister.

'He used to fetch me home from school and make sure none of the other children bullied me.'

He wasn't quite so successful in protecting her in later years, however. By the time she was sixteen, Norris had long since left home to be a professional footballer, and Iris fell prey, not to bullies, but to a teenage Lothario called Nicky Brocken. He was her first love and he got her pregnant.

'I always thought it couldn't happen the first time,' she said, looking at me with hurt and puzzled eyes as if seeking my reassurance, even today, that it shouldn't have been possible.

Being godfearing people with 'respectable' middle-class values, Iris's mother and father joined up with Nicky Brocken's parents to force their children into an unwanted and unsuitable union.

'My mother told me, "We want you properly wed before you start showing and the neighbours start talking,"' said Iris.

The sad thing was, Iris never did show. She lost the baby two months after the wedding and Nicky Brocken, freed from his obligations, disappeared from her life.

'My brother was playing football up in the North East and I left school and went to work at a supermarket on the tills.'

In 1974, she met David Blease and fell hopelessly in love with him. They were married within six months, both aged just twenty.

'He didn't have a real job, did Davey. He picked up a good few quid every week playing semi-pro football, mostly for cash, moving around clubs quite a lot. The rest of the time he lived on his wits, as we used to call it. A bit here, a bit there. He did all right – we were never short. But he couldn't leave the women alone, that was what split us up.'

'When did you leave him?'

'In 1976, two years after we were married. I'd had enough of the competition. Some nights, he wasn't coming home at all and he never cared who saw him when he was out with his women. It was like he was flaunting it.'

'So it was well after you'd left him that he played for your brother's football team?'

'The Wavertree Corinthians, you mean? Yes, about three years after. Norris started the Corinthians in 1975. He'd retired from the professional game, you see. He'd lasted till he was nearly forty, which was pretty good going, but he couldn't give it up altogether so he formed the Corinthians.'

'That seems odd, if you don't mind me saying so.'

'What does?'

'That your husband didn't join them when they first started, when you were still together.'

'Not really. Davey was in the selling game at that particular time and he was out of town quite a bit on business. Norris wanted people who were available every week.'

'But why have him in 1979 when you'd left him? I mean, I

would have thought, after the way he treated you, Norris would have had nothing to do with him.'

'I think he was stuck for a goalkeeper. I'd moved away by then, anyway, and Davey was still hanging around the Wavertree area. He was down on his luck at the time and was running a window-cleaning round. Norris met him one night in this pub and he ended up playing in goal for them. It didn't last long though. Davey went off to London after a few weeks.'

'How did you find that out?'

'What – his move to London? I think Norris must have told me. All I know is, I haven't heard from Davey since the day I left him.'

It was the way the sentence was said that made me realise.

Iris Fewtrell didn't know that her ex-husband, David Blease, was dead.

Chapter Thirty-one

'Mrs Fewtrell,' I said. 'Iris. Your brother has hired me to find David Blease. What do you know about that?'

'It doesn't surprise me.'

'Why is that?'

'It's just that Norris always had a thing about Davey. Thought he should have supported me more. He never sent money or anything after he went.' Again that air of resignation, as if a spark inside her had died.

'Has he told you what his search has turned up so far?'

'I haven't seen him for a while.'

But he rang her most days as I knew from his Friends and Family list.

'He phones you though, I take it? Has he never told you where Davey could be?'

'I leave it up to Norris. If he wants to be bothered, good luck to him. It's all in the past as far as I'm concerned. It's over twenty years since I divorced Davey. I've had George since then. And now he's gone too.'

At least we wouldn't need to search for George.

'What do you think Norris was going to do if he found Davey?'

She shrugged her shoulders. 'Get money off him, I suppose.'

'He's rich now then, is he?'

'I don't know, but he was never poor for long, wasn't Davey.'

'Iris, did you ever know a couple called the Westcotts? They had a butcher's shop in Picton Road.'

'Doesn't ring a bell. Who are they?'

'Your Davey knew them when he played for the Corinthians, and he went to stay with them in London when they moved there.'

She didn't seem interested. 'What's that got to do with anything?'

'That's what I thought you might tell me.'

She shook her head. 'No. I've never heard of them.'

'And you've no idea where Davey might be now?'

'Could be anywhere. To be honest, I couldn't care less. I told Norris, why bother? If Davey'd wanted to help me he would have done so in the first place.'

I looked round the room. 'You seem to be managing well enough without him.'

'I am now, thanks to George. He left me well provided for.'

'You say Davey's never short of money for long, so what about when he dies?' I saw no point in destroying her illusions for the moment. 'Who will inherit his money?'

She looked embarrassed. 'I've no idea. He could have married again. He's the sort of man who'd always have a woman around.'

And more waiting in the wings, I thought.

'Did Davey ever mention his uncle, Arthur Blease? Lived in Ormskirk.'

'Who?'

I repeated the question.

'No, I've never heard that name. Davey always told me he had no relatives. They were all dead.'

'What about Harry Mottram? Have you ever heard of him?'

She hadn't.

There seemed little else to say. I thanked her and left. On the drive back to Maria's, I turned over in my mind the information that Iris Fewtrell had given me. It wasn't much.

Possibly Norris Pond was hoping to secure an inheritance for his sister from David Blease's estate but there were legal channels for that. Why hire me?

It still seemed more likely that Pond was after Blease's killer, Peter Westcott, but for what reason? Revenge? Yet, if Iris was right, there was little love lost between Norris Pond and his brother-in-law. Why should he care who had killed him? Or had Westcott got access to money or possessions that once belonged to Blease, and Norris Pond wanted to get them back?

Whatever it was, I didn't see how Harry Mottram entered the equation other than Westcott might be working for him. Maybe Badger would throw some light on that.

Maria had Victoria dressed and ready when I returned.

'I've made up a picnic,' she said. 'I thought we could have it in the pinewoods.'

'As long as you've done bloater-paste sandwiches.'

'Ugh, how you can eat those, I don't know.'

'Not me. Roly. He loves them.'

'You put the buggy in the car, I'll bring Victoria.'

It was perfect weather for a picnic, hot and sunny. I strapped Victoria into her chair on the back seat and we set off for Freshfield.

'Well,' asked Maria. 'How did you get on with Iris? Was she Digger Blease's wife?'

'She was. She was a strange woman really. She seemed a bit yonderly, as if life had been too much for her and she was living in a haze. Can you believe, she didn't seem to know Digger Blease was dead?'

'If they were divorced, the authorities wouldn't be aware of her to inform her.'

'You'd think Norris would have told her though. After all, it's over a week since I rang him about the fire.'

'Perhaps he did tell her and she didn't want to accept it.'

'I suppose it's possible,' I conceded. 'Anyway, she didn't have much else to say. Mr Fewtrell's dead as well and she didn't seem too concerned about that.'

'So, what's your next move?'

'Back to Pond. If he's just been away for the weekend, he should be home tomorrow.'

'Changing the subject, do you think Leonard Smithson will sign that contract to sell Nirvana?'

'Yes, I'd say there'd be a good chance of it if we let him, although he'd be stupid to do so.'

'It's all he deserves.'

'That's as maybe but blackmailers never stop, Maria. They'll clean him out.'

'So, it's up to you to stop them.'

I knew that, but how I was going to do it I wasn't so sure.

Cars were lined up on both sides of the path when we reached the pinewoods. Sunday drivers were out in force. Small children were running in and out of the pine trees, screaming and shouting; barking dogs vainly tried to catch the red squirrels. Roly jumped out of the back and chased after them. It was like the setting for an Hieronymus Bosch painting.

'Isn't it nice here?' said Maria, uncoupling Victoria from her seat. 'You get the buggy out, Johnny.'

'I prefer it at six in the morning,' I said, 'when nobody's around.' At dawn, before the world has woken, the woods are deathly still and you can hear the sea lapping on the shore nearby.

'Spooky,' said Maria.

We put the baby into her buggy and she chuckled as I pushed her along the uneven path. She was so pretty. I still could hardly believe she was something I'd created. Maria held on to my arm. Affectionately or possessively? Perhaps neither. Perhaps it was only my own response that attributed these emotions to her actions.

We spread our picnic out on one of the wooden tables. Maria had brought cans of Scrumpy Jack, smoked salmon, and Coronation chicken sandwiches as well as the bloater paste ones, broccoli and mushroom quiches, Melton Mowbray pies and sausage rolls. Enough to feed a regiment.

'This is the first time we've been out properly as a family, Johnny, do you know that?' she smiled, lifting Victoria on to her knee. 'Isn't it wonderful?'

I squeezed her arm and kissed her. 'It is,' I said. 'Wonderful.' But I gazed about at the other laughing families around us and it felt more like quicksand and I was sliding in fast.

'Had a good weekend?' asked Jim at the office the next morning, watching Roly settle himself on his blanket.

'Nothing a night at the Masquerade won't cure,' I replied. 'Anything happened?'

'Lennie Smithson's due in at any time. He rang me at home over breakfast. He's received the contract.'

'Anything else with it?'

'He didn't say.'

Smithson was round in person a few minutes later and he looked deathly. 'It's no good. If all this gets out, I'm ruined,' he said. 'I'll have to let him have the club.'

There had been no letter with the contract.

'Mottram covering his back again,' I said. 'No ransom notes, no written blackmail demands, no photos, ergo no evidence. Sign nothing,' I instructed him. 'Hang on to the contract and wait for us to call you.'

When he'd gone, I turned to Jim. 'I'm going to get hold of Badger. Looks like our best chance is for me to get into Mottram's house.'

'No, Johnny, it's dangerous and it's illegal.'

'No other way, Jim.'

I dialled Badger's number and he answered almost immediately. 'Have you got half an hour?' I asked him.

'Sure, man. I'll meet you outside La Tasca in Queen's Square at twelve. You can buy me lunch.'

'I bought you lunch last time.'

'You could always let me live rent free instead.'

'Lunch it is.'

'Well?' enquired Jim.

'He wants me to meet him at La Tasca.' I saw Jim's eyebrows rise. 'It's a new Spanish restaurant in Queen's Square. Funnily enough, I was in one at Canary Wharf when I was in London. Have you seen Queen's Square lately, Jim? You wouldn't recognise it. Full of trendy new wine bars and restaurants.'

'First the Albert Dock, now Queen's Square. Where will it end? Duke Street'll be next, they're rebuilding all round there. The place'll be full of yuppies. A bit different from the old days, eh, Johnny? We used to play at the Pink Parrot in Duke Street and most of the groups would end up at Joe's Café at two in the morning after their gig.'

'In the 1970s, it was the Beachcomber and the Babalou and the Knightsbridge down there.' I said. 'All history now.'

'Those were the days, though.' Jim smiled nostalgically at the memory.

'Let's hope there's enough people around with money to spend to make all these new places pay.'

'Drug money, Johnny. It's the cash culture that the new wealth of cities like Manchester and Liverpool is founded on.'

'Not to mention the black economy,' I added.

Jim looked wistful. 'I remember when the Stork Hotel was on Queen's Square. We did a gig there, back in 1971 I think it was. I took this girl with me, a little fat creature called Judy, and while we were on stage, she pissed off to one of the bedrooms with the bloody hotel manager.'

'Bet that never happened to The Beatles,' I said. 'By the way, I never got a chance to tell you before Smithson came. I found Digger Blease's ex-wife yesterday.'

221

'You didn't! How come?'

'She only turned out to be Norris Pond's sister. She was the one at the top of his Family and Friends list.'

'So *that's* why Pond was so keen to find Blease. He was chasing him for alimony for his sister but, of course, he's dead so she's missed out there. Did she tell you anything?'

'Nothing that helps us find Westcott or finger Mottram. She's called Fewtrell now, after her third husband, that's why we couldn't trace her. She thinks, like you do, that the reason Norris Pond has been chasing Blease is to get her some money off him.'

'Blease could have left a will. I think Glass was chasing that angle. In fact, I'll ring him now and see what he's found out.'

But Detective Chief Inspector Glass had found nothing. There had been no will at Somerset House in the name of David Ian George Blease. He was disappointed that we hadn't any more evidence on Peter Westcott that would allow him to put out a call for his arrest.

'Keep trying,' he said. 'I could use a good result.'

Obviously he wasn't having much success tracking down his armed robbers.

'I'm not sure money *is* the reason Pond is after Blease,' I said, after Jim had terminated the call. 'I think it could be more to do with Westcott or Mottram.'

'Had Pond's sister heard of either of them?'

'I asked her and she said not. I don't think she was lying.'

'What about Pond? Any sign of him?'

'No. I might go round again this afternoon after I've arranged things with Badger.'

Badger arrived at La Tasca minutes after me. We went inside and ordered a selection of tapas and a bottle of red wine.

'Anything new on Mottram then?' I asked him.

'I found out the young bloke's name for you. It's Sean. He seems to be Harry's main man.'

'Sean who?'

'I didn't get that far. I just heard Mottram shout to him.'

'What about the other one, the older one?' The fake Murphy. Westcott.

'No sign.'

'I need to get into the house, Badger, to find those negatives. Are you going there tonight?'

'You're in luck. He's handing the car over to me at nine and I pick him up from Nirvana at two in the morning. So if you come to Livingstone Drive at one-thirty, you can collect the car and tell him I'm sick.'

'He's going to Nirvana? Christ, he's got some face.'

'Sure has.'

'Mind you, what can Smithson do? He can hardly shoot him, it's not his style.'

'He could refuse him admission.'

'Mottram's playing mind games with him,' I said. 'He's gloating, letting Smithson know he can't touch him. Well, let him. Maybe it'll give him a false sense of security.'

'You want to be careful there, man. Are you taking back-up?'

'No. Safer to go alone, but I'll want you to give me the layout of the house.'

I brought out my notebook and Badger sketched me a rough plan of Harry Mottram's Mobberley mansion.

'There's a big safe in his office on the ground floor at the front,' he said. 'That's the most likely place where he'd keep the negatives, but I tell you, man, the whole place is alarmed. Sensors everywhere.'

'I'll bear it in mind.'

After I left Badger, I drove to Norris Pond's house but again there was no reply. Two copies of a free newspaper stuck in his letterbox suggested he hadn't been back since I last visited. So much for stopping the papers when you go on holiday. You might as well put a *Gone Away* sign up for potential burglars.

I went back to the office. Jim was not enthusiastic about my planned trip.

'Stop being a policeman,' I said. 'I'm not breaking in and I'm not breaking the law. I'm just going to have a nose around, see if I can talk to this Sean character, find out if our fake foreman is still on the scene.'

'I've got some news for you about him,' interrupted Jim. 'Clive Ormesher was on the phone before. The security cameras at the Court did pick him up and they've got a probable match. He's a forty-seven-year-old ex-wrestler from Walker called Karl Dwane.'

'Walker – isn't that near Newcastle?'

'That's right. He's a Geordie.'

'The Animals did a song about Walker, that's how I knew.'

'Mottram must have latched on to him when he lived up there. He's got form for GBH and demanding money with menaces among other things.'

'Sounds like Mottram's sort of person.'

'There's a warrant out for his arrest. Nothing to connect him to Mottram, though.'

'I bet if we searched Mottram's house, we'd find him.'

'We'd never get a search warrant, Johnny. It's all conjecture.'

'This puts the kibosh on my theory, you realise. I'd have put money on him being Peter Westcott.'

'Which begs the question, where does Westcott fit into all this now?'

'I don't know, Jim, I'm lost. Maybe after tonight I'll have some answers.'

Chapter Thirty-two

After I'd done the radio show, I took Roly back to the flat and rang Maria to explain I was going to Mottram's house and wouldn't be home till tomorrow night. She wasn't too happy about my excursion.

'You're going to get killed one day,' she said, 'and I don't want that. What would Victoria do without her daddy?'

I told myself that was emotional blackmail and rang off. I needed to prepare for my trip. I microwaved a Marks & Spencer roast duck meal and cooked some sauté potatoes and carrots to go with it. At least I intended to go to my doom well fed. Roly sat at my feet, eagerly waiting for the duck skin. A canine gourmet.

After the meal, I took a long hot bath, listening to the new Linda Gail Lewis/Van Morrison CD, then put on a pair of black slacks, white shirt, tie and black leather jacket, hoping I looked reasonably like a chauffeur. I also took with me a small 35mm camera.

'You're in your own bed tonight, son,' I said to Roly. 'Make a change for you.'

Tommy McKale seemed surprised when I turned up at the door of the Masquerade Club at midnight.

'Christ,' he exclaimed, looking at me. 'It's a bit late for burials, isn't it?'

'I'm supposed to be a chauffeur, not an undertaker.'

'Where's the peaked cap then?'

'In my pocket.'

'You need a proper disguise. A false moustache and a ginger wig.'

'That went out with Sherlock Holmes.'

I explained my mission to him and he became serious. 'You're playing with fire with that man, Johnny. I've told you before, he's dangerous.'

'You remember the kidnapped girl case I was on?'

'Of course. She went inside for killing one of Mottram's men. Should have got the George Cross.'

'Instead, she's in Durham Prison, mainly because Mottram nobbled the jury.'

'We discussed it at the time. He was after Lennie Smithson's club and I said he wouldn't give up.'

'Well, he hasn't.' I told him about the photos and the blackmail.

Tommy whistled. 'He's got him by the short and curlies in every sense of the word, hasn't he.'

'That's why I'm dressed like this. I'm taking the place of Mottram's driver to get into his house.'

'Whatever for?'

'To try and find out who his henchman is and maybe have a look around for the negatives.'

'Fuck me, Johnny. The Israelis could use you in their army. That's the sort of stunt they pull. Them or the SAS. If Mottram susses you, you're dead.'

'Thanks, Tommy. Just the encouragement I need.'

'You're not going yet, are you? Come in and let me buy you a drink in case I never get the chance again. Your bird's inside somewhere.'

'Hilary?'

'The very same. Still seeing her, are you?'

'Sort of.'

'You don't half live dangerously. How's the baby?'

'Fine. And Maria's fine too.'

He shook his head and shouted across the bar. 'Vince! A pint of cider for Johnny. He's going on a kamikaze mission.'

Vince came across looking glum. Without a word, he poured my drink and pushed it across the counter before walking back to the opposite end of the bar.

'What's up with him?' I asked.

'Boyfriend trouble. His little pal's ditched him. He's had to pour lavender oil on his pillow to get to sleep at night, he's so upset. I tell you, Johnny, sex has a lot to answer for in this world.'

Almost on cue, Hilary bounced up. She was wearing a tight turquoise Giant top, revealing her bare midriff, and a pair of equally tight denim jeans with frayed pockets and seams. She still had the slim figure for it. 'Did somebody mention sex? I don't seem to have had much of it lately.'

'I'll leave you two to it,' said Tommy McKale hastily.

'And how's the lovely Maria?' Hilary asked provocatively, after he'd gone.

I ignored the jibe. 'Your flu's better then?'

'No thanks to you. You never came round. And why are you wearing that ridiculous outfit?'

'I'm doing some undercover work. I'm supposed to be a driver.'

'God, Johnny. This detective business has really got to you, hasn't it?'

'You don't understand, Hil. This is dangerous work.' I explained about Leonard Smithson's indiscretion and the blackmail attempt.

'Three in a bed,' she said. 'Sounds fun. I'm lucky if I can get one person in my bed these days.' She looked at me quizzically. 'Are you taking me home with you tonight, Johnny, or will Maria be there? Maybe *she'd* fancy a threesome?' She grinned, reached up and kissed me on the lips and, if I hadn't had Mottram's to go to, I would have taken her to the flat then and there.

'Come on,' I said, taking her arm. 'I've got to go in an hour. Let's have a dance.' I led her on to the dance floor.

227

By one o'clock, we'd had a couple of drinks and Hilary had calmed down.

'We'll go out later this week,' I promised her.

'Friday night,' she said quickly. 'It's my night off. We could go for a meal in Chester and you can stay overnight at mine.'

'Fine,' I agreed, knowing it wasn't really but I could worry about it later. Right now I had to meet Badger.

I took a taxi to Livingstone Drive. A silver Lexus was parked outside the house. I rang Badger's bell and he came straight down.

'You're OK,' he said. 'I've told Mottram I can't make it tonight so he's expecting you.'

'You didn't give my name?'

'Come on, I'm not stupid, man.' He smiled. 'I said you were called Pat Lake. He thinks you're from Dublin so you'd better practise your Terry Wogan accent.'

'Oh great.'

'Here's the car keys and this is a remote control for the electronic gates. He's got a meeting in the morning at eleven at the Adelphi so you'll be back by then.'

Unless something went wrong.

I climbed into the Lexus and started the engine. It was almost silent. I drove back into town and parked a few yards down from the entrance to Nirvana. I put on my chauffeur's cap and a pair of large, black-framed spectacles with plain glass lenses. My only concessions to disguise. The clock on the dash said 01.55.

At dead on two, the familiar figure of Harry Mottram appeared at the door, peered down the street till he picked out his car and walked towards me. I recognised him immediately from the Charity Night at the Golf Club. Now he was wearing a dark suit and striped tie and looked like a captain of industry.

I jumped out and opened the back door. He didn't speak, just nodded. I shut the door after him, climbed back in the driving seat and set off for the M62.

'You know where you're going?' he said brusquely.

'Mobberley.'

'That's it. I'll tell you where the house is when we get there.'

In the rearview mirror, I watched him slump back in his seat and take out a mobile phone.

'That you, Sean? Have you heard from Karl yet?' I pricked up my ears at the mention of the name. Karl! It had to be Karl Dwane. 'Yeah, yeah,' he went on. 'No, he should have been back by now. Never mind. No, I'm on my way home. See you in the morning. Ciao.'

He switched off the phone and I concentrated on the traffic along Edge Lane. So Karl Dwane was out somewhere on a job for Mottram and there was a warrant out for his arrest. If I knew he was inside Mottram's house, how long would it take for Clive Ormesher to get a search warrant?

Nothing more was said for the rest of the journey. I came off the M6 at Junction 19, through a deserted Knutsford until I came to the village of Mobberley whereupon Mottram leaned forward and pointed out the stone pillars that flanked the entrance to his drive.

I pressed the remote control to activate the huge electronic wrought-iron gates and drove for almost a quarter of a mile before I reached his mansion. Rhododendron bushes flanked the roadside, behind which lay newly mown lawns and flower beds, visible in the light of a full moon.

The building itself was impressive, an old manorial house two storeys high with stone pillars flanking the steps leading up to an imposing wooden front door which looked strong enough to withstand the firepower of a Civil War battle, as indeed it probably had.

I pulled up outside the steps, jumped out of the car and opened the rear door for Mottram.

'Leave the car here,' he instructed, as he hauled himself out. 'You'll find a gate round the side, go through that and you'll see your room in the annexe. Have the car ready for me at nine-thirty.' It was already gone three o'clock. Mottram obviously was a man who didn't need much sleep.

I bade him goodnight, I couldn't bring myself to touch my cap, and walked round to the tradesman's entrance. The outbuilding was little more than a converted garage. The door was ajar and a light on in the hall. I went inside and found a large bed sitting-room with a kitchenette off and an en-suite bathroom and toilet. There was food and milk in the fridge, an electric kettle and even a small mini-bar. Just like a posh hotel. The bed was a kingsize one and a satellite TV stood in the corner.

Badger had never mentioned I would be sleeping in separate accommodation which appeared to present an insurmountable difficulty to gaining entry to Mottram's residence. Obviously there was no need for me to go into the house at all as everything was provided for me here in this annexe.

So much for Badger's diagram.

I went outside again to reconnoitre. There were more gardens at the back, a conservatory adjoining the lounge and French windows leading from the dining room. A light burned in an upstairs back bedroom which I took to be Mottram's. Everything was quiet and eerily still.

I went back to my quarters and stripped off for bed. I set the alarm on my watch for eight o'clock, hoping I might get a chance to see Sean before it was time to leave.

I was lucky. I'd barely had time to take a shower and grab a cup of tea and toast when I heard someone whistling outside. I looked out of the window and saw this man in his early twenties, his head shaved, carrying garbage to the bins.

I immediately went outside in time to intercept him on his way back.

'You must be Sean,' I said.

He looked at me aggressively. 'Who wants to know?'

'Pat Lake,' I said. 'I'm the driver, standing in for . . .' I stopped. I didn't know what name Badger might be using.

'Oh yeah. So?'

'You been working for Harry long?'

'What's it to you?'

I couldn't see Sean being a success on *Michael Parkinson*.

'Just wondered what he was like to work for, that's all. I might be looking for a job myself soon, something more permanent like. What is it you do yourself?'

'This and that.' He regarded me suspiciously. 'Ask a lot of questions, don't you?'

I asked another one. 'You don't know a bloke called Peter Westcott, do you?'

'Never heard of him.' The reply came instantly and I felt he was telling the truth.

'Just wondered. He used to live in Mobberley.'

No reply. He turned and walked back to the house. I returned to my room, picked up my camera and went back to the window. A couple of minutes later, he reappeared with more garbage and I took a few shots of him before he went back in the house.

Nobody else came out and I could see no way of getting into the house without arousing suspicion.

At nine o'clock I walked round to the front of the house and climbed into the driving seat of the Lexus. Within five minutes, Harry Mottram came out of the front door and marched over to the car. He was in the back seat before I had time to get out and open the door. 'The Adelphi Hotel,' he ordered. 'And step on it.'

Just as I was driving out of the gates, I saw the postman pedalling up the road on his red bicycle. It was already Tuesday. Tomorrow morning, if I didn't act quickly, he could be bringing Leonard Smithson's contract, signed, and Mottram would own Nirvana.

Despite heavy traffic on the M6 and M62, I got us into Liverpool before ten-thirty. I wondered whom his eleven o'clock meeting was with.

As I pulled up outside the Adelphi, he leaned forward and

231

handed me a brown envelope. 'Leave the car,' he said. 'The attendant will park it.'

I took the envelope and put it in my pocket. 'Thanks.'

He was out of the car before me, bounded up the hotel steps and disappeared into the foyer. I left the keys in the ignition, shut the door and walked up the road to Max Spielman's in Renshaw Street.

'How long to develop this?' I asked the assistant, handing over the film.

'Twenty minutes.'

'That'll do me.'

Whilst I waited, I went for a tea and croissant at La Brioche down the road. When the photos were ready, I took them straight to the office. The ones of Sean had come out clearly.

'Not much to show for a night's undercover work,' commented Jim. 'Who is it?'

'Unless I'm mistaken, that's the second man who helped kidnap Joanna Smithson, shot Mr Patel and took a knife to Graham Duxfield.'

'What's his name?'

'Sean something. Mottram's chief gofer. Run one though the scanner and fax it to one of your police buddies. See if they recognise him. Also, I heard Mottram mention someone called Karl who's supposed to be on his way back from a job he was doing for him.'

'You mean it could be Karl Dwane?'

'I'd put money on it. What's new with Smithson? He didn't sign the contract, did he?'

Jim smiled. 'It's in here.' He indicated the desk drawer. 'He came back after you'd gone last night and I persuaded him to leave it with me.'

'You did well there.'

'Actually, he was a bit the worse for wear. He'd been on the whisky.'

'We've still got all of today to do something.'

'Hardly much time, is it?'

I couldn't think what to do next. 'I'll have another look for Pond,' I decided.

I drove to the flat to pick up Roly and rang Geoff to say I wouldn't be round for my usual Tuesday morning visit. He didn't seem concerned. He could handle things well enough; in fact, he ran most of the property side these days.

I took Roly for a run in Stanley Park before going on to Aintree and Norris Pond's house. Once again, there was no reply, and no sign of life. The estate was quiet, everyone out at work.

It wasn't too far to Croxteth so I thought I'd call at Graham Duxfield's hideout to show him the pictures I'd taken of Sean. I found him and his mother alone in the flat looking after baby Oliver.

'I wondered who it was when you knocked just now,' said Graham, fidgeting nervously.

His mother, looking more than ever like Bette Davis on her deathbed, was wiping up custard that the child had daubed on the walls behind his playpen. Oliver followed her round slapping her and screaming at a decibel level that Iron Maiden would have been proud of.

Roly thought it was a game and joined in, lapping at the custard like he hadn't eaten for a week.

'I've brought a photo for you to look at,' I told Graham. 'Do you recognise this person?'

'Yes, that's him,' he said, studying the photo. 'I'm sure of it. That's the man with the knife who stopped me outside the court. Who is he?'

'He's called Sean. That's all we know at present.' I put the photos back inside my notebook.

At that moment, the doorbell rang and Graham almost jumped out of his skin. 'Who's that?' he said, shaking.

'It's probably Sharron,' I reassured him.

'She's got a key. Anyway, she's working at the Rest Home.'

'It could be anybody, Jehovah's Witnesses, the man to read the gas meter.'

'It's all electric here,' said his mother, tearing herself away from the custard cleaning.

I was beginning to get nervous myself. Since we had his statement, I'd tended to forget that Duxfield might still be in danger. 'Keep out of sight,' I instructed. 'Get in the kitchen and I'll answer it.'

But I didn't get the chance because just then the door flew open with an almighty bang and a burly man in his mid-forties stood on the threshold holding a gun. I had seen him before; he was the foreman of the jury at Liverpool Crown Court. The blood drained from Graham Duxfield's face as he mouthed the word 'Murphy' and I knew unmistakably who the intruder was.

He had impersonated the late Billy Murphy at Joanna Smithson's trial, had possibly killed Murphy and now he had come to seek out Graham Duxfield. To silence him.

Harry Mottram's henchman, the Geordie, Karl Dwane.

Chapter Thirty-three

The first shot whistled past Graham Duxfield's face as he dived behind the sofa. His mother stood in the playpen, dishcloth in hand, screamed, then pushed Oliver down on to the floor and threw herself over him.

I was nearest the door. Dwane seemed to see me for the first time and immediately pointed the gun at me. Before he could pull the trigger a second time, I dived for his ankles and pulled him over. The weapon fell to the ground.

We wrestled on the floor and I tried to grab his arm that was reaching for the gun but he thrust his knee into my groin and winded me before jerking his head forward and butting me squarely between the eyes. A huge noise exploded in my head and I slumped to the ground.

Through a swirling mist and flashing lights, I vaguely saw Dwane take hold of the gun and rise to his feet but I couldn't move any of my limbs to stop him. Then, a brown shape came flying through the air and, with a snarl, fixed its teeth round Dwane's collar, catching him off-balance and pulling him over. Roly.

I shook my head as the room came back into focus. Dwane was trying to scramble to his feet again but the dog stood over him, growling menacingly.

Dwane bought his arm across in an effort to smash his gun against Roly's skull but, just in time, I was able to stagger over and deflect it and, at the same time, jab my fingers into the assailant's eyes.

I've had no training in martial arts or self-defence but I've always instinctively believed that blows to the Adam's apple or the testicles, or fingers in the eyes, tend to disable most men.

I don't know what works with women but, so far, I've not been attacked by one. Perhaps I've been lucky but there's always time.

My strategy worked in this case. Dwane dropped the gun as he fell backwards and brought his hands up to his eyes. Roly immediately leapt at him again, jumping on his chest.

With a roar, Dwane hurled himself to his feet, throwing the dog on to the floor, and swiftly turned towards the door. Before I could stop him, the gunman was running out and down the stairs. Roly barked and set off after him but I called him back. I didn't want him run over and I knew Dwane would be quite capable of it.

I clambered to my feet, dizzy but more or less conscious, as Graham Duxfield emerged from behind the settee and his mother slowly rose up inside the playpen, allowing the crushed Oliver to extricate himself and start howling.

'We might have been killed,' she cried, glaring at me as if it was all my fault.

'Good job I was here, then, or you would have been.' I didn't think there was any doubt about that. Karl Dwane had meant business.

I picked up his gun, thinking it might well come in useful in the days ahead, then dialled Jim Burroughs on my mobile.

'I'm at Graham Duxfield's,' I panted. 'That Karl Dwane's just been here with a shooter. Tried to kill Duxfield.'

'I take it you stopped him?'

'Yes, but he got away. Can you ring Ormesher and inform him? Tell him to get his men down here.'

'Where do you think Dwane's heading?'

'I don't know. It's unlikely he'd risk coming back here but I wouldn't think he'd chance going to Mottram's either.'

'Didn't you get his car reg?'

'Sorry, Jim. I was half-conscious at the time.'

'That's no excuse. Right, leave it to me. Was Pond in when you went round?'

'No. He's not been back. I'm becoming a bit concerned about him now, Jim. If there is a tie-in between Westcott and Mottram beyond landlord and tenant, and Mottram knows Pond is on their trail, then Pond could be in danger too. Haven't you noticed what seems to happen to most of the people who cross Westcott's path, and Mottram's too? They stop living.'

'You could have a point there,' Jim conceded.

'I think I might go over and see Iris again. Pond could be holed up with her.'

'Keep me posted. Ormesher'll want to talk to you, don't forget.'

'I'll be in touch.'

I used Sharron's bathroom to bathe the cut on my brow and give myself a splash of cold water to clear my head. 'Don't open the door to anyone till the police come,' I told Graham. 'I don't think he'll come back but you never know.'

'Thanks, Mr Ace,' he said, holding out his hand. 'You saved my life, and maybe Mum's and Oliver's too.'

'Thank the dog,' I said. 'Without him we could both have been dead.'

Roly wagged his stump and followed me down to the car. I got back on to the A59 and drove through Ormskirk towards Preston. I was still feeling shaken after the attack so I stopped off at the Bull and Dog at Burscough, Norman Thomas's pub, for a sandwich and a glass of cider.

It was three o'clock when I reached Fulwood. I could hear the sounds of the television coming from the front room as I walked up Iris Fewtrell's front drive and she opened the door the minute after I pressed the bell.

'Me again,' I smiled.

'What is it?' She seemed agitated.

'Can I come in? I hope you don't mind the dog. He's well behaved.'

Reluctantly, she ushered us into the front room and switched down the volume on the TV. Roly lay down in front of the unlit gas fire and smiled to himself; satisfied with his morning's work.

'I've been trying to get hold of your brother but he isn't at home,' I said. 'I wondered if he might be here with you?'

'No.'

'You don't know where he is?'

'No.'

'Have you spoken to him at all since I was last here on Sunday?'

'No.'

'Mrs Fewtrell, I'm seriously afraid something might have happened to Norris. Have you no idea at all where he could be staying, because he hasn't been home for at least three days.'

She started to cry quietly. 'I'm sorry.' She took a handkerchief from her cardigan pocket and dabbed her eyes. 'He might be at his cottage. He has a holiday home in Wales, just by Conwy Harbour.'

'Have you tried ringing him?'

'He hasn't got a phone there.'

'You think he's in danger too, don't you?'

'I – I don't know,' she stammered, then, as I looked meaningfully at her, 'Yes.'

'But why? What has he done?' She hesitated. 'You must tell me, Iris, if you want to save his life.'

She took a deep, trembling breath.

And then came the bombshell.

'It's my son,' she said, at last.

'I didn't know you had a son.' A child had never been mentioned and I'd therefore taken it for granted that Iris had never had one. Now I realised my mistake. It was a question I should have asked.

'He was born in 1976.'

'So David Blease was the father?'

She nodded.

'Was he still with you when the baby was born?'

More tears. 'No. He had left six months before.'

'Hang on, I thought you left him?'

'In a way, I did. You see, when I told him I was pregnant, Davey was furious. He wasn't one for responsibility or commitment, you see. Didn't like the idea of being tied down.'

I knew the feeling. Yet how could he just abandon his own flesh and blood?

'So he walked out on you?'

'Maybe he didn't intend to go for good. We had a blazing row and he stormed out of the house. It was teatime. He didn't come home that night but that wasn't unusual. However, I decided I'd had enough and the next day I packed my things and I never saw Davey again. Eventually, I filed for divorce and it went through unchallenged.'

'What happened to the baby?

'I kept it, of course.'

'And he never came back to see it?'

'Not once.'

'What about when Davey played for the Corinthians in 1979 – the baby must have been three by that time. Didn't he try to get in touch with you then? After all, he was playing for your brother's team.'

'I didn't know that then. Remember, I'd moved away from Liverpool.'

'You didn't know he was playing football with your brother?'

'Not at the time, no. Norris never told me.'

'So when did you find out?'

'I don't know. Much later.'

'Did your last husband adopt the baby when you married him?'

'Oh no, he'd grown up and left home by the time I married George.'

'Where did he go?'

She started to sob. 'I don't know, do I? He's not been in

touch. That's why Norris was trying to find Davey, in case the lad had gone to his dad.'

I felt the charade could go on no longer. Sooner or later she'd have to be told her ex-husband was dead and this was as good a moment as any.

'Iris,' I said, 'I've been trying to find your ex-husband, as you know – on your brother's instructions. And I have to tell you, I'm afraid, that David Blease died in a house fire in London in 1979, shortly after he left the Corinthians.'

'Oh no.' She rocked in her chair, the handkerchief clutched to her mouth. 'He can't have.'

'It's true, I'm afraid,' I said. 'I've seen his grave.'

'Does Norris know? He never told me.'

'I told him a fortnight ago. He probably didn't want to upset you.' I hesitated.

'What did he say?'

'He re-hired me to find the man who killed your ex-husband.'

'I thought you said he died in a fire.'

'He did, but it looks like he was probably murdered.' I explained about Peter Westcott and Blease's affair with Westcott's wife.

'You mentioned a Mr and Mrs Westcott when you came before but you didn't tell me about the affair. Typical of Davey though and his women.'

'It seems that this time he got his come-uppance,' I said. 'In the end, it was his womanising that did for him.'

'And you think it was this Westcott person who killed him?'

'It would appear so. But I've also found a connection between Westcott and a man called Harry Mottram who's a known villain in Liverpool.'

'You mentioned him before too, but I've not heard of him. You say you haven't been able to find Westcott?'

'Not yet, but I'm worried he might have found out that Norris is trying to locate him and that's why I need to warn your brother. But you said your son could be involved in this. Where does he fit in?'

'I told you he left home. Well, that was in 1996, when I decided to marry George. The boy didn't take to having a stepfather, you know what teenagers are like, so he said he was going down to London to look for his real father.'

'Did your brother know this?'

'Yes. After George died, I was on my own so I asked Norris to try to find the lad. I thought he might come back home now that I was on my own.'

'When was this?'

'Only a few weeks ago.'

Which was when Norris Pond had first hired me to find David Blease.

'I take it he didn't find him?'

'No, but he found some people who knew him and he told me he was afraid that Sean was getting into bad company.'

'Sean!' I said quickly. 'That's your son's name?'

'That's right.'

I took out my notebook and showed her the photograph I'd taken earlier that morning, at Harry Mottram's house, of the shaven-headed man.

'Oh my God,' cried Iris Fewtrell, going white. 'That's him. That's my Sean.'

Chapter Thirty-four

It wasn't looking good for Mrs Fewtrell. She'd only just learned that her ex-husband was dead and now she would have to accept that her only son was a vicious killer. Norris Pond had been right about her son keeping bad company. It only needed her brother to be murdered as well, and his prospects weren't looking too bright, and it could well finish her off.

'Give me Norris's address in Conwy,' I said. 'I'll go over there now.'

'I'll come with you.'

'Better you don't, Iris. It might be dangerous. I promise I'll ring you as soon as I have any news.'

First of all, I had to ring Ken at the radio station.

'Any chance you can get someone to stand in for me tonight, Ken? I've got a case on.'

'You're out of luck, Johnny. Shady Spencer's gone to the Costa Blanca for a fortnight.'

'Is there nobody else? What about Jeannie in the Newsroom?'

'Who?'

'Jeannie – you know, as in *Aladdin*.'

'The dark-haired one?'

'That's her. Supposed to be having it away with Ricky Creegan.' Creegan was the station head and I'd never believed the rumour for a moment. Jeannie was far too pretty to do it with an ageing creep like him.

'News to me. More of your scurrilous gossip-mongering,

no doubt. A very capable girl that. All right, she is on duty at the station tonight so I'll get her to do it. Only one night, mind. You'd better be back tomorrow.'

'If I'm not killed first. Thanks, Ken.'

I decided to take the motorway route to Wales and avoid the traffic in Preston and Liverpool. On the way, I rang Jim to find out what was happening at his end.

'DI Ormesher wants to see you like yesterday. He's over at Croxteth.'

'What's up with him now?'

'You left the scene of a crime again, didn't you? Anyway, never mind that, have you managed to see Mrs Fewtrell?'

'Yes, and guess what?' I put him in the picture about Sean.

'So you reckon that's why Norris Pond really hired us – to find his nephew? Nothing to do with getting alimony from Blease.'

'Looks like it, and now we've found the lad for him, the question is, is Norris Pond still around to hear the good news?'

'That his nephew's become a contract killer, you mean?'

'No. That we've found him. The rest can come later.'

'You really think Pond may have been stiffed already?'

'Let's just say I'm concerned about his welfare.'

'But like we've said before, Johnny, why would anyone want to kill Norris Pond, for God's sake?'

'Mistaken identity, maybe. Mottram's a man who likes to delegate; half the people he uses don't know they're working for him, but Sean seems to be his right-hand man so if they get Sean, they'll likely get to Mottram. If Mottram knows Pond is on Sean's trail, he'll want to stop him in his tracks.'

'In case Pond is the Law, you mean?' said Jim.

'Yes. Mottram won't know it's a family thing, that Pond isn't the police or a bounty hunter but merely Sean's uncle.'

'It's a good point. So where are you now?'

'Iris said her brother has a holiday cottage in Conwy so I'm on my way to Wales now to see if he's there.'

'Right. Keep me posted then.'

The journey to Conwy took me a couple of hours. It was coming up to six o'clock when I drove over the bridge past the castle and round the back of the town to the seafront. I parked the car side on to the river, leaving Roly on the passenger seat, and walked back till I came to the address Iris Fewtrell had given me.

There was no sign of life. It was a terraced cottage, painted pink and black. I peered through the front window but the lace curtains did their job. I walked round the back and tried the gate. It was unlocked. The back window was above my head but I found an old bucket in a corner of the yard and took it across to stand on. I was now able to see a couple of inches above the windowsill but it was enough.

I'd found Norris Pond but was I too late?

I ran to the back door. As expected, it was locked so I took a step back and kicked my heel hard against the lock. The door jamb split and I was inside.

Norris Pond was lying in the kitchen, face down. There was blood on the floor. I turned the body over and saw the gunshot wound in his forehead.

I rang Jim. He was still in the office. 'Lennie Smithson's just left,' he said, before I could speak. 'Mottram's rung him to make sure he received the contract.'

'What did he tell him?'

'He said he had, so Mottram told him if he didn't get it back tomorrow morning the photos would go to the press and to Brenda Smithson.'

'What's he going to do?'

'Lennie was a bit clever for once. Said he'd already put it in the post box when he realised he'd missed the five o'clock collection so Mottram wouldn't get it until first thing on Thursday morning.'

'Did he buy it?'

'He wasn't happy, Lennie said, but he'd no choice and Lennie did tell him he'd signed the contract.'

'Brilliant. That gives us another day. What about the police? Did you send them Sean's photo?'

'Yes. They've done a check but he's not got a record.'

'What name did they look for?'

'They tried Blease and Fewtrell but came up with nothing and no match on the picture.'

'What about Karl Dwane?'

'Nothing to tie him to Mottram.'

'Talking of Dwane, I reckon we can have him pulled now,' I chose my words carefully, 'for the murder of Norris Pond.'

'Pond's dead?'

'Jim, I'm standing by his body as I speak. Gunshot wound to the head, same as Mr Patel, and my bet is, the gun that was used is the one currently in my pocket. I took it from Dwane this morning at Croxteth.'

'Oh Christ,' said Jim. 'That's all we need. Are the police there?'

'No, and I'm not calling them either. Not with the murder weapon in my pocket.'

'Where exactly are you?'

'In his cottage in Conwy. I had to break in. He's been dead a good while, I'd say.'

'So you don't think it was Sean who was the hit-man this time?'

'No, but he and Karl Dwane obviously both went to the same gun school. Bullet in the head job. I reckon Dwane shot Pond first thing this morning then drove straight down to Croxteth to waste Graham Duxfield. An early-bird double, except he didn't come up on the second one.'

'There's a call out for Dwane but no sighting as yet,' Jim told me. 'Do you think he'll go to Mobberley?'

'If he does, he'll soon be on his way again. Mottram won't want him hanging around too long. Remember what we said earlier about him delegating. He likes to leave as much space as possible between him and his lackeys. In fact, Jim, thinking about it, I'd say Karl Dwane could well be next on Mottram's hit list. He's become a liability to him, far too high-profile.'

'What are you going to do now?'

'Lock this place up and come back to Liverpool. I want you to ring Ormesher, Jim, and let him sort all this out. It's his case, after all. He won't want the Welsh Force getting involved, any more than I do.'

I switched off the phone and looked down at the body of Norris Pond. Somebody was going to have to tell his sister and that someone would most likely be me. But not immediately. I needed to be out of this house fast before somebody came and found me standing over the corpse with the gun that probably killed him in my possession.

Luckily, it appeared nobody had heard me break in. Everything was silent outside. I gave Norris Pond one last glance. His hair was still grey and crinkled, his shoulders broad. Somehow, in death, he looked even larger than in life. I could imagine him being a daunting opponent on the football field. So much for his Corinthian values now. They hadn't saved him. I wondered if his book would ever be published.

I felt we'd let Norris Pond down in our enquiry. We'd found the man he wanted, but dead. We'd found his nephew, but that investigation had led to Pond himself being killed. Hardly the result he wanted and not the best advert for Johnny Ace Investigations.

I left the house quietly by the back way, managing to prop the door back against the opening. So long as the wind kept down it would stay in place, certainly until the police came and that depended if any of the neighbours had noticed anything amiss.

My mouth was parched so I walked down to the Liverpool Arms and had a quick half of cider. Then I made my way up through the entry beside the Library into the main street and bought fish and chips, which I took back to the car to share with the dog.

It was six-thirty. I switched the radio on and listened to Jeannie doing my show. She was pretty good. Luckily, I knew she wanted to be a journalist rather than a radio presenter otherwise I might have been worried.

I watched the boats moored on the river bobbing in the water. Across the bay was Deganwy station and the road to Llandudno. I wasn't looking forward to the night ahead but, when it was all over, I decided I'd take Maria and Victoria for a weekend in Llandudno. Away from all the aggro.

Roly nudged the greasy paper with his nose, searching for the last chip.

'We'd better go,' I told him, 'before the police arrive and arrest us.'

We were back in my flat in less than an hour. There was a message from Maria on the answerphone. I rang her and explained I was going to be out again all night.

'What's happening, Johnny? You've not rung me all day, I've been worried sick.' That's one of the troubles with commitment. You have to worry about other people worrying about you. Of course, if you have nobody to worry about you in the first place, that spells lonely. I'm not sure you can win.

'I've just got back from Wales,' I said. 'Norris Pond's dead.'

'Oh no! How?'

'Shot, just like Mr Patel.'

'How awful, Johnny. What are you going to do?'

'I'm staying at the flat tonight. Things are hotting up, Maria. It's all going to be over in the next twenty-four hours, one way or the other, so I'm staying in town till then.'

There was no doubt that it would all be over – but I had no clue how it was going to end or if I would still be around to see it.

Chapter Thirty-five

Jim rang as soon as I'd put the phone down. 'I've spoken to Ormesher. He wants to see you in his office first thing in the morning. He's not happy with the way you keep disappearing.'

'Not happy? I'm solving his bleeding case for him. Anyway, what are you doing still in the office?'

'Waiting to get hold of you. Rosemary's not pleased either, I can tell you. She's had her meal and gone off to her Spanish class.'

Why a woman in her late fifties who spends all her holidays in Bognor Regis wants to learn Spanish was beyond me. It was beyond Jim, too, but he maintained it gave him a bit of peace and quiet and a chance to watch football on Sky instead of being forced to endure an evening of soaps. The trouble was, there wasn't too much football played on a Tuesday.

'Tell you what then, Jim. Let's go and have a Chinese and we can chat about the case at the same time.'

We met in Nelson Street in the Chinatown area. I left Roly at the flat. He's never been too keen on Chinese food. He prefers Indian.

'They're making a smart job of this,' commented Jim, referring to the redevelopment work in the area and the new archway. 'It'll be as good as Manchester before they've finished.'

We ate at the Jung Wah. I had chicken and cashew nuts, Jim chose the fish in lemon.

'What's the plan, then?' he said, after we'd both finished our meals.

'Tomorrow night, I'm going to Harry Mottram's to get Lennie Smithson's negatives back for him.'

'No, Johnny, listen to me . . .'

'Jim,' I said patiently. 'Somebody's got to pay us. Norris Pond's dead so that's his bill down the chute. Therefore we need Smithson's ten grand.'

'You should leave this to the police, Johnny.'

'You said yourself they won't take any action against Mottram, and once Smithson hands over that contract, that's our ten grand gone. Besides, I want to nail this bastard.'

'You're not going in there on your own?'

'Certainly not. I intend taking a couple of guys with me.'

Jim groaned. 'Don't tell me. The McKale brothers.'

'Got it in one.'

The conversation paused while the waiter brought the China tea. I poured out two tiny cups as Jim asked, 'Where does Peter Westcott come into the equation?'

'I don't know, Jim. Maybe he never did.' But I didn't believe that for a minute. Westcott was central to the whole mystery.

'Incidentally,' said Jim, 'a bit of news I forgot to tell you in all the excitement. DCI Glass rang. He checked Harry Mottram out and, although he has no official police record, apparently he was suspected of being involved in a few shady operations in the Smoke.'

'So he has been in London and it was him who owned the flat Westcott rented?'

'Seems like it.'

'What were the shady operations?'

'Prostitutes and drugs mainly.'

'And Patti Westcott was on the game so she could have known him?'

'Maybe. Anyway, there was a big fuss about one of his girls who'd been raped. She was subsequently found dead of an overdose. Mottram left town in a hurry, never to be heard of again.'

'When was that?'

'Only a year or two ago.'

'That would be when he fled to Newcastle and the same thing happened there. Tommy McKale told me about it. A woman was raped and died but nothing was ever pinned on Mottram.'

'Glass still hasn't found any mention of Westcott. Do you think he's still in London?'

'Could be.'

'I mean, we know it was Karl Dwane not Westcott who impersonated the jury foreman so maybe Westcott's still down there.'

'Maybe.' For all we knew, he could be in Bangkok buying a new wife.

We finished our tea and Jim went straight home. 'Need to get back before Rosemary,' he explained, 'or I'll never hear the end of it.'

I didn't feel like going home. Instead, I made my way to the Bamalama Club.

'Rap night tonight, Johnny,' apologised Jonas at the door. 'Do you like Eminem?'

'Only when they come in little packets,' I replied.

'We still have the blues nights on a Sunday.'

'I'm glad to hear it, Jonas.'

I went inside. The club was packed and the average age couldn't have been more than eighteen.

'Bring back Howling Wolf,' I remarked to the barman, Leroy, a six foot six African Olympic athlete who'd come over to England on a scholarship to study physiotherapy. Bar work helped him pay the rent.

He agreed with me. 'All this lot want to drink is water.'

'It's the E-culture, Leroy.'

'The water's dearer than the beer though so the boss is happy.'

'Is Shirley not on tonight?' I asked him.

'Night off. She's got a new boyfriend, Johnny. She's going out with Jonas's eldest lad, Winston. You lost out there, man.'

'I thought he lived in Toronto.'

'He came back. Too cold for him in winter.'

I wasn't too upset. Shirley and I had never been a romantic item and I was pleased she'd found someone to take care of her. We'd always be pals.

I drank down a couple of ciders but the endless repetitive noise defeated me and I drove back to the flat. There was a message on the answerphone from Hilary reminding me I was taking her out on Friday. I had more to worry about than that.

First thing next morning I rang Badger. 'Not taking Harry Mottram home tonight by any chance, are you?' I asked him.

'No, why?'

'I wanted to take a trip out there, that's all. I wondered what time he'd be likely to be back.'

'What day is it? Wednesday. He often goes to Manchester on a Wednesday,' Badger assured me, 'but he's usually home about two. You won't have much time if you're doing a bit of housebreaking – and don't forget his two minders and the staff.'

'What staff? You never mentioned those before.'

'He has a handyman-cum-butler and a chef. Both live in.'

'Can they handle themselves?'

'The chef's about eighteen stone and the handyman's a martial arts trainer.'

'Shit. And there's his wife as well.' If the staff were anything to go by, she was probably an Olympic gold medal shot-putter. Even if I took both the McKale brothers, the odds would be 2–1 against us.

'Get there early then,' advised Badger.

'Actually, I need Mottram to be home, Badger. I'm going to have a little chat with him.'

'Oh God, then I'll make sure I'm at the crematorium for your send-off.'

'Thanks, Badger,' I said. 'I'll let you know the date in case they have a wake for me.' I put the phone down and set about preparing for the battle ahead, for battle it would surely be.

I still had the gun that I'd taken from Karl Dwane but I hesitated to take that as it was likely to be needed as evidence when the murder of Norris Pond came to trial. However, I was sure the McKales would arrive well tooled up.

It was a reckless action I was taking and I knew it but I couldn't see any other way. Even if the police pulled in Karl Dwane, the odds were he wouldn't reveal any link to Mottram. Similarly with Sean. Mottram might well be questioned but, as before, he'd protest his innocence, there would be no evidence and he'd still have the photographs of Leonard Smithson *in flagrante delicto* locked away for future use.

I left Roly at the flat and set out to find Tommy McKale. He was at his Leisure Centre setting up some new gymnasium equipment.

'Looks expensive gear,' I said.

'All the girls want "fab abs" nowadays, so this little item will provide them.'

'Fab abs?'

'Abdominal muscles. The Dolly Parton look is out, Johnny. Big pecs instead of big boobs.'

'I know which I prefer. I could never fancy a woman who looked like Arnold Schwarzenegger.'

'So what's your problem, Johnny, or have you come for a work-out? I tell you what, come and have a drink at the bar and you can tell me all about it.'

He led the way up to the minimalist bar and produced two bottles of isometric Lucozade. 'Drink this, it'll give you energy.'

'I might be needing it,' I said, taking the bottle from him. 'Tommy, you did say a while ago that you've not been too happy about Harry Mottram trying to muscle in on your territory?'

'That's right, I did.'

'Well, I might have found a way to get rid of him and do us both a favour.' I proceeded to outline my plan.

Tommy nodded approvingly. 'Risky, but it could work. A shooter job, is it?'

'Might well be.'

'Christ, Johnny, you don't half get into some situations. What time had you got in mind for this outing?'

'I thought if we left here around midnight. I'll come down to the club and pick you up. That is, if you can get away so early.'

'Should be able to. Wednesday's not the busiest night.'

'How many men will you be able to bring?'

'Denis and me'll be enough, surely?'

'I don't know, Tommy,' I said doubtfully. Three known murderers seemed formidable opposition to me without the 'staff' as well.

'How many of them are there likely to be?'

'As far as I know, Mottram and his two trained monkeys – this Sean character and Karl Dwane. Both are professional killers and Mottram himself has been known to extinguish the odd person who gets in his way.'

'Three against three then, is it? Shouldn't pose a problem.'

'Hang on, it's three against five,' I warned. 'There's a couple of live-in retainers who sound like they've been in training for *Gladiators*, and Mottram's wife will probably be in the house as well.'

'She'll hardly be much of a threat.'

'Unless she has a Uzi under her bed.'

'I'm relying on the element of surprise, Johnny. Do you know the layout of the place?'

'I've got a diagram of the ground floor.' I took out my notebook and showed him Badger's sketch.

'Looks straightforward,' he said. 'What's the plan then?

We ring the front door bell and rush them, or is it a back window job?'

'I think the former. Too many alarms for breaking and entering.'

'See you tonight then.'

I left the Leisure Club and drove over to St Ann Street for my belated meeting with DI Ormesher.

He wasted no time with polite preliminaries. 'What exactly's going on here?' he barked. 'In the morning you disappear from a flat in Croxteth where a gunman has tried to shoot one of the jurors from the Joanna Smithson trial, and by teatime you're in Wales standing beside the body of a man killed by the same weapon. And at no time did you bother to phone the police.'

'Didn't Jim Burroughs pass the message on?'

'Yes, but that isn't the point. For a start, the Welsh Police weren't any too pleased at you walking away, I can tell you.'

'How come they were involved? I told Jim to ring you direct.'

'A neighbour letting his cat out saw the back door missing and dialled 999.'

Just my luck – it must have blown down in the wind. 'Anyway, you got there, that's the main thing. Did you find out who the dead man was?' I asked him the question before he could ask me.

'I'm surprised you didn't know. It was a man called Norris Pond, a retired footballer.'

'What had he to do with this case?' I enquired innocently.

'I was hoping you'd tell me. There must be some connection. Then, I ask myself, why did Johnny Ace just happen to be in that house?'

I was thinking on my feet. 'As you know, I went to Croxteth in the morning to see Graham Duxfield. I take it you know he's signed an affadavit about the jury rigging?'

Ormesher nodded. 'Go on.'

'Well, while I was there, Karl Dwane burst in and tried to shoot us. He got away but later on I had a tip-off . . .'

'Anonymous, of course?' smirked Ormesher.

'As a matter of fact, yes. This person informed me I'd find Dwane at this hide-out in Conwy.'

'And you never thought to ring me?'

'It all happened so quickly. I drove straight over but when I got there, instead of Karl Dwane, I found this body.'

'Of a man supposedly unknown to you, yes. And you immediately drove straight back again, the second time in a day you'd left the scene of a major crime.'

'I didn't disturb anything.' I wanted to get him off the subject. 'Didn't Jim Burroughs tell you it was Karl Dwane you needed to find?'

'He did.'

'And?'

'And what?'

'Have you found him yet?'

'Oh yes,' said Clive Ormesher, grimly. 'We've found him all right. He was discovered by a railwayman in the early hours of this morning. In Edinburgh.'

'In Edinburgh? What was he doing there?'

'Taking advantage of Virgin Trains Sleeper Service,' replied the inspector with heavy sarcasm, then he resumed his serious tone. 'In actual fact, he was lying at the bottom of an empty goods wagon.'

'You don't mean he was . . . ?'

'Dead? Yes, very. Karl Dwane had been shot twice through the head.'

Chapter Thirty-six

'It makes sense,' I said. 'Once the police knew Dwane's identity, his days were numbered. He was too close to Mottram.'

'You're still convinced Mottram's behind all this?'

'Without a doubt.'

'But you've no proof?'

'Not yet.'

'Because I can't get a search warrant for Mottram's place just on speculation and there is absolutely nothing to tie him to Joanna Smithson's kidnapping or any of these three murders.'

'Give me time,' I told him. 'I'm working on it.'

Ormesher looked at me suspiciously. 'There's nothing you haven't told me, is there?'

The photos and the blackmail attempt on Smithson; the gun in my flat; my plan to raid Mottram's mansion at Mobberley.

'Of course not.'

Then there was the fact that Norris Pond was the uncle of Sean, Mottram's right-hand man. But if I told Ormesher that, he might have the ammunition he needed to raid Mobberley and I wanted to be there first to secure Lennie Smithson's photos. And earn my ten grand. At least, with Dwane gone, the odds were tilted in our favour – 5–3 against.

'Hmmm.' Clive Ormesher rose to his feet. 'I told you before, if you can come up with anything on Harry Mottram, I'll listen to you. But I don't want you breaking the law or taking matters into your own hands to do it and that's an order.'

'Of course,' I promised.

'And if you do find out anything, for God's sake ring me. Is that clear?'

It was clear enough to me. *You do the dirty work and I'll step in to mop things up and claim the credit.* Fair enough. Jim and I get the ten grand, Clive Ormesher gets an extra stripe. I knew which I'd prefer.

But first I had to get Mottram.

I left the car in the police station car park and walked to Rodney Street for some lunch at Café Renouf before returning to the flat.

Roly was waiting at the door, wondering why he'd been shut in for so long. I was tempted to take him with me to Mobberley, remembering his heroics at Croxteth, but I couldn't risk him being shot so I rang Maria.

'Any chance you can have Roly tonight?' I asked her.

'Where are you now?'

'At the flat but I'm going to Mottram's tonight to get Leonard Smithson's negatives back.'

'On your own?'

'No, I'm taking the McKales with me.'

'Johnny, it's suicide. Let the police sort it out.'

'I'll be OK, I promise. You'll be in, will you? You're not working this afternoon?'

'No, I'm busy doing Christmas cards.'

'Bit early, isn't it?'

'If I don't take them round the shops in August to get the orders, I'll miss the boat. I'm not the only one making greetings cards, you know. It's become a cottage industry.'

'I'll be round in an hour then. I'll take him for a walk first.'

We went along the Dock Road and stopped at the Atlantic for a quick drink. Syd Ricketts was at the bar, well on his way to his daily quota of ten pints, mostly bought by other people who would usually get him them to shut him up.

In his early days, Syd used to be a night watchman on the

docks, a job that gave him plenty of opportunities in the home furnishing line and earned him the nickname of 'the George Henry Lee of the docks'. At one time, it was said, he was offering a bigger catalogue than Littlewoods. Then containers came in and Syd's little empire crumpled overnight. In the company of several thousand others, he was made redundant.

Since then, he'd done a bit on the markets, peddled seafood round the pubs and collected glasses at various nightclubs but he still drank on the Dock Road, scene of his former glories, and still kept his hand in as a part-time fence. Unfortunately, most of the stuff he was now selling seemed to be leftovers from his docker's days.

'Johnny, how are you, I haven't seen you for ages. I say, you're not interested in a 16mm film projector, are you, in working order?' Syd never wasted time getting to the point.

'Not for me, Syd, thanks all the same.'

'Only I've got one you can have, reasonable like.'

'Of course you have, you pillock, that's because they went out with the Ark. Haven't you heard of video and digital cameras?'

But Syd was not to be rebuffed. 'How about a couple of night storage heaters then?'

It beggared belief. The bloke was barely five foot two and knocking eighty. Night storage heaters are full of bricks and weigh a ton. How did he carry them around? He never had a car.

'No thanks, Syd. I've got central heating. Tell you what, let me buy you a beer. A half of bitter, is it?'

'Better make it a pint, Johnny. We've a long night ahead.' Didn't I know it? 'I say, that's an ugly dog you've got there. What happened to its tail?'

Roly looked up at him and growled quietly.

'Lost it in the Gulf War,' I replied as Pat came over. I ordered Syd his drink and a half of cider for myself.

'What's happened to you on the wireless, son? There was some bint doing it last night when I put it on.'

'Only for the one show, Syd. I'm back tonight.'

And, if I didn't hurry, I wouldn't make it. I still had to take Roly to Maria's. I gulped down my drink and hurried back to the flat, Roly breaking into spasmodic runs to keep up with me.

Maria seemed worried when I eventually arrived at hers. She'd put her cards away and was preparing Victoria's tea.

'Sit down,' she ordered, 'and tell me everything that's happened.'

'What do you want to know?'

'Well, for a start, who killed Norris Pond?' she asked. 'And why?'

'One of Mottram's men did it – Karl Dwane, the guy who was the jury foreman at Joanna Smithson's trial.'

'Why did he kill Pond? He'd nothing to do with that.'

'There is a connection, Maria. You know Mottram's other henchman, the one called Sean? Well, he is Iris Fewtrell's son by Digger Blease. Norris Pond is his uncle.'

I let Maria absorb this new information. 'I still don't see why Mottram should want Norris Pond killed though,' she said at last.

'He probably mistook him for a private eye or something, someone too close on his trail.'

'Just like you, you mean – a private eye. Johnny, you're mad to go there tackling Mottram. Let Smithson get his own photos. Why should you risk being killed?'

'Ten grand,' I said, 'and I won't be killed. I'm taking Tommy and Denis with me.'

'I don't like it, Johnny.'

'Don't worry, love, I'll be all right. I'll be back home with you and Victoria tomorrow night, I promise.'

'Come back after you've done the show and have a proper meal before you go.'

I didn't argue with that. Even Napoleon didn't go into battle on an empty stomach.

Ken was relieved to see me when I got to the station.

'That girl last night made Anne Robinson look meek,' he complained.

'Who? Jeannie? I thought she did quite well.'

'Maybe she did but she wasn't half bossy. And that phone-in she did!'

'I missed that. I was busy finding dead bodies at the time.'

Ken looked startled but carried on. 'Told this fellow from Dingle who rang in that he'd do well to get off his backside and get a job instead of wasting everyone's time ringing up her show and complaining.'

'Good for her. I like a bit of controversy. In fact, I thought we'd have a phone-in about asylum seekers tonight. Did you know there's thousands who've been refused admission to the country who are still here and no one knows where they are. Hard to credit, isn't it.'

Ken's face paled. 'You're back with a vengeance, I see,' he groaned. 'Just when I thought I'd have a quiet night. Creegan'll sack you again, I'm warning you.'

'It could be my last show anyway,' I said. 'I'm on a mission tonight and Maria reckons I might not come back.'

'As long as they give your job to Shady Spencer and not that girl,' said Ken.

Maria had done a chicken casserole and we opened a bottle of red wine. 'That was a good show you did,' she said.

'Thanks.' As usual, I gave Roly a piece of skin.

'You will take care, won't you, Johnny. I . . . we couldn't bear to lose you.'

'I know.'

'Come back here tonight,' she pleaded.

'No, because I don't know what time it'll be. I'll ring you first thing in the morning, I promise.'

We finished the meal in an uneasy silence. Roly sensed something was wrong and crept off to his basket. When I rose to leave, Maria threw her arms round me and hugged me. 'I love you,' she said.

'I love you too.'
I walked slowly down the path to the car knowing I might never see them again.

Chapter Thirty-seven

I went back to the flat to change. I put on a couple of T-shirts under a thick sweater, protection, a pair of denims and Kickers boots. In the end I decided I would take Karl Dwane's gun and I also strapped a sheath knife to my ankle. Something I'd read about in The Saint books.

At just after midnight, I presented myself at the door of the Masquerade. Tommy McKale was talking to Dolly at the paybox.

'She wants to come,' he said. 'Hasn't had a good dust-up for years. She says it'll give us better odds.'

'We've already got them,' I said. 'They're down to five now.' I informed him of the last journey of Karl Dwane.

'Good. Let the bastards kill each other, it'll save us a trip.'

'Can't wait that long. Are we all set?'

'It's a quiet night, Johnny. We can leave whenever you like. Vince can look after things here.'

'Let's go then.'

'We'll take my car,' said Tommy. 'The windows are bullet-proof. Denis can drive.'

The vehicle was a black Mercedes 320E and Denis McKale drove at a steady 75 mph along the M62 past Burtonwood Services to the M6 in the opposite direction to the journey I'd made nearly forty-eight hours ago. A lot had happened since then.

'What's the set-up?' asked Tommy as we approached the village of Mobberley.

'Electronic gates from the road and a long driveway leading to the house. Don't worry,' I added as Tommy's face dropped. 'I've got the remote for the gates.' I'd decided to hang on to it after my last trip in the Lexus. Mottram hadn't noticed.

Maybe he had cameras rigged up behind the bushes but I figured that, at one-thirty in the morning, nobody would be sitting up watching the CCTV monitor. They'd rely on alarms, which would only be activated by someone breaking in, and we were not breaking in.

'So the plan is,' I told them, 'we walk up to the front door, ring the bell and, when they open it, the three of us storm in like the SAS.'

'Sound,' agreed Tommy.

Denis let the car cruise silently as we approached the house. Outside the front door was parked Mottram's Lexus. We glided to a stop behind it and Denis switched the engine off. Quietly, we all climbed out and walked up to the front door.

I rang the bell three times and waited. No answer. I banged on the door. Silence. It was then that Denis McKale drew my attention to something wedged in the door, two inches above my head.

A bullet.

I tried the door but it was locked.

'Ring the bell again,' said Tommy. 'I want to get at them. I could do with a good work-out. I wonder where the other bullets landed.'

Two of them in Karl Dwane's head, I thought.

'Ssshh, I can hear footsteps. There's someone coming,' whispered Denis.

The two brothers stood to one side as a key was turned and the door swung open. A man with the body of a Sumo wrestler, who could have doubled as Goliath, framed the doorway.

'I've come to see Harry Mottram,' I said.

'He ain't here.' He started to close the door but I quickly blocked it with my foot. He had an Oriental twang to his voice and I guessed he was the chef Badger had spoken of.

'Yes he is, that's his car.'

His response was quick. He stamped on my foot and as I instinctively withdrew it he tried to slam the door but Denis McKale was too quick for him and put his shoulder against it.

At the same time, Tommy jumped forward and thudded his fist in the man's solar plexus, winding him, giving Denis the chance to rush in with a fierce uppercut to the chin, which sent him sprawling on to the polished hall floor.

Tommy ran into the hall, picked up a mahogany carved chair and slammed it down on the man's skull. 'That should keep him quiet for a bit,' he said. 'Who's next?'

He hardly had time to ask before a figure clad in black T-shirt and shorts appeared by the banisters at the top of the landing.

When he saw what was happening he leapt down the stairs three at a time, landed at the bottom and, in the style of a Thai boxer, kicked Denis McKale in the throat with his bare feet, knocking him, choking, to the ground.

As he turned round, Tommy caught his other ankle and pulled him over and I quickly grabbed the mahogany chair and repeated Tommy's action on his colleague.

'Two down, three to go.'

'Don't anybody move.'

We looked up to see Harry Mottram standing halfway down the stairs. He wore the same suit he'd worn at the Golf Club. In his hand was a gun. Behind him was the shaven-headed Sean, also holding a gun.

'It's him,' Sean said to his boss, 'what drove you the other night.'

Mottram smiled maliciously. 'So it is. Taken up burglary now have you, Mr . . . Lake, wasn't it?' I said nothing. He reached the bottom step. 'Stand apart,' he barked and fired a shot inches from Tommy McKale's scrotum.

The two of them advanced and, covered by Sean, Mottram relieved Tommy of the gun in his inside pocket.

'Yours too,' he snapped at Denis who silently handed across his weapon. Mottram put them both in a cupboard in the corner of the hall and locked it before coming back to me. 'Now you, scum.' I took Karl Dwane's pistol from my pocket and threw it on to the floor. Mottram stepped forward and slashed me across the face with the back of his hand. 'Don't try to be clever with me,' he snarled, picking up the pistol and putting it in his pocket.

At this point, the Karate Kid stirred and staggered to his feet. The chef remained recumbent on the ground.

Mottram took up his own gun and pointed it at Tommy and Denis. 'Lock them in the garage,' he said to Sean. 'Follow him, one at a time,' he told the McKales, 'and don't try anything. I like a bit of gun practice. Keeps my hand in.' And he fired a shot at their ankles to start them moving. 'You,' he said to me, 'in my study. Take him in, Lee, while I lock these two away. Sean can ship them out tomorrow.'

Lee pushed me towards a door that led into a large room overlooking the front drive. When he switched on the light, I could see this was Mottram's office. Two banks of metal filing cabinets stood at one end but the room was dominated by a huge oak desk on which were a computer, multi-office machine and a couple of telephones. In the corner was the large steel safe Badger had mentioned. A large leather Chesterfield took up almost the whole of the wall opposite the bay window.

Mottram returned a few minutes later. 'Go and sort Tony out, Lee. He looks like he's had a nasty bang on the head.' He glared at me. 'Someone will pay for this.'

Lee left the room and Mottram closed the door after him and turned to me.

'Right,' he said. 'Let's talk. I know who you are. You're Johnny Ace, the so-called private detective. I know this because young Sean went to see his mother today and she told him all about you.'

I realised I'd still not told Iris Fewtrell about her brother Norris's death. It seemed now that I wouldn't need to.

'Before I kill you,' went on Mottram pleasantly, 'I want to know just why you've been hounding me.'

'Lenny Smithson hired me,' I replied. 'First because you kidnapped his daughter and now because you're trying to blackmail him.'

'Not trying to, I am. I'm surprised you waste your time on trash like Smithson. A stupid man, leaving himself so vulnerable. He deserves all he gets.'

'And I suppose his daughter does too?'

'The murderess, you mean?' Mottram laughed. 'I shouldn't mock her, she saved me the bother of attending to Dewhurst myself. He was becoming a liability.'

'Yes, I've noticed you like to cover your tracks by disposing of your own employees. Karl Dwane for example.'

'Not a great loss to society. He'd served his purpose.'

'Did he kill Billy Murphy or was it Sean?'

'Sean. The only person Dwane killed was Norris Pond and that was made easy for him.'

'Easy?'

'I lured Pond to his Welsh hideaway with a message that Sean would be waiting for him there. He was trying to find Sean, you see. Iris hadn't heard from her son since she got hitched to the geriatric. When the old man died, she wanted her little boy back so she asked Pond to find him.'

'And he traced him to you.'

'Eventually.'

'And you didn't want anyone interfering with your set-up, Sean being an integral part of your team?'

'My right-hand man.'

'So you had to get rid of Norris Pond.'

'You're catching on fast,' approved Mottram. 'Pond fancied himself as the boy's guardian and he thought Sean was getting into bad ways. He had to go, but I couldn't ask the lad to kill his uncle so I gave the job to Dwane.'

'So you knew all along that Pond was Sean's uncle then?'

'Oh yes.'

'And while Dwane was at it, you thought he might as well kill Graham Duxfield as well, did you?'

'Seemed a good idea. The last of the dissenting jurors, so to speak.'

'But what you don't know is that he'd already signed an affadavit disclosing everything about Murphy and the jury rigging so you would have been too late.'

'Not to worry. Dwane cocked it up anyway.'

'He certainly paid for his mistake.'

Mottram shrugged. 'Some you win, some you lose. He lost.'

'Tell me, where does Peter Westcott come into all this?'

Mottram smiled again. It was a smile that would have blunted the jaws of a piranha fish. 'You really don't know very much, do you, Ace?'

'I know you rented a flat to him in Limehouse in a block called Première Place.'

'Did I?'

'And his wife was on the game in Shadwell, just down the road.'

'I can't imagine there'd be too many takers for that lady, though I shouldn't speak ill of the dead.'

'So you admit you knew Patti Westcott? Do you know who killed her too? Was it the same person who killed Sean's father in a similar fire? Tell me, is Peter Westcott involved in your operation on Merseyside or did he stay in Newcastle?'

If I thought the mention of Peter Westcott's name would evoke some response from Mottram, I was wrong. He just laughed.

'Enough. I can't stand the strain. Do you want to see Leonard Smithson's photos before I dispose of you? You see, I don't leave all the killings to Sean. I intend to deal with you personally.' He took a bunch of keys from his pocket and threw them on the floor in front of me. 'Here, open up that safe.'

I picked the keys up and walked over to the corner where

the safe stood. Mottram's gun was trained on me all the while. 'It's the one with the round top,' he said.

I found it, turned it in the lock and swung the heavy door open. On the ledge in front of me was a thick white envelope sealed with green packing tape. I took it out.

'Are these they?'

'Go on, open it.'

I tore open the wrapping. Inside were a dozen colour photographs of a naked Leonard Smithson having intercourse and oral sex with two women in various permutations. I didn't see the Coca Cola bottle mentioned by Badger but I hazarded a guess where it might be.

'Well?' said Smithson. 'What do you think of your respectable client now?'

'We all have our weaknesses,' I said. 'No reason to take his club from him. He's worked all his life for that.' I felt inside the envelope and pulled out three strips of negatives. I held them up to the light. They matched the photographs. I replaced them and the photos in the envelope and started to put it into my pocket.

'Hang on,' snapped Mottram. 'Back in the safe if you don't mind.'

It was now or never. I had the photos I'd come for. I wouldn't get another chance, but he was still holding the gun. I took a step towards him and held out the envelope. 'You take them,' I said and, as he instinctively hesitated, I threw the envelope at him and dived for his feet. He fired but the shot whistled over my head as we both fell to the ground and I heard the gun clatter to the floor.

Mottram wrapped his hands round my arm and bent it backwards. Belying his forty odd years, the man was strong and in fine physical condition. I knew the arm could break. Desperately, I reached up with my other hand and jabbed my fingers in his eyes. That had saved me in the fight with Dwane and it worked again with Mottram. He yelled out, let go of my arm and rolled backwards.

I seized my chance and threw myself across the floor to where his gun had fallen. He was right behind me but I had the move on him and grabbed it before he could reach it. I scrambled to my feet, the gun pointing at him as he knelt before me.

I thought of Joanna Smithson's ordeal, of the wrecking of my Kirkdale house and the attack on Shani Patel. And the shooting of Shani Patel's uncle and the luckless Billy Murphy, who'd had the bad fortune to be picked for the wrong jury. And Norris Pond trying to save his nephew from bad company. Not to mention the women in London and Newcastle who had died after he'd raped them.

All of those lives lost and more. I seriously considered pulling the trigger and ridding the world of this man who seemed totally unrepentant about the evil he'd done. In fact, he seemed to regard it all as rather amusing.

My finger tightened on the trigger and I pulled up the safety catch. For the first time, it occurred to Mottram that I might actually shoot him and he opened his mouth to protest but suddenly the door behind him flew open and Sean appeared on the threshold, gun in hand.

Before I could move, he fired at me. The bullet grazed my cheek and I automatically fired back. It was a wild shot, I hadn't had the chance to take proper aim and so I missed Sean completely.

But only because the bullet hit the chest of Harry Mottram, sending him crumpling to the ground.

And then Bedlam erupted. Tommy and Denis came running through the hall as Sean dropped his gun and knelt down beside the stricken man.

'What's happened?'

'Mottram's been shot. How did you get out?'

Denis answered. 'When the shooting started, Sean ran out and left the door open. Tommy managed to put that Lee bloke out and the other one's been asleep since he hit him with that chair.'

'The rest'll do him good,' said Tommy and we turned our attention to the man lying on the floor with Sean beside him, cradling his head in his hands and sobbing.

I felt Mottram's pulse. There was none.

'You bastard,' Sean cried, tears streaming down his face. 'You fucking bastard. You've killed him, you've killed my dad.'

'Your dad!' I exclaimed. 'Harry Mottram's your dad?'

And I suddenly understood. Sean Blease. It all fitted into place. How could I have been so wrong?

My big mistake had been to accept as Gospel that it really was David Blease buried in that grave in the East London Cemetery. Understandable in a way. After all, his name had been on the headstone and headstones didn't usually lie.

This one had.

But now, at last, I'd finally found the man I'd been searching for. Harry Mottram alias Peter Westcott alias the missing goalkeeper, David Ian George 'Digger' Blease!

Deceased.

Chapter Thirty-eight

'Norris Pond had always regarded Blease as a bad lot,' I said, 'so when his sister told him Sean had gone to London to look for his dad, he was afraid his nephew would fall in with the wrong crowd and so he hired us to find him.'

It was the next morning and Jim Burroughs and I were at the police station in Detective Inspector Ormesher's office after having managed four hours' sleep since the fracas at Mobberley.

I'd called DI Ormesher as soon as I realised Blease was dead. Lee and Tony were safely locked up in the garage and Sean had been too grief-stricken to put up anything like a fight, though with Denis and Tommy on hand, he wouldn't have stood much of a chance.

I took the opportunity, before the police arrived, to find out from Sean the missing pieces of the jigsaw. 'Digger' Blease must have had some charisma because the lad quite obviously idolised his father and was quite happy to boast to me about their various exploits.

'A natural-born killer', Jim described him.

We'd left the SOC team and Forensic people behind us when we finally departed shortly before dawn. Ambulances had eventually taken away Blease's body to the mortuary for a post-mortem examination, and Lee and Tony to hospital. Sean was in police custody.

I'd made sure to remove the incriminating photos from Mottram's safe to give to Leonard Smithson. They were our fee.

I also rang Maria, waking her up, to tell her I was safe.

'Why did he invent the Wavertree Corinthians story?' asked Jim.

'He didn't. He was actually compiling the book when Iris asked him to find Sean, and it seemed a good idea to use the biography as an excuse. Find the father and you find the son. Saved a lot of explanations. He knew something was up but he didn't quite know what. Until then, Blease's entry in the book would have simply been on the lines of "played in goal 1978–9. Left area soon afterwards".'

'So it was just a coincidence that we were involved with Mottram through the Joanna Smithson case?'

'Yes.' DCI Glass wasn't right all the time about coincidences.

'Can we start at the beginning, please,' asked Clive Ormesher. 'Otherwise you've lost me.'

'Right,' I said. 'Let's go back to when David Blease met Iris Brocken. Blease was always bad news, even back in 1976. His wife soon found this out and walked out on him, despite being pregnant. Everyone knew him as a Jack the Lad, a conman who'd chase any bit of skirt he could get his hands on.'

'Like Patti Westcott?' said Jim.

'Precisely. Blease was having an affair with Patti who was the wife of a local butcher. When the Westcotts left town to run a guest-house in London, Blease went down to stay with them.'

'Didn't Peter Westcott think it was odd, Blease showing up down there?'

'Apparently, Blease had ingratiated himself as a friend of the family. He'd involved Peter in a couple of deals he'd done but, of course, Peter had no idea Blease was carrying on with his wife.'

'And the affair continued?'

'Blossomed, you might say, in as much as the two lovers decided to get rid of Peter Westcott. I would imagine it was Blease who first put the idea about running a guest-house into Peter's head. Fewer questions asked after the event if they went somewhere nobody knew them. My guess is, they got him drunk, put him to bed, set fire to the bedclothes then went off to the theatre and let the flames take their course. No reason for anyone to be suspicious. After all, the man had had a few drinks then obviously he'd lit a cigarette and fallen asleep – happens all the time.'

'And they got away with it,' said Ormesher.

'Yes. But the clever bit was pretending it was Blease who got killed in the fire. The body was badly charred, remember, and it was Patti who was able to identify "their guest" by his ring. From thenceforth, Blease passed himself off as Peter Westcott. So easy.'

'Why not just say Westcott had died in the fire?'

'Might have looked suspicious if people found out later he was living with Patti. Also, it was Blease himself who sent the newspaper cutting of his death in the guest-house fire to Uncle Arthur.'

'Why?'

'To break any contact with the past.'

'He would have been expecting Arthur to pass the message on to Iris.'

'He may have hoped so. Even though he'd never taken Iris to meet his uncle, he might have expected they would get together at some time. He wasn't to know they never met. But even when I told Pond that Blease was dead he still wasn't a hundred per cent convinced. He insisted I carried on with the case. I thought it was because he was after some sort of inheritance but now I think he was beginning to believe there was something odd about the death – either it was murder or a cover-up and Blease wasn't really dead at all.'

'And he was right.'

'He was, though he never lived to know it. But to get back to the Westcotts, as Blease and Patti were now known. They moved to a different part of London and Blease became involved in various activities outside the law, mainly drugs and prostitution. He eventually started using a new alias, that of Harry Mottram, possibly around the time he was thinking of ditching Patti. Police suspected Mottram of various illegal deals but were unable to pin anything on him.

'Going by Blease's previous track record, I'm sure he'd had countless other women while he was with Patti but they stuck together till 1996 when, it seemed, he finally grew tired of her and he threw her out. Patti, as we know, went on the skids and ended up selling her body from a cheap flat in Shadwell.

'It was after this that Blease, as Mottram, bought the flat in Première Place, where he installed his latest girlfriend, the young woman who was to become "Mrs Mottram".'

'What happened to her, by the way?' asked Jim. 'She wasn't anywhere in the house last night.'

'According to Sean, she was staying with some friends of theirs in South Shields. Someone will have to inform her that she's now eligible to join the Widows Association. Your job, Clive.'

'It's already in hand,' replied the inspector.

'Wasn't Blease afraid Patti Westcott might shop him?' interceded Jim. 'I mean, she knew so much about him and he's shown how he likes to get rid of potential traitors.'

'I don't think he ever imagined she'd dare betray him.'

'A woman scorned though.'

'I don't think it was so much scorned as desperate. Patti was destitute. Her income from soliciting was declining alarmingly with the passing years. She needed a nest egg and so she found out where her ex-lover was living and demanded money from him, probably by threatening to expose him as Peter Westcott's killer.'

'But she was just as guilty as him,' objected Jim.

'Maybe, but she could always talk her way out of that by swearing that Blease had arranged the fire without her knowledge then threatened her if she didn't identify the body as his. She'd get away with it, Jim, mark my words.'

Clive Ormesher nodded in agreement. 'He's probably right.'

'Anyway, it was a risk she was prepared to take. I suppose she thought she'd nothing to lose.'

'Except her life,' Ormesher remarked grimly.

'At first Blease went along with her. He started to call on Patti at her Shadwell flat, giving her money to keep her quiet but only until he could arrange to silence her completely. In fact, his visits became so regular, the neighbours mistook him for a client. In the end, he relied on his old fire trick, which had worked for them with Peter Westcott, to get rid of her.'

'Why change a proven method?' said Jim, ever the cynic.

'It was about this time, too, that Sean left his mother after she'd married George Fewtrell and came to London to look for his father. He wouldn't want Patti around then. She knew too much about him.'

Jim frowned. 'How did Sean find him? Blease had been so careful to cover his tracks.'

'Simple. He didn't. Blease contacted Sean. Remember, Iris had kept his name right up until she married George Fewtrell so Blease, being a man who liked to keep tabs on everything, knew where they were. That was part of his success. Control, information is power and all that. After all, it wasn't that difficult, they'd lived at that house in Fulwood since Sean was born.'

'How did he know that Sean would want to see him?'

'He didn't. He just knew the lad was coming up to twenty and he decided he'd like to get in touch with him. My guess is he phoned one day, out of the blue.'

'What if he got Iris?'

'He'd put the phone down and try another time until Sean answered.'

'He picked the right moment.'

'He certainly did. Just as Iris was about to marry George Fewtrell and the lad felt unwanted at home. Sean told his mother he was going to London to look for his father but he didn't tell her he'd already spoken to him. Next thing, he's moved in with Blease, they shared a house in Kew, and he soon became his father's right-hand man and partner in crime.'

'Norris Pond was certainly right to be worried about his nephew getting into bad ways. But if Blease was doing so well in London, why did he leave?'

'His usual trouble. Women. He'd raped some girl who then took an overdose and he saw things were getting a bit hot for him. He had contacts in Newcastle so he moved up there, taking Sean and Sandy, Mrs Mottram, with him but, within two years, a similar thing happened. He couldn't leave women alone and would never take no for an answer. This time, however, he had the local mob after him and he had to leave like yesterday. That's when he decided to come back to his old stomping ground on Merseyside.'

'He was lucky nobody recognised him here.'

'It had been a long time, over twenty years.' Although I remembered that when I first saw 'Mottram' at the Golf Club, I'd had the feeling I'd seen him before and, of course, it was on the Wavertree Corinthians club photo that Nobby Wharton had shown me.

'Did Pond know Blease was Harry Mottram?' asked Jim.

'No. But Blease knew Pond was getting close to him. Pond had been making enquiries among some of Sean's old mates and they'd passed the word on to Sean who'd still kept in touch with one or two of them.'

'So Pond had to be silenced.'

'Correct. Karl Dwane had been brought down from Newcastle to take Billy Murphy's place on the jury so Blease also used him to kill Pond, frightened that Sean might botch the job, Pond being family. I'm sure Blease never intended Dwane to return home alive. Dead men can't talk.'

'What'll happen to Sean?'

DI Ormesher was in no doubt. 'He'll get life for the murders of Mr Patel, Billy Murphy and Karl Dwane, all of which he's admitted to. He's also confessed to kidnapping Joanna

Smithson, in partnership with Anthony Dewhurst, so Joanna will soon be on her way home with a full acquittal.'

'What about the two staff at Mobberley, Lee and Tony?'

'Tony's in hospital with a fractured skull,' Ormesher looked pointedly at me, 'but he'll live. He and Lee Ying were responsible for smashing up your house in Kirkdale and attacking Miss Patel so they'll go down for that.'

'So those two were Auschwitz 101?'

'Yes.'

'All ends tied up then,' smiled Jim. 'We'd better be going.'

'Thanks for your help,' said DI Ormesher. 'We should be able to wind up Blease's "Conqueror" operation now, a protection gang masquerading as a security firm, and there's enough hidden away in Mottram, sorry Blease's, office, to close the files on a few dozen other cases both here and in Newcastle and London.'

I'd never been thanked by a police officer before. It was an edifying experience. And the McKales would be pleased to get 'Mottram' off their backs.

'I'll forget about the breaking and entering at Mobberley, the GBH on Blease's men, illegal possession of firearms, leaving the scene of a crime,' Clive Ormesher added. 'Have I missed anything out?'

Only the blackmail attempt on Smithson and the revealing photographs, I thought, and he'd never know about them.

As soon as we got back to Dale Street, Jim rang Leonard Smithson. He was round in an hour and I presented him with his invoice.

'The photos?' he said.

I pushed the envelope across the table. 'All there.'

Smithson took out his chequebook. 'I can't thank you enough,' he said.

'You can,' I replied. 'Just write the cheque.'

'I'm calling it a day,' I told Jim after a relieved Leonard Smithson had left. 'Why don't you go home yourself? You look shattered.'

'I think I will.'

'I might have a few days off, Jim,' I said. 'Take Maria and the baby to Llandudno for a long weekend.'

'Why not. You've earned it.'

We both had. With the retainer and expenses on top of our fee, Leonard Smithson had written us a cheque for not far short of fifteen grand.

Maria was delighted at the idea. 'Victoria will love it at the seaside, not to mention Roly.'

'That's settled then.'

Friday morning dawned bright and sunny. I packed the baby's buggy and our suitcases in the back of the RAV4, fastened Victoria into her child seat next to Roly and we set off through the Mersey Tunnel.

'This is our first family holiday together,' smiled Maria, squeezing my arm. 'Isn't it exciting?'

'It's wonderful,' I said. As we reached the M53 I noticed the road sign for Heswall and I remembered that Hilary was expecting me to take her out tonight.

Too late now. But it was something I was going to have to deal with when we got back. I didn't want to completely lose touch with Hilary.

I turned to Maria and kissed her. 'Yes, it's wonderful.'